THE OTHER SIDE
OF THE PILLOW

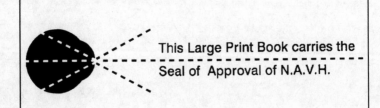

This Large Print Book carries the
Seal of Approval of N.A.V.H.

THE OTHER SIDE OF THE PILLOW

ZANE

THORNDIKE PRESS
A part of Gale, Cengage Learning

GALE
CENGAGE Learning·

Farmington Hills, Mich • San Francisco • New York • Waterville, Maine
Meriden, Conn • Mason, Ohio • Chicago

GALE
CENGAGE Learning·

LIBRARY OF CONGRESS CATALOGING-IN-PUBLICATION DATA

Zane.
    The other side of the pillow / Zane. — Large print edition.
      pages cm. — (Thorndike Press large print African-American)
    ISBN 978-1-4104-7424-7 (hardcover) — ISBN 1-4104-7424-0 (hardcover)
    1. African Americans—Fiction. 2. Large type books. I. Title.
    PS3626.A63O85 2015
    813'.6—dc23
                                 2014034256

Published in 2014 by arrangement with Atria Books, a division of Simon & Schuster, Inc.

Printed in Mexico
1 2 3 4 5 6 7 18 17 16 15 14

*Some people never get
to meet their heroes.
I gave birth to mine.*

For my children.

■ ■ ■ ■

JEMISTRY

■ ■ ■ ■

PROLOGUE

"Violence can only be concealed by a lie, and the lie can only be maintained by violence."
— Aleksandr Solzhenitsyn

2000

It had been three weeks since the abortion. What a way to kick off the new millennium. At a time when I should have been happy — recently getting my master's in Education, working as a high school Social Studies teacher, and making decent money — all I felt was ashamed.

Wesley had been making an attempt to improve his behavior. He had no idea that I had been pregnant. As far as I was concerned he never would find out that I had killed our child. I didn't want to do it, never thought that I would find myself in that place, not to mention that I had never imagined that I could go through with it.

But I had, and not another living soul knew about it with the exception of the people at the clinic. I had not shared it with any of my family or friends. I could not bear to have them think anything negative about me.

"What's for dinner?" Wesley asked as he walked into the kitchen of the town house we were renting in Georgetown. "I'm starved."

"I made some chicken and noodles, and a spinach salad," I replied, washing the pots in the sink. I always preferred to clean up before eating. Afterward I would be too stuffed to do it and I did not believe in leaving dirty dishes overnight. "I'll get you a plate. Why don't you go wash up and I'll have everything together by the time you get finished."

After I had served both of us, I sat down across from him at the dining room table.

Wesley started digging into his food like there was no tomorrow. I stared at him and even though he was incredibly good-looking, that was not enough to overshadow all of his actions.

You're too good of a woman to keep putting up with his shit!

He was guzzling his beer, having not noticed that I had yet to touch my plate, when I blurted out, "I'm leaving you."

He almost spit the liquid out but managed to swallow it as he placed the bottle back down. "Don't be ridiculous, Jemistry. You and I both know that you're not going anywhere."

"I am . . . going. I'll leave tonight and come back tomorrow, or this weekend for my things. If that's cool with you?"

"No, the shit is not cool with me!" he yelled out in anger. "You're not going anyplace. I won't allow it."

I sighed. "I'm grown and I can do what I want. We're not married and —"

"Yet!" he interjected. "We're not married yet, but we will be."

"Never!" I exclaimed, getting loud myself. "It's over, Wesley!"

He smirked and took another bite of his food. "All you've ever wanted was me. Now you think that you're going to walk off into the night like everything is everything? You sound foolish."

"No, I've been foolish, and that's the point. I've allowed you to walk all over me for two years and I will not do it another day. Not even another second."

I had truly reached "that second." The second that I realized that I would not tolerate his bullshit for another second of another

11

hour of another day.

"You act like you can keep doing whatever to me and I'm going to take it," I added.

He smirked again, his gray eyes staring me down as if I were an enemy, which is how he treated me half the time, like a gladiator he was facing in an arena. "You've been taking it. What's the difference now?"

"Wesley, I'll admit that I have been weak. I've held out hope that one day you would wake up, a light bulb would turn on in your head, and you would understand that cheating on me, beating on me, and treating me like your property isn't appropriate."

He sighed. "I haven't done anything lately, Jemistry. Give me a break."

"It's true, and ironic, that I've finally arrived at this point when you're actually acting decent. But it's only a matter of time before you fuck around on me again, or have me getting bandaged up on an emergency room table."

"I thought you were over that," he said matter-of-factly.

"Over it? You put a pillowcase over my head and beat me half to death. How does one get over that exactly?"

The bastard actually laughed. "You tell me. You dropped the charges, came back home, and went right back to sucking my

12

dick every night. Seems to me like you got over it pretty damn quick!"

"You disgust me!"

In truth, I disgusted myself because he was right. I had relinquished all my common sense and self-respect in the name of love. I used to scoff at women who stayed with men who cheated on them, or hit them. Yet, there I was with one who took pride in doing both.

I got up from the table and headed to the kitchen to get my purse and keys. I didn't plan to stay there another minute. I would get a hotel room for a few days and figure things out from there. Look for an apartment that was available immediately or at least within the next few weeks.

Before I could even get the strap of my purse situated on my shoulder, Wesley was punching me in the back of my head. I dropped to the floor and covered myself to prevent his rage from causing too much damage.

"You filthy bitch!" he screamed. "No one leaves me! I leave them!"

He hit me until he lost his breath and, eventually, his footing. That was all the opportunity I needed. I got up onto my knees and grabbed the cast-iron skillet out of the drainer in the sink, then stood up, and with a swinging motion, hit him across the temple.

He was caught completely off-guard and stunned and then dropped to the floor, wincing in pain while I grabbed my keys and headed to the door.

I paused and looked down at him. An expression of shock was still on his face. "You'll live," I said. "I did, and I hope this makes you think twice before you put your hands on another female. I'll be back here tomorrow with a sheriff to get my things. Now you can go to the emergency room and say that you fell."

When I got outside into the fresh air and started walking toward my old 1987 Buick Century, a sense of pride overcame me. It had been a long time coming, but I was reclaiming my life, my dignity, and my heart.

I refused to believe that all men were like Wesley. I had simply made the wrong choice and had attempted to change him. I now realized that it was never about me. It was about a sickness within him and a need to humiliate and control women.

Little did I know back then that Wesley was only the first of a string of men who would run ramshod over me. It would be a cycle that would continue for the next twelve years. *Shame on it all!*

CHAPTER ONE

"People put up walls. Not to keep others out, but to see who cares enough to break them down."

— Socrates

2013

Poetry night at The Carolina Kitchen near the Rhode Island Metro station was packed. There were a handful of people there that I recognized from Howard, but most were strangers. That gave me a feeling of relief. I had never recited my poetry live before. Actually, I was not a poet at all; I was a venter.

I had placed my name on the list to read a piece that I had appropriately titled "Bitter." It was the way that I felt, so it made all the sense in the world to select it for my first — and probably last — time reading in public. I was nervous, but sipping on a chocolate martini was helping.

15

There was a young Rastafarian up at bat reciting something about women with big booties who believed that their sex was their best asset. He was going on and on about how women need to stop acting like a THOT — That Ho Over There — and needed to demand respect for themselves. I was feeling him and wished that my room-mate were there to hear it. I was far from celibate, but Winsome was straight wilding out the majority of the time.

He finished up his piece to mass applause and finger snapping. I was hoping that they would call at least two or three other names before mine so I could finish my drink. Even though I spoke in front of my students and faculty all the time, this was different. My words would be personal and from the heart.

Queen Aishah, the comedic host for the evening, came back on stage working her fabulous hips, rocking her attention-getting hairstyle, and grabbed the microphone. "That was hot, Brother Hakeem. I hope some of the young ladies in this joint tonight take heed of your words." She shielded her eyes and glanced out at the audience like she was trying to find someone in particular. "Yeah, I see some chicks dressed like THOTs tonight. Ya'll advertising, and that's all I have to say about that."

Most of the audience laughed but I noticed some of the scantily clad chicks were offended. I could barely keep up with all the terminology meant solely to degrade women. THOT was a new one. Ho, chickenhead, bird, and the good old-fashioned *whore* were tossed around on the regular. The sad part was that a lot of women had started to embrace the monikers and often called one another those names.

Thank goodness that I had chosen a simple outfit: black jeans, black boots, a black sweater, and a black beanie studded with little silver stars. I was in a militant mood so my clothes reflected my attitude.

"All right, we're going to move on." Queen Aishah looked down at the tablet in her free hand. "Next up is Jemistry. Damn, love that name."

So much for finishing my martini. I sighed and navigated my way to the front as people looked at me strangely, as if to say, "You'd better bring it after Brother Hakeem put it down!" No doubt he was a tough act to follow.

I took the stage and Queen Aishah handed me the microphone, grinned, and sashayed off. She was so confident in herself; I wish I could have said the same.

17

I cleared my throat and tried to imagine that the room was empty, that I was simply practicing like I had done several times at home earlier that day.

"This piece is called 'Bitter.' It's for all the sisters out there who have been hurt, despite giving their all and being all that they can be for men who do not appreciate them."

Several women yelled out things like, "That's right!" "Amen, Sister!" and "Preach!"

Several men hissed and booed and acted like I had called them out by their government names.

I cleared my throat again and then start spitting out the words — slowly, concisely, and from the pit of my soul where all of my own personal pain and bitterness collided.

Hurt
Pain
Anguish
Bitter
That is how I feel as a woman
A woman who has been
Deceived
Betrayed
Disrespected
Humiliated

Dismissed
Used
Demeaned
Abused
Mistreated
It makes no sense . . .
No sense at all
I am a good woman
A brilliant woman
A compassionate woman
A loving woman
An educated woman
A beautiful woman
A romantic woman
A unique and special woman
So why do men overlook me?
Or come into my life and play games?
Use Jedi mind tricks?
Spit out bullshit lies?
Expect me to share dick?
Expect me to tolerate their shit?
Say one thing and do another?
Call me names and expect me to be their
    lover?
Hit on me and then try to kiss me?
Talk shit behind my back?
Hurt
Pain
Anguish
Bitter

Those are the words that describe me
Those are the terms that define me
Now it is time for me to find me
Before it is too late
And my heart can no longer participate
In what people call love
In a true relationship
Bitter . . . that's me

I opened my eyes, which I had clamped
shut at some point halfway through, and
there was an eerie silence over the entire
place for a few seconds. Then there was
mass applause and cheers . . . from the
women. A few men clapped and many were
shaking their heads and crossing their arms
in defiance. Their egos were bruised, but
they knew that I had spoken nothing but
the truth. They were going to learn that day.

As I walked off the stage, Queen Aishah
came up to announce the next poet. She
grinned at me and whispered, "You said
that! That was some real shit right there!"

When I returned to my seat at the bar,
there was a man sitting on the stool next to
mine. I hadn't noticed him before. I wondered if he had come in while I was per-
forming. He was almost like a giant — at
least six-five compared to my five-two
height. Even though he was sitting, I could

tell that he was like a tree. He had a smooth, dark-chocolate complexion, eyes the shade of almonds, a polished fade, and he wore rimless eyeglasses.

The bartender came over to me. "Need anything else?"

"Can I have another chocolate martini, please?"

The guy kept staring at me and I wondered if he was about to go off on me about what I had said onstage.

After another minute or two, once my fresh drink was in front of me, I could not take the stares anymore. There was an older woman onstage reciting a poem about the joys of menopause and moving on to the next stage of life. He was not paying attention to her at all. He was too busy watching my every move.

"The entertainment is that way." I pointed toward the stage. "I'm finished with my performance."

He grinned and exposed a beautiful smile and straight teeth. "I enjoyed your piece. 'Bitter,' wasn't it?"

I rolled me eyes. *Here it comes!* "Yes, it was called 'Bitter.' That's what I am."

"I kind of figured that, and it's such a shame."

He looked me up and down like I was on

display. I was hoping that my face wasn't shiny from having been underneath the hot lights, even momentarily.

"You're too beautiful, sassy, and intriguing to be bitter over a man from your past."

"Actually, you stand corrected. I am bitter regarding *several* men from my past. *All* of the men from my past. Not a single one of them appreciated any of the goodness in me until after I was gone."

"So now the rest of us men can forget it, huh?"

I took a sip of my drink and analyzed what he was implying with his question. The Virgo in me kicked in. One thing is a definite trait among Virgos — we overthink and overanalyze like crazy. On the one hand, I was sick of men to a degree. At least the whimsical fantasy that one man could make a commitment to one woman and do the right thing by her. On the other hand, I loved sex and the specimen sitting beside me was most certainly a candidate for some freaky sex.

He kept looking at me as the menopausal broad left the stage. "Well?"

"I never said that no man has a chance with me. All I'm saying is that I'm not going to be so quick to throw my heart on the line again, unless a man presents himself correctly and is done with playing games. You feel me?"

"Somewhat." He took a long guzzle from his draft beer. "But you have to realize that not all men have to be done with playing games. Some of us have never played them."

I smirked. "That's what you all say. All of you proclaim to be honest, trustworthy, and interested in settling down, up and until you get into a woman's panties and move on to the next one."

"Wow, someone *has* really hurt you!"

"Several *someones* have trampled all over me. They've treated me like a piece of disposable pussy or a deer that has already been hit in the road. Instead of picking me up and trying to resuscitate me, or better yet, leaving me the hell alone to suffer in silence, they run over me again and try to finish the job that the previous dude started."

He shook his head and frowned. "It would probably be in my best interest to move to the other side of the bar and wish you a good evening."

I shrugged. "Probably would be."

He sat there for a few more seconds, still staring.

"Probably would be," I repeated.

"Yes, probably." He chuckled. "But in-

23

stead, I'd like to pay for your drinks and ask if you'd like to head someplace quieter so we can continue this fascinating discussion." He reached out his hand. "I'm Tevin Harris."

I shook his hand. "Jemistry Daniels. I'm not so convinced this is a fascinating discussion, though."

"I'm fascinated!"

I smirked and continued drinking. Another brother had taken the stage but I was really drowning him out. He was talking about some kind of impending "race war." That always amused me when people said things like that, as if we were still in the 1800s. I had always wanted to ask at least one person spouting that foolishness whom they planned to start a race war with, considering that most families were mixed with several different ones.

"So, Jemistry, would you like to take me up on my offer?"

He is not giving up!

I hesitated to respond. He seemed harmless enough, but so do most serial killers. Most are also charming as all get-out.

"Um, tell you what. I'm not trying to hurt your feelings or anything, but I'm not the most trusting person, as you might suspect."

He chuckled. "Yeah, that's kind of evident."

"I prefer to close out my own tab. I ordered the drinks, so I'll pay for them. It is kind of noisy in here to talk so I can meet you somewhere else." I held my index finger up in his face. "*But* I'm not getting in a car with you. Nor are you getting into mine."

I already had it in my head that the only thing that talking could possibly lead to was fucking. I would make "arrangements" with him as I had with two other men at the time to come over and have some "drive-by sex" when the urge hit me. I was attracted to him. He was tall and had big feet, so I was guessing that he had a big dick.

What the hell!

"Fair enough." He threw a twenty on the bar for his beers. "Do you have a place in mind?"

"How about Oya over on Ninth and H?"

"Never heard of it, but I'll meet you there in a few."

He stood up. Yeah, he was a giant, but a fine one. I could not help but drop my eyes to see his dick imprint in his slacks. I suppressed a smile.

"Would you allow me to walk you to your car, Jemistry?"

"No, no thank you. I'll be fine. I'm going

to pay for my drinks and then head that way."

He walked off as he said, "I hope you show."

I watched him leave out and wondered to myself if I would show up. The key to the entire thing would be to make sure I didn't catch any feelings. That was always the hard part: having a big heart, desiring to be loved, and trying to avoid falling too hard for a man, especially a man like him. People always said that you have to judge each person by their own character, but it was not easy to keep tossing my heart on the line all the time. Most men I could brush off without a second thought, but there was something different about this one.

Heaven help me!

CHAPTER TWO

"One day you'll meet someone who
doesn't care about your past because
they want to be with you in your future."
— Anonymous

As I valeted at Oya, I was on my cell with
Winsome. She was freaking out because I
was actually taking a chance.

"I can't believe you didn't tell him to beat
it," she said through my headset. "Normally,
when dudes approach you, you act a fool
and dismiss them before they can get two
words out."

I laughed. "I'm not that bad."

"Jemistry, please. When we're in the store
or whatnot, you throw so much shade
toward anyone who even blinks at you, that
they're too intimidated to speak." She
paused and giggled. "I don't believe it.
You're lying."

"Well, I'm not lying so believe it. I'm actually meeting up with a man. I wanted to alert you to my whereabouts in case something happens."

Winsome laughed from the other end. "You are so damn paranoid. You met him in a public place and you're meeting him in another public place. How do you ever expect to settle down if you think every man is a sociopath?"

"He might be a damn sociopath. Time will tell and it's not like I've never attracted them before. Did you forget about Paul?"

"Paul wasn't a sociopath. Paul was a man whore."

"Same difference."

We both laughed as the valet handed me a ticket.

"So, is he fine?" Winsome asked.

"Have you sucked more than ten dicks in the past year?"

The valet stared at me like I was crazy. It probably made his dick hard, though.

I smiled and kept walking toward the entrance.

"Fuck you, Jemistry."

"I'm about the only person you know that you haven't fucked."

"Bye, heifer!"

Winsome hung up and while my words had been stated jokingly, I really did need to have a talk with her about slowing her roll. Winsome was bisexual, so she was doing the most. She was exceptionally beautiful and that only escalated her ability to get random people into her bed. She was originally from Trinidad but she relocated to the States to attend Howard, which is where we met. She had flawless skin the color of a coconut, dark brown eyes that seemed to stare right through you, and deep dimples that complemented her five-foot-two, petite frame. Men and women were constantly drawn to her like moths to a flame. While I was good at deflecting people, Winsome had this "come hither" look about her.

I enjoyed sex but she loved sex, and my issue was that she always had numerous people trying to get into her panties. We were both single so it was whatever. Yet and still, she was prone to bring strangers to our place and that was when the drama started. Some felt like they could drop by whenever, some never wanted to leave, and others simply looked suspect to me. Like they might jump off the edge of a cliff and go off if things did not go their way. Her business was only my business because we were roommates and I would often walk into some mess, or wake up to some mess, and it was just . . . messy.

Tevin was sitting at the bar near the entrance of Oya. I loved the spot because it had a Miami type of feel in the heart of downtown DC. With all-white leather seats, white tables, and white-and-gray-marble floors and walls, the atmosphere was intimate and relaxing.

"You showed!" Tevin exclaimed. "I didn't ask for a table yet. I didn't want to take a walk of shame if you stood me up."

"Walk of shame?"

"Yes, when a person sits at a table looking crazy and staring at the door to the point where people at other tables start watching the door to see if the person is going to be stood up or not. Then they have to try to make an uncomfortable exit while people snicker at them under their breath."

"That actually makes sense. Walk of shame. I have to remember that one." I giggled and looked into his eyes. Damn shame, he was so sexy. "I'll be honest. I had a little debate with myself about coming, but you seem harmless . . . so far."

He shrugged. "The best thing about having a debate with yourself is that you always win."

We both laughed.

"That's true," I said.

An uncomfortable silence fell between us for a few seconds.

Then, he said, "Once you get to know me, I hope you come to a final conclusion on whether I'm harmless or not. We just met and I don't even know anything about you . . . except that you're fine and extremely cautious about my fellow brethren. I have no reason to mislead you."

"No one else had a reason to mislead me either."

Tevin frowned. "Listen, Jemistry. I love your name, I love your vibe, and I want a fair chance to get to know you. But if all of the drama from your past is about to take a seat at the table with us, I'd rather call it a night now."

He was right. I was taking it too far.

"I apologize. You have a point, Tevin. I can't promise that I'll never mention another word about my past. It's a part of who I am. I'm not sure how we can truly learn about one another without discussing some elements from both of our pasts. That is what has shaped us into the two people standing here in this moment. However, I'll try to keep my bitterness about days gone by in check."

31

Tevin stared at me for a few seconds, like he was having his own internal debate. Like he said, he was going to win either way.

He finally said, "I agree. All I'm saying is that if you're going to automatically disqualify me because of what I have hanging between my legs, it's pointless."

When he mentioned what he had between his legs, my pussy thumped. Currently, I was going back and forth between two lovers, but it was all about sex. Nothing more, nothing less. I was about to interview Tevin to see if he could be the third person in my rotation, but he didn't need to know all of that.

I held up my index and middle fingers. "I, Jemistry Daniels, do solemnly swear that I will not unjustly discriminate against Tevin Harris for the simple fact that he is a man."

Finally, I got a bona fide laugh out of him. "Cool beans. Let's grab a table."

CHAPTER THREE

"The only abnormality is the
incapacity to love."
— Anaïs Nin

I pulled into the building garage for the
condo that Winsome and I shared on Six-
teenth Street in Adams Morgan about two
AM. Getting to know Tevin had been an
enlightening experience. Turns out that he
was a vascular surgeon at Sibley Memorial,
which made him smart as shit. I was about
to be in serious trouble because I loved an
ambitious and smart man, not to mention
smooth, which he definitely was.

We had shared a late dinner and amazing
conversation. Gazing into his eyes over the
candlelight and being serenaded by his
deep, sensual voice was too much for me.
Even the way that he ate sushi turned me
on.

I sat in my 2011 Nissan Rogue for a moment and digested it all.

"This is how it always begins," I said aloud. "You fall for a man too soon and then the proverbial shit hits the fan."

I had agreed to see Tevin again, but did not commit to a specific day or time. I told him to call me the next day at work. I could not believe that I had stayed out so late on a Wednesday when I had to be in my office by eight. Being a high school principal was not an easy feat, but it was a rewarding one. Teens had a bad rap overall; most of my students were simply trying to get an education amidst the pandemonium created by the five percent of students who had been failed by their parents and believed that making a spectacle of themselves would be their claim to fame. I was not having it, not at Medgar Evers High School.

Tevin said that he was thirty-four, and I was thirty-seven. Not a big deal, but I preferred to date men at least my age or older. Then again, I didn't want to actually date him. I only wanted to fuck him, so it didn't matter. As long as I kept repeating those intentions to myself, I would be fine.

When I walked into the front door of our condo, I couldn't believe my eyes. Then again, I shouldn't have been the least bit astonished by anything Winsome did. After all, she worked as a fake-review writer from home. Yes, it was actually a paid position. Companies such as hotels, restaurants, and retail chains paid her to post positive comments on all the major review websites like Yelp, TripAdvisor, and Zagat. She made her own schedule and only had to send in a weekly list of all the reviews that she had posted in order to get paid. That was one of the reasons why I never paid attention to reviews — at least not the positive ones. A lot of those were fabricated. I was sure that Winsome was not the only one working those sites on the regular. The sites were not at fault since they were simply offering consumers the opportunity to vent about their experiences and to make recommendations.

I was planning to kick off my shoes, sit on the sofa, and watch the latest episode of *Paternity Court* on the DVR after I'd tossed my purse and keys on the small table in the foyer and walked into the living room. When I first heard that they were making a show with that title, I talked major shit. It was mind-boggling to me that the paternity of so many children could be in question that it warranted an entire show on the topic. *Maury* already covered that topic about three days a week on the regular. But the thing that fascinated me the most about *Paternity Court* was Judge Lauren Lake's hair. It was always flawless. Half the time I could not even concentrate on the cases since I was staring at her hair. I kept meaning to ask my stylist if she thought it was her real hair, a wig, or a weave. Whatever it was, it was banging, and it made me want to step up my game.

As much as I proclaimed that I would never watch a show like that, I was all into it. I would often get emotional over some of the guests and when they showed the little kids playing in the toy area on the screen, I would want to pick them up and embrace them one at a time. Then they had adults who would make an appearance in order to finally discover whom their biological fathers were for once and for all.

Part of my issue with men was that my father had died before I was even born. The one man that I should have been able to count on to love and protect me never even got to meet me. He was a Metropolitan Police officer and he died in a high-speed car chase at the infamous intersection of Minnesota Avenue and Benning Road. My mother was never the same. Well, I can't say if she was the same or not, but that was how everyone else in the family described her.

Never the same. All I know is that she was depressed for my entire childhood, sedated by all kinds of medications, and never loved another man up until she died of breast cancer when she was fifty-two.

I heard the moaning before I saw the action. Then I saw nothing but tits, asses, and one big-ass dick. Winsome was having a threesome with a man and another woman. I had never laid eyes on either one of them before. She was in the middle and enjoying her own little slice of heaven, lying on her back as the man fed her his dick and the woman ate out her pussy.

I kicked off one of my black boots and threw it at Winsome's tits. "What the fuck are you doing? I can't freaking believe this!"

The chick stopped eating her out immediately and looked petrified. I was betting she thought that I was Winsome's woman coming home, catching her in the act. That exact scenario had happened before and I had to make it clear that I had zero interest in Winsome's coochie. I simply didn't care to see it under any circumstances. The man could not have cared less and probably thought that after a few seconds of bitching, I would want to join in since his dick was so big. Nope. Wasn't hap-

37

pening. He was still trying to shove more of his mandingaling down her throat, trying to get his.

Winsome pushed his dick away from her and sat up. "Damn, Jemistry! Why you throwing boots and all of that? It's not that serious!"

"Not that serious?" I rolled my eyes. "It's two in the damn morning and you have strangers up in here fucking you on the sofa that I bought. The one that I sit on to eat my oatmeal every morning and watch my favorite shows on at night. The one that my company sits on to chill. You got musty dick and pussy juice drizzling all over it and you don't think it's serious?"

Winsome stood up, tits swinging. "First of all, they're —"

"Don't first of all me like I've done something trifling. I spoke to you a few hours ago and you said that you were here chilling and working." I looked the guy in the eyes and then the broad. "You a call girl now? Did they find you on Craigslist or some shit?"

"No, I'm not no call girl and you know it. All I was *trying* to say is that they're not strangers. I've known them for a minute." She ran her fingers through the woman's reddish-brown hair. "This is Kay Kay."

"What's up?" Kay Kay said nervously, still probably shocked that I walked in.

Winsome ran the fingers of her other hand down the man's chest. "And this fine thing right here is Dominic."

Dominic stared at me, up and down, and licked his lips. "What's good, cutie?"

Winsome folded her arms in defiance. "See, they're definitely not strangers."

"The fact that you happen to know their names doesn't mean that they're not strangers. Put on some damn clothes and get them out of here." I walked past the sofa toward my bedroom and waved them off. "You can miss me with all of that." I paused and turned around, glaring at Winsome. "On the sofa, though? You're buying a new one. I'm never sitting on that shit again!"

I went into my room and slammed the door.

After undressing, I went into my bathroom and hopped into the shower. By the time that I threw on a nightgown, Winsome was poking her head in my door.

"How did the date go with that dude?"

I rolled my eyes at her. "His name is Tevin. He's cool. I plan to hang out with him again sometime."

"Thank goodness! You need a man!" Winsome came in and sat down on the edge of my bed. She had on a black T-shirt that had BEAT ME, WHIP ME, FUCK ME, CUM ALL OVER MY TITS, AND THEN GET THE FUCK OUT printed in white letters on the front, and a pair of white sweatpants. "I'm tired of you disrupting my flow!"

"Winsome, you're a trip. I'm not disrupting a damn thing that doesn't need to be disrupted. You are sexing way too many people at the same time. And from what I saw tonight, with no damn protection."

"Oh, come off it. We were doing oral when you came in. You *will not* make me believe that you use dental dams and condoms when you're serving up your pussy or slobbering on a dick. Don't even try it."

"I'm not going to try, but the difference between you and me is that I only have sex with a couple of people." I paused and started analyzing what she had said a moment ago. "And I could have a man *if* I wanted one, and you know it. I'm sick of the bullshit, so I'd rather stay single and do me. Relieve my sexual tension when I feel like it and keep it moving."

"You push men away the second they start talking about getting serious. There are a lot of chicas out there who want a man to tie them down and you push them all away."

I climbed underneath my comforter and

turned on the news. I really wanted to go watch *Paternity Court,* but I was serious about that sofa. I was donating it to a nonprofit and making Winsome purchase a new one, but not before I laid down some ground rules.

"You can't be fucking all over the place, Winsome. That's not cool. You're getting a new sofa and you'd better not have done anything on the dining room table."

She sucked her teeth. "I'm not that damn nasty!"

"At this point, I wouldn't put anything past you." It suddenly hit me. "You've never fucked someone in my bed while I'm at work, have you?"

"No, don't nobody want to fuck in your scraggly little queen-size bed when I have a California King. As much as you play in your pussy, ain't nobody got time for that."

I laughed, picked up a pillow, and threw it at her head. I did have quite the toy collection to knock the edge off. "Get out of my room. I have to be at work in five hours."

She got up and headed out. "What did you think about Dominic and Kay Kay?"

I shrugged as I reached for my lamp switch to cut it off. "What is there to think? You were just doing them, right? Or are you contemplating doing some kind of polyamorous nonsense?"

"I don't even know what the fuck that is," Winsome responded sarcastically.

"The Devil is a liar. You know exactly what it is."

She grinned. "We were just doing it. They're actually siblings, though."

I stopped worrying about the lamp switch. "Siblings? That's disgusting."

"It wasn't disgusting for me, and it's not like they did anything together."

"Didn't they?"

"No, they did not. You didn't see no shit like that going down. Both of them were doing me, but that's it."

I glared at Winsome like she was crazy. "You need to chill before you end up with some incurable disease and come crying on my shoulder."

"Get some sleep. I'll holler."

Winsome closed the door and as I was reaching for the lamp switch again, I noticed a text message that must have come in during my shower. It was from Tevin.

JUST CHECKIN ON U TO MAKE SURE U GOT HOME

Damn, even surgeons are using text shorthand, I said to myself.

42

But it did make me blush and that was a feeling that was both unexpected and unwelcomed. There was no way that I was trying to catch feelings for him, but it was going to be a challenge unless I refused to ever see him again.

I opted not to respond to the text, cut off the light, and laid there in the dark struggling to fall asleep. I got maybe two hours total before I had to get up and head to school.

Chapter Four

"The giving of love is an
education in itself."
— Eleanor Roosevelt

"All students, please report to your home-rooms immediately."

Lilibeth Parker was the school secretary. I am not sure why she felt the need to make that announcement every school day. There was not a single student in the entire high school that didn't realize their asses needed to be in their respective homerooms by eight thirty-five AM or they'd be considered tardy.

"Lilibeth, did we ever get those test scores in?"

"No, not yet, Ms. Daniels. Do you want me to call the school board and check on them?"

I stood beside her desk, considering how I wanted to respond. "No, that's okay. Hopefully, they'll arrive by this afternoon. I'll be

44

in my office if you need me."

"Gotcha."

I went into my office, closed the door, sat down at my desk, and waited to see if any drama would start so early in the morning. I had instilled fear in the majority of my students by implementing a zero-bullshit tolerance policy and making examples out of people who tried to come for me before I came for them. I was among the youngest of principals in the DC Public Schools system and I was determined not to fail in the position that I had held for the past three years. That was why I was concerned about seeing the test scores; I didn't want to appear to be in an all-out panic, though.

The federal No Child Left Behind Act had forced the DC Public Schools to comply with Adequate Yearly Progress (AYP) rules or face major consequences. A lot of the schools failed miserably on a yearly basis. We had failed the first year that I was here, but I turned it around by threatening to put foot to ass with any of my teachers whom I felt had funky attitudes. I did not literally kick them, but I made it clear that heads would roll if they did not start assessing the students who were struggling and offer them additional assistance. I did not care when they did it — before school, during

45

recess, or after school — but if they truly cared, it should not have been a big deal. Teachers customarily have a shorter work-day than most and get summers off so it was what it was.

I was about to eat my vanilla crumb muffin and drink the coffee that I had purchased at a local organic market on my way to work when my cell phone rang. It was Tevin. This was going to be a test to gauge how he received being neglected via text messages. Honestly, he was about to get a piece of my mind.

I smirked and answered the phone. "Good morning."

"Good morning, Jemistry. It's Tevin."

I acted as if his number wasn't already saved in my phone, rather less already embedded in my memory. "Oh, hey. I didn't recognize the number. How are you?"

"I'm fine. I take it that you arrived home safely last night. I sent you a text."

"Wow, did you? I didn't see it. I'm not too hype on texting. It seems kind of detached and impersonal to me."

He got quiet for a few seconds. "I see. Well, I wasn't sure if I should call you that late. I didn't want to risk waking you up."

"Then your plan worked because I was sleeping like a baby." I took a sip of my coffee. "But in theory, the chime from the text message could have woken me up as well." My tone reeked of sarcasm. "I'm just saying."

"True. Anyway, I'll keep in mind that you are not a fan of text messages."

"Let me ask you a question, Tevin. Before there was text messaging, how did you communicate with people who were not right in front of you? How did you let them know you were thinking about them? That they were special to you?"

"Well, I would call them like I'm doing right now."

I played with my muffin, which looked and smelled delicious, but I didn't dare put even a morsel in my mouth. I didn't feel like we were at the point where I wanted to be eating on the phone while we spoke. That was kind of a trifling habit, but with my schedule, it was not unusual for me to engage in it.

"That's how I would communicate," he continued. "As for letting a person know that I am thinking about them, I would probably send them flowers with a card letting them know my sentiments."

"I like flowers, so maybe I'll receive some one day."

"Maybe you will."

Both of us got quiet, as though we were searching the caverns of our minds to come up with a topic. We had spoken for hours the night before, so it was quite awkward.

"I'd better go check and make sure the hallways are empty, except for security guards. Some of my students will do the most when they think they can get away with it."

"You have a lot of students play hooky?"

I giggled. "Yeah, there are some usual suspects. Most will straighten up once I alert their parents and they get in trouble. The ones with parents who don't care are a different issue."

Lilibeth was knocking on my door.

"Come in!" I winced when I realized that I had screamed in Tevin's ear. "Sorry for yelling."

"It's cool. I'll let you go so you can go hold down the fort. I have some patient files to look over. My first surgery isn't until around noon."

"Sounds good." I gasped when Lilibeth entered with a bouquet comprised of a few dozen roses and several clusters of baby's breath. "Oh my goodness!"

"What happened? Is everything okay?" Tevin asked from the other end of the line.

I snickered and grinned from ear to ear.

"My secretary just entered with a beautiful bouquet of flowers. Thank you."

Lilibeth set the vase down on my desk and handed me the card that was attached to a plastic stick.

"You're assuming they're from me?" he asked. "They could be from one of your other admirers."

"Oh, I'm sure they're from you." I blushed, even though he couldn't see my face. "That was very sweet of you."

"So am I forgiven about the texting?"

"Yes, you're forgiven."

Lilibeth smiled and left out as I opened the card. It read:

Jemistry,
I realize that we just met but I want to be "the example" of what a man should be instead of "another example" of what a man should never be. You are beautiful, smart, and entertaining and I hope to see you again.

xoxoxo
Tevin

"These are wonderful. Thank you," I repeated.

"Well?"

"Well what?"

"Can I see you again?"

I could tell that he was somewhere between anxious and nervous about my reply.

"Um, sure. I told you last night that we could hang out again."

"I don't want to *hang* with you. I want to court you. There is a difference."

I sat there in silence for a moment. "Tevin, I agree that there's a definite chemistry between us, but I don't necessarily think that I'm relationship material right now. Do you not remember my poem from last night?"

"Yes, I remember your poem. I also remember the painful expression on your face as you recited it. I want to be the one to change that expression to something more exhilarating, more gratified, and more surreal." He paused. "And while I definitely agree that there is chemistry, I see more than that. I see a possibility."

Dammit, this man is about to take my breath away! I thought to myself. Then that thought was immediately followed by fear . . . the fear of being hurt again. Tevin's word game was tight, but I had been hoodwinked by the crème de la crème of slick talkers before.

When I didn't say anything, he added, "But we can take things slow. How about dinner tonight?"

I couldn't help but laugh. "That's what you call taking it slow?"

"That's what I call breaking bread together and continuing to get to know each other. You can pick the spot."

"No, you pick it this time," I insisted. "Your choice of restaurant will tell me something about you."

"Hmm, the only thing that it might tell you is that I like good food. How about The Oceanaire Seafood Room on F and Twelfth Streets about seven-thirty? Ever been there?"

"Not yet, but I've heard nothing but great things about it. Count me in."

For the rest of the school day, I felt like I was hiking on air. There was something about the man that turned me on. However, I didn't want to risk actually falling for him so I did the one thing that any confused woman attempting to avoid falling in love would do: I went over to Anthony's place after work and fucked the shit out of him.

CHAPTER FIVE

"You never lose by loving. You always
lose by holding back."
— Barbara De Angelis

"Where have you been?" Anthony asked the second he opened the front door to his house.

"I don't have to report to you." I entered, kicked off my brown leather pumps, and let my tan suit jacket fall to the floor. "We're friends with benefits, remember?"

As I walked straight upstairs to his bedroom, he shut the door and followed me. "I understand all that. Friends with benefits, cuddle buddies, whatever. But does that mean we can't socialize outside of my bedroom?"

"What the hell do you want to socialize for, Anthony?" I stood in front of his bed and started removing all of my clothing. "We start socializing and you might catch feelings, or I might catch feelings, and then that fucks up the entire arrangement."

He crossed his arms in rebelliousness, but as soon as I took my bra and panties off, his eyes were glued to my body.

"I don't like the term *arrangement*. You make it sound like I'm a male escort or something."

"The only thing that I want you to escort me to is a hellified climax so I can hop in the shower and keep my dinner appointment."

"Appointment or date?" he asked vehemently.

I smacked my lips and didn't bother to respond.

Anthony was about five-nine, much shorter than Tevin, had a few extra pounds on the belly, light-skinned with a bald head, and a gorgeous smile. We had met about a year before in the produce section of Shoppers Food Warehouse. Before I actually picked up a man in a grocery store, I always believed that it being a hot spot was nothing more than an urban legend, or a marketing ploy for certain major chains. But there he was, grinning at me as I selected some limes to make a homemade key lime pie.

I had made it clear to him from the beginning that I was not interested in dating him.

But we did hang out — movies, dinner, walks in the park — until it came time for me to cut the bullshit and confiscate the dick. I made sure that we were both tested for every STD known to man before we actually did anything. He bitched about it at first, but when I informed him that getting tested meant the possibility of one day fucking me and not getting tested meant that he might as well lose my number, he got the tests done.

"Are you going to stand over there staring at me, or are you going to come over here and commence to fucking?" I asked and then turned around, making a show of exposing my entire caramel ass as I climbed on top of his bed. "I love the way that you hit all of this from the back. My pussy is in distress. Please . . . put it out of its misery."

I could hear him approaching behind me, removing his wife beater and shorts along the way. "This is the last time I'm doing this, Jemistry."

"That's what you said the last time, and the time before that, and the time before that." I turned over, lay on my back, spread my legs, and started playing in my pussy with my fingers. "See how juicy Abigail is?"

Anthony laughed. "You and your dumb-ass nicknames for your pussy. Every time you come through, you name her something different. Who the fuck is Abigail?"

"Abigail Adams, wife of the second president of the United States, John Adams. Mother of John Quincy Adams, the sixth president of the United States. Mother of six, and if I want to call my cooter Abigail, then you need to shut the fuck up about it."

"You're so mean, but you're smart. I love your bedroom trivia facts." Anthony climbed on top of me, butt-ass naked, and started sucking on my breasts. "And I love these."

I glanced at the alarm clock on his nightstand. It was already five.

"Where are the condoms?" I asked. "That's enough foreplay."

Anthony sat up on his elbow and stared at me. "Listen, this is getting kind of old for me."

I gazed into his eyes and then down at his rock-hard, eight-inch dick with a five-inch circumference. Yeah, I had measured that billy with a tape measure before. "Doesn't look like Marcus Junius Brutus is getting tired of fucking me."

Anthony couldn't help but chuckle. "I'm not even going to ask."

"Marcus Junius Brutus? The Roman politician and traitor who conspired to kill Julius Caesar and then later committed

55

suicide." I grabbed hold of his dick and started giving him a hand job. Pre-cum was already leaking from the head. "Yes, your dick has betrayed you. You may want to holler at him about that after I leave for dinner."

"Do you have a dinner appointment or a dinner date?"

Oh, hell to the no! You're going to question me?

"Since you feel the need to keep asking the same irrelevant question, I'll simply say that it's the same thing."

"No, it is not the same thing. I'll bet you have a date. You want to fuck me but date someone else? That's some crazy-ass shit. I've always been good to you, Jemistry. At least I've tried. You're the one who insisted on making this all about fucking."

I sighed. "Anthony, not to offend, but you're beginning to sound like a side chick. You need to stay in your lane and continue to accept the role you signed up for. We agreed to be fuck buddies. So when I'm horny, I come over here to fuck you."

He sighed like he was mad, but the Negro was fingering my pussy at the same time. He was weak for my snapper and he understood it.

"I don't disrespect you, or come over here

56

unannounced," I continued. "I already told you. When and if you meet a woman you want to commit to, simply tell me, and it's over. I'll go cold turkey off your dick. Now do you want me to leave or are you going to break out the condoms so we can have a party?"

Anthony got a condom out of his night-stand and ripped it open with his teeth. I put it on with my mouth and sucked him off for a few moments. Winsome was wrong. I did suck dick with condoms but she was right about the dental dam thing. There was no way that I was serving up pussy through plastic.

I sucked on him until he was about to explode in the condom and then stopped. "Lie down on the bed," I ordered.

"I thought you wanted me to hit it from the back," he said.

"Just do what the fuck I say!"

He laughed. "Look at you, trying to go gangster."

"I am gangster." I pushed him down on the bed. "You're moving too damn slow."

"What you gonna do? Ride this dick?"

"Yeah, I'm going to ride it until you bust wide open like my little bitch. Now spread your fucking legs."

Anthony looked shocked. "Spread my legs?"

"Just do it!"

I picked up his left leg and tossed it to the side. Then I climbed on top of him, put my left leg between his legs behind me and placed my right leg on the outside of his right arm with my foot up by his head. Then I went to town on the dick and got my workout on at the same time.

Anthony started panting, gasping, and sweating.

"You like this pussy?" I asked. "Tell me how much you *love* this pussy!"

"Oh, yeah. I love it," he managed to get out between trying to navigate my hips up and down and lift his bottom half to pound up into me. "You love this dick?"

I didn't respond, fucking with his ego.

"You love this dick?" he asked again.

"Hmm, it's mediocre," I finally said. "You're still a rookie in training, but you're improving."

He laughed. "I'm going to put you over my knee and spank you after I get this nut out."

"You'd better not bust too quick or that's your ass!"

"You talk more shit than —"

Anthony couldn't even get the remainder

of his sentence out because I started grinding and pounding harder on his dick at the same time while I dug my nails into his chest. I caught my rhythm and he completely lost it then.

"I talk shit because I can back my shit up," I said, starting to lose my senses as well as I tightened my pussy around his dick and squeezed.

People always ask what the benefit of dildos is over vibrators. It is not about the fact that vibrators work on batteries and do most of the work. It is about the fact that dildos are more lifelike, and make the people using them learn how to do most of the work. Most chicks never figure that shit out and that's why they lie there and wait for the men to bang them out instead of truly knowing how to blow some minds.

I tightened up on Anthony's dick even more. "Yeah, boy, this is how a pro rides a damn dick. You like that? You feeling me?"

Anthony couldn't even speak at that point. I could feel his body convulsing and knew the bastard was about to come too damn fast. I hopped off his dick and sat beside him on the bed. He looked to the side and glared at me, then down at his dick. "What the fuck are you doing?"

"You're not pulling that three-minute shit

with me. I'm waiting for you to calm down a bit and then I *might* let you have some more of Abigail's brown pudding."

Anthony sighed and started playing with his dick. "Jemistry, you're a cold piece of work. How you gonna stop fucking me right before I nut? And it wasn't no three damn minutes either."

It really wasn't even about Anthony and his sexual skills. For some ridiculous reason, I was sitting there, naked and covered with his sweat, feeling guilty over the fact that Tevin probably was in an operating room at the moment, saving someone's life, while I was continuing to fuck mine up by screwing a man that I didn't even want to have a decent conversation with.

"Jemistry?" Anthony was getting angry. "Jemistry, are you for real?"

He was right. I was being shiesty, shitty, and straight-up stank.

I climbed over him, stacked two of his pillows, and laid over them, positioning my ass up in the air. "Come get this."

Anthony didn't hesitate as he grabbed the sides of my hips, maneuvered his dick into me, and went about his business.

It was crazy. I had it all figured out. I was going to be a stone-faced, heartless, bitter woman for the rest of my life, fuck a couple of men when I felt like it, who could be trusted not to be throwing their dicks all over the city every night, and concentrate on my career. Now Tevin had entered my world and was about to throw a monkey wrench into all of my plans.

Anthony grabbed my ass cheeks and started slapping the right one. He was saying some dirty shit, but I drowned it all out. All I could see was Tevin's face, remember his words from the night before and earlier that day, and wonder to myself, *Could he be for real?*

CHAPTER SIX

"A man is already halfway in love with
any woman who listens to him."
— Brendan Francis

When I arrived at Oceanaire, Tevin was
already waiting for me in a booth. My pussy
had served as a sleeping pill for Anthony so
I left him knocked out on the bed. After I
took a shower and redressed, I laid two
twenties on his pillow as a joke. It would
piss him off when he woke up, but I truly
didn't appreciate how he had come at me,
trying to change the rules in the middle of a
"situationship" that we had both agreed on.
I had been coining my connections with
men as "situationships" for quite some time.
They definitely would not classify as relationships, in the old-fashioned sense.

Tevin stood as I approached. He was so
fine that I felt weak in the knees. He had on
a navy pinstriped suit with a white shirt and

red tie. "Hey, Jemistry. Thanks for coming."

"Thanks for the invite." I gave him a soft hug — his cologne aroused me — and then sat down in the booth.

"I noticed that you are a martini fan, but I thought you might enjoy some wine this evening." He sat back down and placed his napkin across his lap. "I took the liberty of ordering a bottle of Cakebread."

I grinned and put my napkin on my lap. "Not sure what that is but it sounds interesting. Is it wine that tastes like cake?"

"You're a funny woman." He took my hand and my first instinct was to pull it away, but that would have been rude. Holding hands was romantic; I had been avoiding romance like the Bubonic plague. "Cakebread is a Cabernet Sauvignon from the Napa Valley."

"That didn't make it much better. I don't know what a Cabernet Sauvignon is either."

We both laughed.

"You look beautiful today."

Damn, he's saying too many of the right things!

"Thanks. I appreciate that."

He let go of my hand, thank goodness, and then picked up his menu. "While we wait for the wine, do you want to decide on dinner?"

I picked up my menu as well. It was expensive on my salary, but since it was on him, I planned to try out something good. The waiter brought the wine and Tevin sniffed a small amount that was poured into a glass, swirled it around, and then tasted it. "That's fine," he told the waiter who then poured us both glasses.

The waiter set the remainder of the bottle down. "Would you like to order now, sir?"

"Give us a few moments. We're still deciding."

He walked off and I asked, "If I'm not being too nosey, how much does Cakebread cost?"

Tevin shrugged. "About three hundred for the bottle."

I almost leapt out of my seat. "Three hundred for something to sip on!"

He chuckled and pointed at my glass. "Aren't you even going to taste it?"

I took a sip of the wine and I had to admit, "It's amazing!"

"You're amazing!" Tevin gazed into my eyes. "I only hope that you one day realize that . . . or realize that again."

"What do you mean by that?"

"You're so busy trying to construct walls around something so special that needs to be exposed to the world. There is a vulnerability in you that you refuse to set free. You believe that every man is going to use, hurt, or abuse you in some way. Not all men are alike."

"So you keep saying."

"I keep saying it because it's the truth." He paused and drank some more wine. "Jemistry, why do you think that you're not worthy of being loved? Truly loved by a man who desires the same thing as you?"

"My only desire is to live my life, drama- and disease-free. I want to keep working hard, prove myself, and move up to a higher position in the school system. I've only been a principal for a few years, but I truly believe that I can become superintendent one day. If not here in DC, then possibly in one of the local suburbs in Maryland or Virginia. Even if I have to relocate across country to realize my dream, I will. That's another reason why I don't need to be tied down."

"It's not about someone tying you down. It's about someone lifting you up even further than you already are."

"You do realize we met last night, right?" I asked jokingly.

"I go after what I want."

I blushed. "But you don't even know me like that. Tevin, you're a tall, handsome surgeon. I'm quite sure that women fall all over you wherever you go. You have this commanding presence and, even in the brief amount of time since we've met, I've seen how women stare at you." I looked around the room. "Even in here."

"So, that means that I have to entertain them because they look?"

"No, but —"

"Men look at you as well. I looked at you when you were on that stage last night pouring out all your emotions. You want to be loved, Jemistry, and I want to be loved. We both want the same thing, so I say that we mark that as our goal and make a road map to get there."

This man has rendered me speechless!

I cleared my throat, drank some wine, and concentrated on the menu. He was determined to turn this into some kind of fairy tale and I was going to fight it tooth and nail. I realized that nothing was holding me there and I could have gotten up and walked out. But there was no way that I could do something mean like that to a man who had shown me nothing but attention and kindness thus far.

It's only a matter of time before he fucks up and gives me an excuse to stop speaking to him!

Dinner was fantastic! I had the fried red chili calamari as an appetizer and the stuffed shrimp with pasta as my entrée. Tevin had the jumbo lump crab cake for an appetizer and the Greek branzino for his main meal. That wine was all up in my head so I passed on the chocolate chip cheesecake, even though it looked delicious.

The conversation had remained deep, but interesting. Tevin opened up to me about his past relationships. He had been married before, but everything fell apart when his wife had her third miscarriage. He said the pain had become too much for both of them; she had shut down emotionally and it eventually led to a divorce. When he said that, I was wondering why he would want to become involved with another woman who was already emotionally shut down . . . me.

They had attempted counseling; he had taken her on a series of Caribbean vacations to try to get the spark back, but nothing had worked. One thing that I could ascertain clearly was that he had loved her with all his heart. That made me jealous and I could not help but wonder if I could ever replace her. Then again, I should not have even been contemplating all of that. I was going to refuse to fall for him.

"Thanks again for dinner," I said as Tevin walked me to my SUV. I had lucked out and found a space a couple of blocks away. They offered valet parking, but if I could ever find a space in DC, I grabbed it.

"You're very welcome." He came up behind me and put his hands on my shoulders. "When can I see you again?"

I hit the key fob to unlock the doors, then turned to look up at him. "I'm going to be busy for the next couple of days. Can I give you a call?"

His eyebrows scrunched up. "Are you really going to call me?"

"Yes, I am." I had no idea whether I was lying or not. "You're a great guy so we can hang out again."

"I told you before. I'm not trying to hang out with you. I'm trying to fall in love with you."

I laughed uncomfortably. "You are something else."

"Give me a hug."

I embraced him and scared myself because I hugged his waist tighter than I had hugged anyone in years, even the men that I had been fucking. His chest was like an iron vest and I could feel his dick against my midriff. Even soft, I could tell he was packing a big gun.

He kissed the top of my head. "You smell so good."

"So do you," I replied, telling nothing but the truth.

Then he went and did it. He gave me a French kiss that I felt from my scalp to the tips of my toes. Kissing was too personal. Sucking dick was an act. Kissing meant a true connection. His thick tongue explored my mouth and I explored back.

Our kiss lasted a good two minutes and then Tevin sucked on my bottom lip and I felt it in my pussy. A lot of people don't realize that sucking on a woman's bottom lip can cause that reaction. It's something about pressure points and there is some kind of anatomical correlation.

"I have to go." I pulled away from him and climbed into the driver's seat. "I'll text you to let you know that I got home okay."

He placed his hand over his heart, feigning a heart attack. "Did you just say that you're going to text me?"

I couldn't admit that I was too scared to talk to him any more that night. The last thing that I needed was to end up lying in my bed having some kind of whimsical conversation into the morning. It would lead to me fantasizing about him, masturbating thinking about him, and that would be the beginning of the end. That was how it always went in the past. I would get caught up, start believing the hype, fall in love, and then get dogged out by various breeds of men.

"It will be a quick text saying that I got there."

I was about to close my door when he held it open. "One last question."

"Sure."

"I'll be honest enough to admit that I was last intimate with a woman a few months ago. It was nothing serious and I couldn't see it progressing to anything real, so I stopped seeing her."

"You don't have to ex—"

"No, I want to be honest. I don't want you to get the wrong impression. I'm a busy man so I'm not out here picking up random women and trying to get them into bed. When I was younger, sure, I thought a lot with my dick, but that's not where I am now. I don't want another girlfriend. I can get another girlfriend anyplace. I want something that lasts."

"Well, at least you know what you want."

"Yeah, there are too many diseases and

too much foolishness out there, especially in DC since there is a shortage of available men. I'm not trying to get caught up in that funnel cloud." He paused and stared at me. "So when was the last time you were intimate with a man?"

About three hours ago!

I definitely couldn't tell him the truth. The man had dropped nearly five hundred dollars on dinner and was telling me how he considered me to be wifey material.

"It's been awhile, and I'm definitely not seeing anyone else."

"Good. Good. Then that gives me a fair chance to get to know you without competing for your time and attention."

He leaned in and kissed me on the cheek. "I'll be waiting for your text."

He winked as he closed the door. He stood there and waited for me to pull away before he started walking back up the block.

I drove home in silence. No radio on. I was sure that if Winsome were doing the do, she would either be in her bedroom or someplace else. The next morning, I was going to look online for sofas that I liked and that she could afford. I planned to be chilling out in the living room watching my favorite shows on my DVR within the next few days.

CHAPTER SEVEN

"Trust is such a huge word. It either
makes something or destroys it."
— Unknown

A few weeks passed and I was still torn and
confused, and sounding like one of those
insecure women with low self-esteem who
write in to advice columns to figure out
something that is common sense. Tevin still
had not given me any reason to distrust
him, and believe me, I was searching for
one. He seemed like a perfect man and we
all know that true perfection does not exist.
Everyone has flaws, dammit. Where were
his?

We had been on several dates, and no, he
didn't force me to go. Every time I considered sending his calls to voice mail or blocking him altogether, I couldn't justify it. Plus,
I really did think that he was thebomb.com.
What I appreciated about him was that once

I had said something about text messaging, he had made it a point to show me attention either in person or via phone. He had never asked me for my email address or asked to connect with me on a social network. In an age when so many people communicate virally, it was a welcomed change.

I had Facebook and Twitter accounts, but I rarely posted anything at all. I was not about to risk my livelihood over posting some foolishness online. Several teachers and principals had failed to recognize that and were fired. They should have been the main ones avoiding doing it, considering that students were getting suspended or expelled for cyberbullying daily. Added to that tragedy was the fact that many of my seniors over the years had lost full-ride scholarships over trying to pretend to be baby gangsters on their pages. Posting themselves smoking weed, holding guns, or even talking crazy and making idle threats had cost many of them their futures. Some of them came from very good homes and their parents — single or married — had struggled to provide them with a stable environment, had attended every PTA meeting and parent-teacher conference, had made sure they completed their homework and that they were attending school. It was truly sad to have to explain to them that all of it was for nothing. That they would have to send their kids to community college instead of driving them to a major university that had previously offered them close to two hundred grand in scholarship money.

So no, hell no, I was not about to get caught up like that. Especially since I was so opinionated, like all Virgos. I could envision how it all would have gone down. I would have run across something that pissed me off in my newsfeed and ended up in a debate. The only reason I had the accounts was to go on and attempt to prevent some of my staff and students from going too far. I would often pull kids into my office and tell them to take things down before they ruined all of their opportunities. I also had my four guidance counselors constantly on the prowl.

The Internet was a powerful tool for gaining knowledge, following world news, and cutting down on having to fax and send important things via snail mail, but it was also a curse for many who could not control themselves and wanted to capture their fifteen minutes of fame. That was proven by the fact that the African-American site with the most web traffic at the time was World-StarHipHop where people sent in videos of people acting a fool, and millions of people watched them daily. A lot of them ended up facing charges and jail time behind those videos, especially the parents who taped themselves whipping their children with belts or electrical cords because they had been twerking on YouTube. Instead of punishing them in a responsible way in private, they decided to post a retaliation video of them practically maiming their own offspring to prove a point. Many of them were now proving that point on lockdown while their kids were still twerking and doing them, but with the added malice toward their parents.

There was always drama at Medgar Evers High School. On this particular day, it came in the form of Uniqua Mays, mother of Brian Mays, a junior who had maintained a good GPA all throughout school and was looking forward to applying to Morehouse College in Atlanta in the fall of his senior year.

"Ms. Mays, how can I help you today?" I asked as she sat across from me in an outfit that looked like she had just finished working the pole at The Stadium Club off New York Avenue. "Mrs. Parker said you have some concerns about Brian." I scanned through his school records. "His midterm report card has him making honor roll yet again."

"You damn right my boo is making honor roll!"

I wasn't going to have a lot of patience with her. She already had a fucked-up attitude; she was glaring at me like she wanted to jump me, and I was not that chick. I wanted to ask her what kind of mother calls her son her "boo," but it was a waste of time. Unfortunately, a lot of single mothers acted like their sons were their men instead of their children. All of that led to them trying to run young women away from them, fearing them fleeing the nest, and leaving them abandoned. The sons either ignored them altogether or allowed the mothers to completely emasculate them. Brian planned to get the hell away from her and now I could see why.

"So, what seems to be the problem then?" I asked, trying to maintain some composure.

"I want him moved to another math class."

I glanced down at Brian's records again. "He currently has an A in AP Algebra. Mr. Adkins is one of our best instructors and Brian seems to be —"

"Mr. Adkins is a fag and ain't no fag going to be teaching my son." She sat up on the edge of the chair and grasped her fake designer handbag tighter. "Men like him should not be allowed around young boys."

Oh yes, I'm about to be tested today!

"Ms. Mays, I would appreciate it if you would not use such a nasty and disrespectful term like *fag* around me. That is very hurtful and inappropriate."

"What the fuck ever! Is *homosexual* better?"

I could feel my blood pressure rising. "Yes, that is better, but your delivery is still full of implications. But, to address your main point, Mr. Adkins is an excellent teacher and Brian will remain in his class."

"So you just gonna sit back and watch that man molest my son and other people's sons?"

I sighed. "Mr. Adkins has been teaching in DC public schools for more than twenty years and there has never been a single complaint or accusation lodged against him about doing anything inappropriate with a student. You will not come in here and slander his name, nor accuse me of any type of conspiracy to molest children."

"Well, that's exactly what the fuck I am doing, bitch!"

It took every ounce of restraint in me not to get up, walk around my desk, and try to knock her block off.

"You will not address me in that tone." I stood up and walked to the door, then opened it. "You need to leave my office. Not now, but right now."

She stood up and brushed up close to me. "You're the principal. You're supposed to be in charge."

"I *am* in charge and I addressed your concern. Brian is not being moved and I will not have any further discussions with you about Mr. Adkins's sexual preference. It is none of your business and it is none of mine. If you would like to discuss the matter any further, you can contact the school superintendent."

You can go be his fucking problem!

She smacked her gums and rolled her eyes, then sashayed out. I could smell her pussy as the draft from the outer office door hit it. Either she had just crawled up out of some funky dick's bed or she hadn't washed in days. Yet, she was worried about Virgil Adkins who had been in a loving, committed, same-sex relationship for nearly thirty years.

Lilibeth looked on as I stood there fuming. "I considered alerting security for a moment. Glad she's gone."

"She needs to get a life."

Lilibeth giggled.

78

"What's so funny?"

"Nothing. It's just the way that you use the teen terminology sometimes. You know, they get all of that from the Internet and reality shows."

"I'm sure. My life is a reality show, so no time to watch someone else's drama. But listening to a gaggle of kids daily roaming the halls talking like that rubs off on a sister."

She and I shared a laugh.

"Do you think she'll be back?" Lilibeth asked.

"I doubt it. She'll talk junk about me, tell Brian that she's going to go over my head and get me fired, and then drop it once she realizes that she can't run this school. She acts stupid, but she's not dumb. She probably just discovered that Mr. Adkins is with another man and freaked out. She tried me, and failed, and knows her issues won't hold any muster. Still, it's no excuse for her behavior."

"Brian seems like a great kid."

"He is, and he's going to be fine. He's done well in spite of his mother's attitude. I'm sure she means well, and only wants the best for him. But everyone's not cut out for parenting. We both know that from experience."

Lilibeth was nodding in agreement when a deliveryman walked in with another vase of roses for me.

"Hmm, he must really like you," Lilibeth said. "Roses every week. What did you say his name is again?"

I laughed. "I never told you his name." I signed for the flowers. "Since you're dying to know, his name is Tevin Harris. Dr. Tevin Harris."

"Oh, a doctor! What kind?"

"A vascular surgeon."

It felt like I was bragging about a man that I was not prepared to claim. Not a good look.

"When do we all get to meet him?"

"Lilibeth, I am not in a relationship, so there's no reason for you to meet him."

"Why can't he come up here and have lunch with you one day?"

"In the teacher's lounge? Not going to happen." I giggled. "Besides, he's so fine that I would have to beat Ms. Landry and Ms. Jacobs off of him."

"It would make for an interesting afternoon. If I wasn't married, I might have to throw my hat into the ring."

"Yeah, right. Your husband cherishes you. We all know that."

Lilibeth blushed. "He does indeed, and he

brings me lunch twice a week. You should have Dr. Harris do the same."

"A, the man is a surgeon and has no time to bring me lunch, and B, you snatched up a good man when good men still existed. My generation and the generations after us are screwed. Men only want to play a bunch of games."

"Not that I know much about your business, Jemistry, but can I offer you a little motherly advice, being that I am old enough to be your mother?"

I didn't respond, but I'm sure she read the curiosity on my face.

"Don't push a good man away trying to prove a point that you can have a cold heart. We've shared a few things and I understand that you've been hurt in the past, but most women have been. Most men have been as well, truth be told. It doesn't mean you have to become some kind of stone statue for the rest of your life."

"It doesn't mean that I have to become some kind of sacrificial lamb and breakdance into the slaughterhouse either."

"Is that what you really think about love? Taking a chance? Baby Girl, you are an amazing woman and you deserve to be happy. Give it a shot. You cannot win a race until you get in it."

I took the vase of flowers, went into my office, and closed the door as Lilibeth turned back to her computer screen. She had a point and she and I both realized it.

I removed the card and read it:

Jemistry,
I hope your day is going well and that you'll consider going away with me this weekend. I want to spend some time alone in isolation with you. No pressure. Just good conversation and exploring life together. Call me.

Tevin

I read the card at least a dozen more times that afternoon, wavering in my decision to take him up on his offer or refuse. Tevin definitely didn't give off the kind of vibe that he would force me to have sex. In all honesty, I was more worried about being able to control myself. Taking what we were doing to a sexual level meant catching feelings. I would not be able to disconnect myself emotionally like I did with Anthony and Gregory, the other dude that I had been sleeping with on and off for about a year. I had not gone to be with either of them since that last time with Anthony when I started feeling guilty.

What was there to really be afraid of? If I got officially involved with Tevin, and it did not work out, it was not like the entire world would know it. It wasn't like it would end up in a book, or anything ridiculous like that. Outside of Winsome and Lilibeth knowing that Tevin had run a game on me like every man prior to him, no one would have to know.

Up to that point, Tevin and I had only shared kisses. Many, many awesome kisses. One time I even had an orgasm and it scared me. I had never had an orgasm from a kiss, which made me petrified about what he might do to me with his dick.

There was a cold, hard truth staring me in the face that could no longer be ignored: I wanted him.

CHAPTER EIGHT

"True love isn't easy but it must be fought for, because once you find it, it can never be replaced."

— Unknown

Winsome and I were walking out of the Regal Theaters at Gallery Place.

She was shaking her head in disbelief. "If I had known that was what that movie was about, I wouldn't have come."

"I heard that it was going to be sad, but I wasn't quite ready for all that either."

We had gone to see *Fruitvale Station,* based on the true story of Oscar Grant III, a twenty-two-year-old Bay Area resident who was shot and killed by BART police on New Year's Day in 2009.

"That entire cast was amazing," I added. "If that movie isn't nominated for the Academy Awards, something is wrong."

"I haven't cried in a movie since I can

remember. I felt that mother's pain and I'm not even a mother."

"Well, one of us better hurry up and have a baby before our pussies dry up," I said jokingly. "It would be good to have at least one kid around."

"Jemistry, you're around kids day in and day out."

"They're teenagers; not the same thing. Most of them had to grow up so fast that they could damn near hang out with us."

We both laughed.

"I'm not cooking, so want to grab something to eat?" Winsome asked.

"Lazy ass. It's your turn to cook."

"Exactly, and that's why I'm saying that I'm not doing it. You'd better either grab something on the way home, eat that Greek yogurt in the fridge that expired last week, or starve."

I slapped her playfully on the arm. "Let's go pig out somewhere and then go to the gym and ditch the calories."

"Sounds like a plan."

We decided on Five Guys. Cheap, quick, greasy, and fattening. If we were going in, we might as well go in all the way.

We grabbed a table with high stools and started digging in like two hungry three-hundred-pound men.

"I'm starving. I skipped lunch today," I said, trying to make an excuse for gorging myself, even though Winsome was doing the same.

"I had a big-ass lunch, but this food is my guilty pleasure." A sliver of greasy fried onion fell down into the center of her breasts and she ignored it. "This shit is so good."

"Aren't you going to dig that out?"

"Dig what out?"

"That piece of onion that fell between your tits?"

Winsome took a sip of her Coke through a straw. "I'm not digging in my ta-tas in front of all these people."

The place was crowded for a Thursday night, but no one probably would have noticed.

"That's nasty." I handed her a napkin. "Take that out."

"Jemistry, listen, you have your etiquette rules and I have mine. We both have some nice racks and food will topple down there every now and then. I'm not going to draw attention to being clumsy with food by digging shit out in public. I wait until I go to the restroom, get home, or at least get in my car to do all that. If you want to yank your tits apart, clear out your bra, and do maintenance, do you."

I fell out laughing and threw the longest fry that I could find in my collection at her face.

"You're so childish!" she exclaimed.

"No, childish would have been aiming for the cavern between your tits and letting it keep that poor piece of onion company while your nasty ass leaves it down there suffering."

"You are completely shot-out, Jemistry! Shot-out and sprung!"

I took a bite of another fry. "I'm not sprung. You're tripping!"

"I saw Tevin dropping you off the other night. Why didn't you invite him up?"

"Chile boo! Invite him up and have him walk in on you butt-ass naked doing a man, a woman, or both? I don't even think so!"

"You still rubbing that shit up in my face after all this time. You have a new sofa, and I even threw in some new end tables and an entertainment center. Yet you're still flapping your gums."

"That's because the visual is still implanted in my memory! It was traumatic!"

"Chick, please. As much porn as you have watched in your lifetime, that shit was minor. Stop acting all innocent, like you don't get down. You still fucking Anthony *and* Gregory while Tevin is sweating your drawers?"

"Not that it is any of your business since I never fuck in front of you, but no, I am not."

Winsome grabbed at her throat. "You gave up your side dick action for Tevin! Damn, he must be blowing that back out!"

Winsome started moving her hips and ass back and forth on the seat and moving her arms in the air like she was fucking.

"Interesting! You're worried about someone seeing you dig a piece of onion out your tits, but you'll yell out about dick and make fucking motions on a chair up in this mickey."

"Damn!" Winsome reached down in her boobs, took the piece of onion out, and tossed it on the table. "Now I have set the motherfucking onion free. But back to what I was saying. Is the dick good?"

"I haven't a clue. We've only kissed."

Winsome rubbed her hands together and squinted at me.

"What's that look for?" I asked.

"I'm happy for you. It's been a long time since I've seen you like this."

"Like what?"

"Contemplating the possibilities. Treating a man with basic human kindness instead of like a wildebeest. Not drowning all your pent-up emotions in your career and using men for sex in some kind of twisted protect mode."

"Winsome, if that is not the pot calling the kettle black. Who are you to say that about me when you refuse to commit to anyone either?"

"It's different for me. I'm bisexual."

"That's some straight bullshit. You want to sit here and pretend like I don't remember you being in love before. You were crazy about Cynthia and now you want to act like it never happened. At least I'm willing to admit to my fucked-up, toxic relationships."

Winsome finished off the last bite of her burger. "Cynthia was a great gal and, yes, I felt like we had something that could've lasted a lifetime . . . but it didn't even make it to year five. You win some, you lose some."

I laughed. "I hate when you do that with your name. Win some and lose some. Whatever. You loved her and she loved you, and it all ended over trifling behavior that could have been avoided altogether. You like women and you deal with men to try to act like it's not the truth."

"I like men, too. Did you see the way that I was sucking Dominic's dick like it was a slab of baby back ribs?"

I tossed my burger down. "I've lost my appetite. Even though I've seen a lot of people having sex, I'm not trying to see you having sex. You're my friend, my best friend, and I could have done without all that."

"Stop acting like I molested you or something." Winsome ran her hands through her shoulder-length locs. "Okay, I will admit that I prefer women, but you're wrong if you think that I'm not into men. The issue is that most lesbians avoid sisters who are bisexual because they assume we'll cheat. But if I ever do commit to someone again, male or female, I won't be stepping out like that."

"I realize that. You're not the type. We both have been disconnecting emotionally from our lovers in an effort to prevent being hurt. I'm a work in progress and I had an epiphany earlier today to that effect."

"What epiphany?"

"Tevin asked me to go away with him this weekend."

"And?"

"And I'm considering it."

"Since it's Thursday night, I'm assuming you need to stop *considering* it and make a decision."

"If I have sex with him, I might fuck around and fall in love with him. I've been doing so good at disconnecting my emotions from sex, but this is different. He's different."

"That's a profound-ass statement coming from you." She paused and stared at me. "What would be so wrong with that? You deserve love. We both deserve love, and you got one thing right. We both have to stop trying to orchestrate our own inevitable fate. Neither one of us is getting any younger. Shit, we're practically middle-aged. AARP is right around the corner."

We both giggled.

"If either one of us is going to have kids, we have to start making moves, exploring options, and most importantly, let our defense mechanisms down."

"True enough."

"It's obvious that you're feeling Tevin. Go away with him and let him prove how much he is feeling you. And if it leads to sex, then so be it. You're a grown-ass woman and he's a grown-ass man."

"So if I give Tevin a chance, you'll give someone a chance to actually be with you? Like actually date?"

"Why does it have to be a tit-for-tat situation? Sure, there are some people who've tried to actually get at me, but I'm not feeling any of them like that. However, I will start being more approachable and see what happens. Cool?"

"Cool."

"You already have your low-hanging fruit so call him and tell him that you're going."

"Right now?"

"No, next week. Yes, right damn now."

"If I do this, you realize everything is going to change?"

Winsome nodded. "All good changes."

"All good up and until something happens and he breaks my heart."

"You're assuming that something negative is going to happen."

"It's inevitable."

"So why do it then?"

"Because you said I should do it."

"I said you should do it because you want to do it."

I closed my eyes and contemplated my next move.

"What are you doing? Praying?" Winsome asked.

"No, but I need to be. I was thinking about how much ice cream and chocolate we need to stock up on so that when I get hurt, I don't have to run out to the store."

"Speaking of fattening shit . . ." Winsome looked at the time on her cell phone. "It's nine-thirty and the gym closes at eleven. We need to get moving. I'm not going to sleep with all this grease in my stomach so my ass will feel like lead in the morning."

We gathered our trash to throw it away. Winsome reached over and took mine. "I'll throw this away. It's loud in here. Go outside and call Tevin and ask him what time you need to be ready tomorrow."

I grinned. "Okay."

"And also tell him that he has to meet me tomorrow to get my approval before he takes you out of town. I'm sick of only seeing him from the window."

"Yes, Mother!"

Winsome headed toward the trash receptacle while I went outside on the pavement to call Tevin and accept his offer. It was time for me to take a chance.

CHAPTER NINE

"One day, someone will walk into your life
and make you see why it never worked
out with anyone else."

— Unknown

"This view is breathtaking!" I exclaimed, trying to catch my breath.

Tevin had taken me to Shenandoah National Park to go hiking and we were on the Appalachian Trail at the Panorama.

"It's great how you can see everything for miles from here."

"And in every direction," Tevin added. "So do you like hiking?"

I looked up into his almond eyes. "I do now, but this is honestly my first time."

Tevin chuckled. "Your first time? Why did you agree then?"

I shrugged. "Why not agree? At some point, everything is someone's first time. Good thing that I've been going to the gym on the regular or I wouldn't have been able to hang."

He looked me up and down. I had on all kinds of hiking gear that I had rushed to purchase at Arundel Mills Mall the second he had told me the plans. In addition to the clothes, I had utilized Google to find out what essentials I needed for hiking.

"You had all of that in your closet already?" he asked.

"No, not at all, but I like to be prepared. I did my research and once I found out that this park has five hundred miles of trails, more than a hundred of them being the Appalachian Trail, I wanted to make sure that if we get lost, we're covered."

Tevin was carrying my heavy-ass backpack for me. He set it down on the ground. "What's in here?"

"Let me see." I looked upward while I tried to recite the list of everything tucked inside. "The essential list is: a map, a compass, a flashlight, eye protection, extra food, extra clothes, a first aid kit, a pocket knife, waterproof matches, a fire starter, water bottles, a whistle, insect repellent, and sunscreen."

Tevin chuckled. "Are you serious? We're only out here for a few hours. I rented us a yurt."

"What the hell is a yurt?"

"Aw, something that the school principal with a thirst for knowledge doesn't know already! I'm shocked," he joked.

"You should have told me so I could look it up."

Tevin didn't understand how upset I was that I didn't know what a *yurt* was. I didn't like it one bit.

"So what is a yurt? Is it a tent, or some other kind of pop-up shelter?" I paused. "We're not going to sleep near bears, are we?"

Tevin took my hand, lifted it, and kissed it. "I'm the only bear you have to worry about. A yurt is a round cabin."

I finally exhaled. "Whew! I'm so relieved!"

"Well, yes, you can relax. Actually, the yurt has a stainless-steel kitchen, two bedrooms, two bathrooms, a stone fireplace, a living room, and an outdoor deck and grill."

"That sounds lovely."

"Not as lovely as you."

He was still holding my hand and pulled me closer to him so that he could kiss me. Boy, did he plant one on. It wasn't even cold outside, but I was trembling.

He broke the kiss and stared right into my eyes. "I love you, Jemistry."

My mouth fell open. I wasn't prepared for

that . . . not at all.

"I love you and you don't have to respond. I don't want you to tell me until you mean it." He let me go and picked the backpack up. "I'm a confident man and I can see it in your eyes. You're falling for me . . . hard."

He started walking down the hill. "We need to get back before dark." He paused and looked back at me. I was planted in place. "You coming, or you need me to leave this survival backpack for you so the flashlight and matches can help you fight off bears?"

I snapped out of it. I had been joking about the bears but we were in the middle of the wilderness. "Oh my goodness! They do have bears out here, you know."

"Yeah, I know, and I'm prepared." Tevin pulled a handgun out of his jacket pocket. "This is how I fight off bears and anyone or anything else."

I giggled. "That definitely works."

I started walking so we could head back down toward his car, about three miles away. "You weren't kidding about spending time in isolation, but I'm having fun."

When I caught up to him, he took my hand. "That's a good thing."

We got settled into the yurt, which was nicer

inside than just about any hotel room or suite that I had stayed in . . . ever. The rental community was in Gordonsville, Virginia, and they had it all: cabins, lodge rooms, a manor house, campsites, RV sites, chalets, and yurts. They had all kinds of activities as well: basketball, billiards, a gym, horse-drawn carriages, miniature golf, and a lake to go fishing.

Tevin had found a small, local grocery store where we purchased everything necessary to grill hamburgers and hot dogs, as well as some food for breakfast the next morning. He turned out to be a great cook. He had asked me to come over to his house for dinner on numerous occasions, but I had avoided it. I didn't want to put myself in a situation where I would be tempted to sleep with him. All of that was about to change. I was prepared to go all in with him to see what could actually become of it. But it would be a challenge and I wanted him to know that. I could no longer convince myself that a "friends with benefits" situation would work with him. We had spent way too much quality time together and I cared about him too much to disconnect from my emotions.

"These burgers are banging." I took another bite of mine as Tevin cut off the grill. "Where did you learn to cook like this?"

"My mother taught me how to cook. By ten, I was cooking dinner three times a week." He sat down across from me at the picnic table on the deck. "You probably thought that I was lying when I said that I could burn."

"No, I took it more literally, like you were burning food and jacking it up." We both laughed. "You haven't told me much about your parents. Are they still living?"

"Yes, they both are. Again, sorry to hear about the loss of yours."

I looked down at my plate, trying to avoid eye contact and to prevent myself from tearing up. "It is what it is. Sure, it would be nice to still have my parents in my life, but I'm not going to throw a pity party. There are many, many people in worse situations than me. I have a couple of degrees, a career that I am passionate about, and . . ."

Tevin was waiting for me to finish my sentence. When I continued to hesitate, he asked, "And what?"

"And a man who loves me."

He grinned. "Yes, you definitely have that."

We stared at each other for a moment. He had told me not to reciprocate what he had said until I meant it, so I would not. But my feelings for him ran deep. I could not call it being in love quite yet, though.

"Tell me more about your parents."

"Well, they're divorced, but they only took that step after all of us were grown. I have two sisters. One lives in New Jersey and she owns a few retail stores. My other sister lives in Florida and she's a dentist. Mom lives down in Florida near Alexis and my father lives in Sweden."

"Sweden?"

"Yes, my father is a vascular surgeon as well. I got it honest. He decided that he wanted to move out of the country after the divorce because he needed a change."

"That's one hell of a change!"

"Indeed! He loves it, though. He learned their language, moved over there, and landed a position at Karolinska University Hospital in Stockholm. He comes back three to four times a year to visit the States."

"I've always found it intriguing when people take such a leap of faith. Moving to another country is not a simple undertaking."

Tevin laughed as he took a sip of his beer.

"What's so funny?"

"It's just that, for a woman who has such a thirst for knowledge, I'm surprised you have that outlook."

"What outlook?"

"Thinking that it seems like a massive undertaking to move to another country. Then again, a lot of us Americans have that same view. It seems more strenuous or daring for us to move somewhere else, but people from other countries uproot their entire families all the time — relocate to the United States, and manage to figure it out."

"You have a good point. I have never thought of it that way. A lot of them even leave everyone else behind to come here and try to make things work."

"Yes, they do. Many never see their family members again."

"You know, I couldn't imagine being a mother in a war-torn country and letting my children be smuggled out to have a better chance at life. I would like to think that I would let them go, but it is unthinkable to me."

"We really need to appreciate the United States, as messed up as so many things are here."

I giggled. "A patriotic conversation and it's not the Fourth of July."

Tevin wiped his chin with his napkin. Even that seemed sensual to me.

You're going to fuck him tonight and you know it!

"I will say this," I added. "This has given me some food for thought. A lot of my students have been offered opportunities to study abroad or stay with foreign families. I have never been too thrilled about the concept, but when you get right down to it, it's dangerous here in the States."

"Yes, there have been a lot of school shootings lately. It's crazy."

I took a deep breath. "Tell me about it. We've had to rethink our security and take more precautions. There's no way to tell when or where someone might lose it. I guess when it's your time, it's your time."

Tevin looked into my eyes and grinned. "Okay, enough of the dismal stuff. This is our time . . . to get to know each other."

"Indeed."

"What else would you like to talk about?"

I shrugged.

"How about we discuss why you're so bitter toward men?"

"Didn't you just say 'enough of the dismal stuff?' " I got up from the table to throw my plate in the trash bag we had near the grill. "So this makes sense to you? Taking me away from the hustle and bustle of the city to a peaceful, secluded place only to turn

102

around and ask me to conjure up all of the negativity that I'm attempting to leave behind?"

"Now that you put it like that, no. It makes no sense at all." I felt his presence behind me a second before he put his arms around my waist and whispered in my ear, "But in order for me to avoid the same mistakes the other men made, I need to know what you expect."

"It's not really all about expectations. It's about human decency and not trying to cause the next person to self-destruct."

He gazed into my eyes. "That definitely is not my intention." He kissed me on the cheek and let me go. "Instead of going into everything from your past in minute details, how about an overview?"

He sat down on the bench of the picnic table, facing outward toward me. "I can make some assumptions, based on that poem you recited."

"What kind of assumptions?"

"Well, I can assume that you've been cheated on, yelled at before, possibly beaten on."

I glared at him, trying to decide how to respond.

"Okay, I am going to give you a quick *overview*. Yes, all of those things have happened to me before, including the domestic violence. I always told myself that no man would ever hit me and get away with it . . . until it actually happened."

I walked over and sat down beside Tevin. "I was engaged once. It turned out to be a nightmare. His name was Wesley and I thought he was the moon, the sun, and the stars when I first met him. We met in grad school at Georgetown. He was from what they call old money, originally from Boston. I loved everything about him, from the way he walked with such confidence to his authentic Boston accent. He was just . . . cool. He was charming, brilliant, and said all the right things.

"Most of the women on campus wanted to at least sleep with him once, and I was no exception. Crazy, but the truth. Like a lot of younger women, I believed that my pussy was better than anyone else's and after he got one taste of it, he would be mine forever.

"I actually competed for his attention. I can laugh about it now, but it was ridiculous back then. It's amazing what people can accept as normalcy when toxic situations are all that they have ever witnessed. Looking back at it now, I'm not sure if I ever had any relatives or friends growing up that did not live in complete dysfunction. So if you only comprehend that type of behavior, something better is damn near impossible to relate to."

"I understand where you are coming from. I've run across quite a few women who felt like I was too good to be true because I wasn't hitting them, cheating on them, or yelling at them like they expected. It's true that good men usually finish last."

"It took me a long time to realize that. When I would meet a *seemingly* nice man, I always expected something crazy to happen. Most of the time it did, but now that I look back on it, I realize that I kept hooking up with guys similar to Wesley over and over again.

"Men who looked great on paper. Men who women would fall all over each other to get to. Men who could never actually do right by another human being because it wasn't in their nature. Then I started believing that all men had to have some kind of crazy mentality about them. I was attracting the wrong type of men because I was wearing my pain, low self-esteem, and negative outlook on my face."

Tevin glanced over at me and took my hand. "I know that extremely well."

I felt ashamed because he was right. It was

the expression written all over my face the night we met, not to mention the "Bitter" poem.

"So why even approach me? Why even ask me out if you saw all of that?"

"Because I wanted to be the one to change your outlook. Color me stupid, but I believe it's actually working . . . somewhat."

I blushed. "Yes, it is."

We shared a long kiss and I was ready to let him take me right there on the deck, but I stopped him.

"I have to warn you about something," I said.

"*Warn me?* You're not really a man, are you?"

I slapped him on the thigh and we both laughed.

"Now that would truly turn this situation-ship into an adventure," I replied. "No, I'm not a man."

"I was just kidding. You're way too beauti-ful to be a male."

"Please, there are some trannies that would put every woman that I know — including me — to shame."

"Not a topic that I'm interested in, but I'll take your word for it."

His comment made me concerned so I asked, "You're not homophobic, are you?"

"Absolutely not! Everyone should do them. I'm just not interested in the lifestyle of transsexuals. Nothing against them, though."

"Good, because Winsome is bisexual."

"Your roommate?"

"Yes."

Tevin had met Winsome when he came to pick me up. It was not going to go down any other way. Winsome had made it a point that if she did not finally meet him, she would give me hell when I got back.

Tevin shrugged. "Cool with me. So she's involved with both a man and a woman?"

I giggled. "I wouldn't say involved. I would say she is simply doing her. She's more scared of putting her heart on the line than I am, but her issues are different."

"Like what?"

"A lot of men get excited about her being bisexual because she can help them live out their fantasies. A lot of women don't trust her because they think she'll go chase after dick behind their backs. The truth is that being bisexual doesn't automatically mean that you'll always want to have your cake and eat it too. It means that you find something attractive and exciting about both."

"Got you." He paused and licked his lips.

"Wait; whoa, back up. What exactly is a 'situationship'?"

"It's a word that I use to describe what I usually end up in. A situationship is like a relationship but one where there is so much outside bullshit, so many emotional hang-ups, and so much that will inevitably go wrong, that it ends up being a hot mess."

"Are you saying you still expect something to go wrong with us?"

"I sure hope not."

We stared at each other for a few seconds. He was probably trying to see if I was going to shut down on him suddenly, after he had made so much leeway with me. I was going to try my best not to do that. I wanted him, and not only in a sexual way. But I was still scared half to death to get my feelings hurt again.

"It's getting chilly. Let's go inside." Tevin took my hand and led me inside.

CHAPTER TEN

"Love is when you look into someone's
eyes and see everything you need."
— Unknown

Later that night, we had both showered in
separate bathrooms and met back up in the
living room of the yurt. Tevin had put our
bags in different rooms to let me know that
there was no pressure to sleep together. He
had no idea that fucking him was definitely
on my itinerary for the weekend.

"Don't you look cute," I teased, talking
about his flannel pajamas.

I had on a black two-piece set that showed
a little bit of boobies and accentuated my
ass.

"I didn't want to come out here like I usually sleep," he said.

"And how is that?"

"Completely nude."

I giggled as I sat Indian-style beside him

on the sofa. "Aw, so you're a ten-percenter."

"What's a ten-percenter?"

"That's the percentage of people globally who tend to sleep naked."

"You and your encyclopedia head. I like the fact that you're a thinker. Not every woman can stimulate me intellectually."

Oh, I plan to stimulate you, all right!

"I still need to warn you."

"Oh, yeah," he said. "I forgot about the warning you wanted to issue to me earlier."

"I hope you don't take any of this the wrong way."

"One way to find out. Issue the warning and let me decide how I take it."

I got up off the sofa and went over to the TV that had an iPod dock attached to it. My iPod was already there, charging.

"I need some theme music."

"Theme music?" I could hear Tevin chuckling. "To talk to me?"

"Yes. Haven't you ever noticed that there's usually at least one song that explains and expresses what you're thinking at any given moment in time?"

"Never really thought of it like that, but it makes sense. So what's your theme song for this moment in time?"

" 'Things Don't Exist' by Goapele. Ever heard it?"

110

"No; never. What's it about?"

"Just listen to it and then I'll pour my heart out to you afterwards."

"Pour your heart out? Maybe I should pour us some wine."

We both laughed nervously as the song started. It seemed silly, but I really wanted him to be able to relate to how I was feeling. "Things Don't Exist" summed it up perfectly.

Tevin sat there and listened to the nearly five-minute song that described a woman who was blue and who admitted that she was her own worst enemy. She sang about how when she looked into her current man's eyes she saw a love that she had never known, and about how things still existed in her heart that she hoped to get rid of so she could embrace love.

"Deep song," Tevin said after it ended. "Let me analyze it, even though I am not a Virgo."

I giggled. "No one ever said that only Virgos can analyze things, only that we tend to go overboard sometimes."

"Sometimes?"

"Okay, all the time." I rubbed Tevin's cheek tenderly. "I wanted you to hear that song because it truly does sum up the woman that I am, in this moment, here with you. I see something in the way that you look at me that I actually do believe is real, but I'm broken. I'm broken and hurt, and as much as I wish that I wasn't, it's the truth.

"I'm not sure why you made the decision to even try to establish anything real with me. I'm a good woman and I know it, but I've always been a good woman. I was a good woman when Wesley decided to commit to me over all the others. And I was also a good woman when he cheated on me, gave me chlamydia, got me pregnant, and put a pillowcase over my head and beat me half to death. I decided to abort the child without him ever knowing. Don't judge me for that, please."

Tevin took me into his arms. "Oh, baby, I'm so sorry."

"The dummy actually believed that using a pillowcase wouldn't leave any bruises. Can you believe that? He actually told that to the police at the emergency room when they came to arrest him. Like using a pillowcase should get him a pass for putting his hands on me."

"I wish that I could get my hands on that motherfucker. I'd kill him."

I could tell that Tevin was serious. It was a pleasant thought, but not a realistic one.

"Trust me, I considered killing him myself, but that would have allowed him to take everything from me . . . including my freedom. He damaged me enough. I call what Wesley did to me my initial 'hit and run.' Then other men came along, saw me as a wounded deer in the middle of the road, and ran over me again. Used me for sex; used me for money; used me as a punching bag. Then it became normal. It is what I came to expect.

"I started wondering if the way that romance and love were portrayed in books and movies from the past was all a myth. If you look at the current novels and theatrical releases, the romantic comedies and love stories, they all make it seem like two people can meet, fall in love, and live happily ever after. Yet, most of my friends are struggling to even find a man to fuck that isn't already doing another one of our friends."

"I take it that it's been a while since you've been with someone, Jemistry, and I want you to know that I don't want to rush you." He sighed. "No, let me rephrase that. I don't want you to think that you're obligated to do anything with me. Of course, I'd love to make love to you, but that has to be what you truly want."

"I know that you would never force me to

do something with you, Tevin. And the fact of the matter is that I've changed to some degree. I made a promise to myself that I would never allow another man to hurt me ever again. He might get one shot in, but after the first red flag, it's over. I wouldn't be here with you if I thought you were capable of *intentionally* hurting me. Yet, in the back of my mind, I don't put anything past anyone."

"Well, I appreciate your *somewhat* faith in me. I'm willing to prove what type of man I am, and it's going to take time and consistency. I get that. You can trust me. I would never lie to you. Anything you ask me, I'll be truthful. That's the only way this could ever work. We have to tell each other the truth . . . about everything."

I sat there thinking about what he had just said.

"Then I need to tell you something," I said.

"What's that?"

"When I met you, I was sexually active with two different men."

I felt Tevin clench up a little. I am sure he never expected that and I damn sure knew that I couldn't tell him that I had fucked Anthony right before I met him for dinner. I did feel it was imperative for me to come clean. Secrets tended to show up in the most unexpected places, and DC was so small, there was a good possibility that Tevin and I would run into either Anthony or Gregory at some point. For all I knew, he actually could have been acquaintances with one of them, considering the fact that all I ever wanted in regards to them was their dicks.

"Let me explain. I was having sex with them, but I wasn't emotionally connected to either. And that was on purpose. Even though both of them wanted to pursue something more, I refused. Having sex with them was a way of taking care of my needs and proving that I could exercise some type of control over my emotions.

"There was a time when my vagina was directly connected to my heart. If you didn't have my heart, then you couldn't even think about touching my pussy. But then, after each failed relationship, I became more and more disillusioned when it came to loving a man, or being loved by one.

"I even considered becoming a lesbian, but I'm not attracted to women, and from seeing Winsome go through drama with chick after chick, that's definitely not the answer. So I wanted to be touched; I wanted to touch back."

Tevin rubbed his hands on his thighs uncomfortably.

"I'm only telling you this because you expect honesty, and that's fair. I stopped sleeping with both of them after our first official date at Oceanaire. I blocked their numbers and haven't contacted them since."

"That's kind of cold, isn't it?" Tevin asked.

"I don't see it that way. Both of them understood that there was nothing there, and that eventually it would come to an end. I met you and I felt guilty about them. Crazy, but true. We'd just met and I already felt some kind of obligation to you."

"And why do you think that is?" he asked.

I shrugged. "Fate, maybe. The feeling that everything that I had ever been through and endured might have brought me to you. The fact that even though you watched me spew out all of that venom, you still asked me out. The chemistry I felt with you the second we laid eyes on each other.

"Part of me felt like it died a long time ago. But there was another part of me that was still alive."

I kissed Tevin lightly on the lips.

"I want to try. I want to try to make this work . . . whatever this is. As much as I am flattered about being the woman that you want, it's more important for me to be the woman that you need . . . in all ways."

"You are the woman that I need, Jemistry."

"I want to be, but you're going to have to be patient with me if we take this further, and I don't mean waiting for sex. I want to make love to you . . . tonight. But once we get into this, I don't want you to feel slighted or get angry with me when I voice my insecurities or shut down from time to time while I try to climb onto the next plateau. It took a couple of decades to turn me into this mess; the cleanup is not going to happen overnight."

"I understand everything that you're saying, and I'm prepared. I'll do whatever it takes to make you happy, so that I can be happy."

I eyed him seductively. "So why don't you take me to bed so we can discover our happiness?"

CHAPTER ELEVEN

"Love is of all the passions the strongest,
for it attacks, simultaneously the head,
the heart, and the senses."
— Lao Tzu

"Are you sure about this?" Tevin asked as he laid me down on the king-sized bed after carrying me into the bedroom where my luggage was located. "I can wait."

"Wait for what?" I responded. I stood up on my knees and started unbuttoning the flannel pajama top. "Wait for global warming to end the world, which could happen tomorrow? Wait for one of us to come up with an excuse not to do it? We came up here to be alone, and we are. Our cell phones are off; you're not on call; so all we have between us is space . . ." I licked a trail down the middle of his chest, ". . . and opportunity."

I pulled his top down over his massive,

muscular shoulders, and then let it fall to the floor. Then I pulled my own over my head and tossed it beside his. I started unfastening my bra.

"I want you, Tevin. I want you to devour me, partake of everything that I have to give. I want you to make all of my pain go away . . . all of my fears. I want you to make me forget my past. I want you to make me even more excited about the future than I am already."

I let my breasts fall out of my bra and then tossed it over his shoulder. I grabbed each one of my breasts in a hand, and then lifted my left one and licked it with the tip of my tongue.

Tevin remained silent, taking in my every move, and my every word.

"I want you to suck my breasts as though you've never done it before. Like you've been waiting since forever to do this, like a teenaged boy waiting for his first time get-ting lucky."

I stood up completely on the bed and unfastened the string on my pants, then let them fall so Tevin could see my black-lace thong.

"I want you to rip my panties off with your teeth and then eat my pussy like it is the sustenance you need in order to wake up in the morning. And then I want you to feed me your dick so I can wake up with a smile on my face in the morning."

Tevin grinned.

"What?" I asked.

"Nothing. I just feel so blessed right now. Even though I'm crazy about you, and I love you, I never expected you to be so freaky in the bedroom."

"We haven't done anything yet."

He grabbed one of my ass cheeks in each hand and pulled me closer to him. "Exactly, and my dick is already hard enough to split bricks. Everything about you is turning me on. Keep looking at me like that and talking dirty to me. What do you want me to do after I feed you this dick?"

"Well, after I hum out several tunes on your mic, I want you to stick it in me and fuck me until I come all over it."

He grinned from ear to ear and then set my ass free.

"Let me go get my condoms out the next room," he said, and started to turn away.

"We've both been tested."

I had delivered my speech to Tevin a couple of weeks earlier and he had agreed to be tested. I was tested as well. We were both clean.

I could tell that he seemed a bit apprehensive so I wanted to clarify that he was the exception.

"I don't want you to get the wrong idea, Tevin. I did use condoms with the others, who shall remain nameless. If we are going to be together, I want us to be together. I want to taste you and I want you to taste me. I want you to be able to lick your breakfast and taste all of this good-good."

I let go of my breasts and reached my right hand down into my thong while I was grabbing Tevin by the back of his neck, drawing his face closer to me, and starting to kiss him. I played in my pussy for a moment; it was hotter than the flames of hell.

Then I took my two damp fingers and put them in between our mouths so we could both suck on them together.

"You like that?" I asked, breathing directly into Tevin's mouth.

"Ummmmmmm hmmmmm," he mumbled. "I love it."

I lay down on the bed and reached for him to get on top of me. "Kiss me again."

Tevin didn't hesitate a second and he was on me, tonguing me down and grinding his dick between my legs.

We continued the kiss until I felt like I was about to scream. I had to come up for air. No one had ever kissed me like that

121

before . . . ever.

"Damn," I whispered. "I can tell you have a humongous dick, even through your pants."

"Want to see it?" he asked, and then grinned.

"I want to see it, touch it, lick it, suck it, and then fuck it."

Tevin stood up and took off his pants. He had no underwear on and what popped out damn near made me jump off the bed. He indeed had a huge dick — ten inches minimum and the girth was *outlandish.*

He sensed my apprehension. "I hope you don't run from this. I probably should have brought this up before, but I didn't want to disrespect you by talking about my size."

"I'm not going anywhere, but I can imagine that it has been an issue with some women."

He chuckled. "Somewhat."

I sat up on the edge of the bed and pulled him toward me by his hips. "Since I plan on being the last woman who ever does this to you, it should no longer be an issue."

I took his dick in my right hand, directed the head to my mouth, and started sucking on the head. "Ummmm, you taste so good."

Tevin started moaning while I took him in and out of my mouth, more and more each time until I caught a rhythm. Then I started picking up the speed and giving him a hand job on the part of his dick closer to his scrotum. I used my other hand to caress his testicles.

"Damn, baby. That feels so good," he whispered.

I let his dick go and then lay down on my back, turning my head so that it was dangling off the bed. "Come here," I said, then joked, "but don't come too quick."

I opened my mouth and allowed him to place his dick back in it and move it in and out. It allowed my throat to open up more and also let him see my tits bouncing up and down as he watched the way that I was playing in my pussy.

I had to take frequent breaths, and each time that I did, I used my tongue to lick and suck on his balls from underneath.

"Oh shit!" he exclaimed about five minutes later, before he exploded inside my mouth. I let every single drop go down my throat, then turned over and sucked on him gently, admiring and worshiping his dick: my new best friend.

"My turn. I want to taste your pussy," Tevin said, still trying to catch his breath.

I sat up, pulled him down on the bed, put a pillow under his head, and then yanked my thong off.

"I thought you wanted me to rip those off with my teeth."

"There's always next time." I giggled. "Right now, I'm about to feed you dessert."

I climbed on top of his face, leaned back, and placed my hands on each side of his thighs. Then I started riding his tongue like I was in a cunnilingus rodeo. He grabbed the front of my legs and started eating me like I was his last feast. It was some amazing shit. His tongue was at least half as long as his dick. He made me come all over his tongue within minutes.

I fell off of him. "I need a break."

He chuckled. "No; no breaks."

"I don't think I've ever come so hard!" I exclaimed.

"You'd better get used to it then." He lay beside me and we cuddled so that our chests were touching and we could gaze into each other's eyes. "I'm planning on making love to you as much as possible, and I haven't actually even done it yet."

"All of it is a part of making love," I replied, playing with his hairless chest.

"Yeah, but here comes the good part."

"Oh my!"

That was all that I got out before he was inside of me.

"Oh, Jemistry!" he whispered right after he entered me. I was trying to deal with the initial pain of his dick being so big. "You feel so good!"

Now I will say this. In my lifetime, I had only been rendered speechless by one other dick. I had screwed this guy back in college off the cuff one night and he put it on me so bad that I couldn't even find the words. Tevin was the second man to render me speechless when he started slowly grinding his dick into me.

I spread my legs into a wide V because it was all that I could think of to try to give him the most access possible. He started going deeper and deeper and I was moaning like crazy . . . but could find no words. And I was considered a "shit talker" in the bedroom. Not that night.

It seemed like Tevin fucked me for hours. It was really more like thirty minutes, but it was like being in heaven. Getting that first nut out when I sucked his dick made Tevin last a long-ass time. I planned to keep that in mind in the future. Saving the oral until after so he would come faster.

When he finally came, he looked like he was having a seizure. He clenched his face up and let his head fall down by my right thigh.

He then looked up in my eyes, said, "I love you, Jemistry," and then climbed off of me.

When he went into the bathroom to clean up and get me a towel, I laid there someplace between bliss and wondering if I could actually make a relationship work for once in my life. I wasn't prepared to consider it love, yet, but it was definitely something worth exploring further.

■ ■ ■ ■

TEVIN

■ ■ ■ ■

CHAPTER TWELVE

"The art of love is largely the art of
persistence."
— Albert Ellis

Two Months Later

It was a rainy day in May and the traffic
was ridiculous as I tried to get to work. Sibley Memorial was in a quiet area, but getting into the vicinity meant driving through
downtown DC from my house near Rock
Creek Park. People in DC started panicking
and driving crazy when it rained badly; during the winter, snow created absolute havoc.
Whenever there were several days of bad
weather, I would stay at the hospital like
many of the other staff.

Being a doctor meant going into work
when I was supposed to be there. When I
didn't show up, someone could literally die.
I had a scheduled surgery that morning. A
seventy-eight-year-old woman had vascular

dementia. She was already suffering from Alzheimer's when she had a stroke that ended up blocking the blood flow to her brain. I planned to go in and clear out the blockage from her veins and, hopefully, improve her ability to function.

When I first became a doctor, I had it embedded in my mind that I could save *anyone's* life. Becoming a vascular surgeon made all the sense in the world to me; growing up, my father would always seem so prideful when he would sit at the dinner table and tell us all how he had prevented yet another person from dying. In our presence, he never mentioned the ones who didn't make it, although I am sure he did to my mother.

I could appreciate him wanting to shield us from the fact that we are all dying. It is only a matter of the hour and the day. Even when I did realize that inadequate blood flow could damage and eventually kill cells anywhere in the body, I was still inspired to try to allow as many people as possible some additional time. If it ended up being ten more years, ten more days, or even ten more hours, it all counted.

Watching people deal with sickness and death still bothered me, even though I paid witness to it daily. Delivering the news of death was the worst, even though I never made promises that I could not keep. I was always honest about the complications that might arise, the percentage of people who survived certain things. I understood the importance of being realistic.

Still, Mrs. Sparrow Turner had touched my heart when I met her, and I prayed that she would survive the surgery. She was a sweet older woman, a widow who had been married for more than forty years before her husband dropped dead of a heart attack a few years prior. She had four children, eleven grandchildren, and two great-grandchildren. It always made it harder when people came from larger families. The waiting room would be packed with people pacing the floor, or clinging to one another, and sometimes a relative or two actually had to be admitted for observation because the stress would overwhelm them.

I will never forget one time when a woman was visiting her husband, who was on life support, after a repair of his abdominal aortic aneurysm. He had been without oxygen for a long time. She was so distraught when I told her that we were checking to see if he was brain dead, and advised her to start considering removing him from the machine, that on the way to the elevator she fell out. She ended up dying from an undiagnosed brain tumor and he ended up recovering. Having to tell him about his wife's death was one of the hardest things I ever had to do in my entire life.

Being a doctor had truly humbled me as a person. A lot of my colleagues were arrogant and often made mistakes because of their egos and not wanting to be team players. I was the type who loved to consult with others to get the benefit of their expertise. I realized that different people viewed things in different ways. Being confident was one thing; thinking you were God was quite another. After all, that job was already taken.

As I pulled into the parking garage in my white E63 AMG Benz, I noticed Katrina Maxwell getting out of her Ford Mustang. She waved and then waited for me to park and get out. Katrina was cool but she was overstepping being professional to try to get me into bed. It was not about to happen. I loved Jemistry and, as I had promised, I would never do anything to hurt or disrespect her.

"Hey, you," Katrina said as I walked up beside her. "Don't you look sexy this morning! Then again, you always look appetizing to me."

"Good morning, Katrina."

We walked toward the elevator together. I tried not to seem irritated by her, but it wasn't easy.

Once we got on, she tried to step closer to me. "I've got tickets to see Kem at Constitution Hall next weekend. You want to go with me?"

"No, but thanks for letting me know he's coming to town. I didn't realize that. Jemistry loves Kem; I'll have to try to snag some tickets."

Katrina looked disappointed but she shouldn't have been surprised. In the six plus years she had been trying to get me to date her, I had never agreed.

"Well, I'm sure some man will be happy to have me on his arm for the night." She rolled her eyes. "Even though you think you're too good for me."

I glanced down at her. "Katrina, I don't think that I'm too good for you. I simply don't want to date you. We work together. I've been around you enough to be able to gauge whether or not we make sense, and most importantly, I'm already taken."

"Oh yeah?"

I chuckled as the elevator ascended to the fifth floor. "Yes, indeed. She's an amazing woman and I love her. That's the end of it but I wish you well."

Katrina rolled her eyes and sucked her teeth. "I'm sick of men turning down all of this." She rubbed her hands over her body. "I'm too fine to be single."

"I agree. You're too fine to be single and maybe if you let men approach you, you could easily tell who's interested and who's not."

"Men approach me all damn day, but all they want is sex. I need a provider. Someone who wants to be with me and only me."

"Well, like I said, I really do wish you the best," I said as I started to get off on my floor. She was going up two more floors. I used my hand to hold the elevator open for a few additional seconds. "And if for some reason you can't find a date, I'm willing to buy the tickets off you for what you paid for them plus twenty percent."

As the doors closed, Katrina looked like I had slapped her.

Seven hours later, I was sitting in my office, trying to regain my composure. Mrs. Turner had died on the operating table. While I realized that I had done my very best to help her, it wasn't enough. Even with Alzheimer's she had this amazing spirit about her, and a kindness that was hard to find.

My cell rang; it was Jemistry. I answered,

"Hey, baby! I miss you!"

She giggled. "I crawled out of your bed about four o'clock this morning. How could you miss me already?"

"You left at four, and by five, I was ready to bawl my eyes out. I buried my head in my pillow to fight back the tears."

"Now you're exaggerating, but I have to admit that I miss you, too. So what are we doing for dinner tonight?"

As much as I wanted to see Jemistry, I didn't want to carry my pain from work to her doorstep. "Maybe we can chill tonight. I had a long day."

"What's wrong?"

"Nothing."

"Don't lie to me. I can tell when something's wrong with you, baby."

"I lost a patient today, and it's hard on me. I wouldn't be good company tonight. I promise you that."

"Let me be the judge of that. You're always there to comfort me when I have a hard day at work with all those rug rats I have to deal with. Let me reciprocate."

"Sounds tempting." I sat back further in my chair, took off my glasses, and rubbed my eyes. "It's going to be nearly impossible for me to relax, or be a good conversationalist."

"We don't have to go out anyplace. How about I come over to your place, cook you a quick dinner, and then we can curl up on the sofa and watch a good movie. You don't have to talk if you don't want to, and I can rub your back, your head, and even your dick for you until you fall asleep. How does that sound?"

I couldn't help but smile. "That sounds very relaxing."

"Exactly!" She paused. "Tevin, you have such a kind heart and I'm sure that you did whatever you could to save your patient."

"I did."

"You tried and that's all that matters. But our lives must go on. One day, one of us will have to say good-bye to the other. Let's not waste any time."

"I'll be home by seven," I told her. "Use your key."

"Bye, baby."

I hung up and thought about all that had happened since Jemistry and I had become official two months earlier. My life had changed in that yurt up in Virginia, and while our sex was what legends were made of, it was more than that.

When I first met Jemistry, she was obviously upset with the world, but with men in particular. My common sense told me not to say a word to her, to let her sit there, finish off her martini, and sulk off into the night. But my heart instructed me to say something to her, to pursue her. There had only been a few times in my life when a woman had appealed to me right off the bat. The last woman who had that effect on me, I married.

Estella was like my fantasy woman. Fine, smart, attentive, passionate, and on track to become extremely successful. We had only dated less than six months before I popped the question. I was convinced that it would be the two of us against the world. We would face every challenge, every obstacle together, and raise a gaggle of children in a mansion fit for a king.

But God had other plans. The first miscarriage made us seemingly closer. The second miscarriage had us wondering what we had done to deserve it. The third miscarriage made us angry . . . her at me, and me at everyone else. I could barely function as a man, much less a doctor, and took a leave of absence to try to pull myself together. Estella went into a shell and completely withdrew from communicating with me, her parents, her coworkers, her friends, and everyone else.

I tried for two years to bring her smile

back, but it never came. Every time she looked at me, all she saw were the children who would never be. She went behind my back and had her tubes tied. I was upset that she had robbed me of the possibility of being a father without my consent. Looking back, I understand why she did it. She never wanted to experience that type of pain again. I was not the one who had carried those fetuses inside of me. I was not the one who'd had to deal with their mangled bodies ejecting out of me. I was not the one who had to feel like a failure because my body could not carry a baby to term. Estella had been through more than I could ever realize until much later.

Just as I felt like a failure at the moment for not being able to save Mrs. Turner, despite all of my efforts and doing all of the right things, Estella had felt the same when she could not carry any of our children to term.

It had been years since I had spoken to her, but something made me pick up my office phone and dial her number. Remarkably, it was still the same number and she answered on the third ring.

"Hello, this is Estella Daniels."

"This is Tevin Daniels."

Silence.

"I was calling to check on you. I had no idea that you still carried my last name. Didn't you ask for your maiden name back during the divorce?"

"Yes, I did. Just never got around to going through all of the paperwork." She paused. "Besides, you never did anything to hurt me. Most of my friends who demand their names back do it out of spite. Daniels has grown on me, so no point in trying to get people to call me something else."

"True." I started playing with a pen on my desk. "I was only calling to check on you."

"I'm fine. How are you?"

"I'm good."

There was yet again an uncomfortable silence between us.

"Tevin, I need to get back to work, unless you needed something," she finally said.

"No, no. I don't need anything."

"Well, then, take care and —"

"Wait a second, Estella. I do need to get something off my chest."

She seemed irritated. "And what's that?"

"In all these years, I've never apologized to you."

"What would you need to apologize for? We never hated each other. Sometimes two people grow apart. Sometimes there is simply way too much water under the bridge, to the point where the cars on it get flooded. Sometimes life throws us curveballs that we can never catch."

"And I agree with everything you said. I do. But now that I've had time to mature, evolve, and think about it all, I realize that I could have been more understanding about what you were going through. I could've been a better man and a better husband."

"No, you were a good man then and I'm sure you're a good man now. I was not mentally prepared to handle the loss of our babies. Not three. It was a pain that I had never imagined to be possible, and you tried to stand there by my side. I pushed you and everyone else away."

"So how are you doing now?"

"I'm making it work. I've resigned myself to the fact that I'll never give birth naturally. My fiancé and I are considering adoption, though."

I had no idea that Estella was engaged. Then again, there was no reason why I should have been privy to that information. When we broke ties, we also broke ties with mutual friends. She had her circle and I had mine.

"Wow, congrats on the engagement!" I told her. "He's a lucky man."

"Thanks, but I'm the lucky one. He accepted me, flaws and all, and I'm grateful for that." I could hear her moving around on the other end of the phone. "Do you have someone special in your life?"

"Yes, I do. It's only been a few months, but I've never felt this way before." I suddenly felt guilty for saying that, even though it was the truth to a great degree. "I mean . . ."

"Tevin, you don't have to explain anything to me. I'm glad that you have found love again. Both of us deserve to be happy."

"Yes, we do. Well, I don't want to keep you. This is my office number, if you ever need anything."

"I'll keep that in mind. Thanks for checking on me, Tevin. I'll keep you in my prayers."

"And I'll keep you in mine."

We both hung up and I got up from my desk, took off my white coat, replaced it with my suit jacket, and walked out the door. Life was hard, but it was never meant to be easy. I was determined to make Jemistry and me work out. So far, so good.

CHAPTER THIRTEEN

"We waste time looking for the perfect
lover, instead of creating the perfect love."
— Tom Robbins

Jemistry cooked some chicken and pasta for
dinner, popped open a bottle of Moscato,
and was making an attempt not to talk too
much. I felt bad and flattered at the same
time; she was really trying to please me.

She had on this purple dress that made
her fineness shine bright and these sexy-ass,
bone-white pumps. Some women don't get
that men are truly turned on by the heels.
Hell, I wished women would have kept them
on in the bed from time to time. Then
again, I enjoyed playing with and sucking
on a pretty set of toes. Jemistry had beautiful feet; she was on point from head to toe.

We were sitting across from each other at
the dining room table in my five-bedroom
home. I didn't need all of that space, but it

made sense for me to purchase real estate. I owned three other homes in the area, but loved living near the park. During the summer months, I loved riding my bike through the trails, hiking, and playing basketball at pickup games.

I thought back to Jemistry bringing all of that gear hiking on the Appalachian Trail in Virginia. It was often hard for her to simply go with the flow. Everything tended to be a production; she was always concerned about having everything she needed to do something.

I sat there chuckling and thinking about it.

"What's so funny?" She glanced down at my plate, which was still half full. "I hope you're not laughing at my cooking."

"No, it's good. Not as good as what I can throw together, but good." I grinned as she drank a sip of wine with much attitude. "I'm only playing with you, baby. I don't have much of an appetite."

"I understand, and I'm sorry for talking so much."

"You've barely said two words to me since you got here."

"That's because I said that I wouldn't. I just want to be here for you . . . when you need me."

I got up from the table, walked over to her, then took both of her hands and stood her up. "And I appreciate that."

I started to lead her into the living room. "Wait! I need to clear the table and do the dishes."

"All of that can wait," I said. "Let's go pick a movie to watch."

"I've got that covered. I brought a Blu-ray with me."

"Oh yeah, which one?"

"It's called *Dysfunctional Friends*. It's about a group of friends that are forced to stay together in the same house after a mutual friend's death. They all agree because his lawyer won't read his will until they do it."

"Aw, so greed makes them deal with one another?"

"Exactamundo! They had all drifted apart because of drama, or just being busy in life after college."

"Sounds like my friends."

"Mine, too. I've been thinking about hosting monthly networking events to try to bring my crew back together. Remember how we used to make fun of our parents for being busy with life? Now we're all stressed out over work, some are popping out babies, and scrapbooking or taking yoga classes."

I sat down on the sofa while Jemistry put the movie into my Blu-ray player and grabbed the appropriate remote.

She was about to turn it on when I stopped her. "If it's okay with you, I would like to talk about what happened to me at work today."

"Of course, baby."

We held hands.

"I've lost a lot of patients over the years, but something really struck me today about Mrs. Turner's death. Even though I'm well aware of my mortality, I realize that I'm still relatively young. There are things that I still want to do before I leave this earth."

"I feel the same way. Life is a one-shot deal. What you make of it, or don't make of it, ultimately becomes your legacy. That's why I'm so determined to make a difference with the kids at Medgar Evers. A lot of them don't have anyone else who believes in them."

"I love the fact that you're so passionate about what you do. There are many people who don't have that kind of excitement about their jobs."

"Hell, Tevin, most people are only going through the motions to get a paycheck. I see it in the teachers at my school, especially some of the younger ones. They're underpaid, underappreciated, and thought that they would change the world when they started. Then they got a reality check."

"Well, the same goes for a lot of doctors, keeping it real."

"Don't get me wrong. There are a lot of great teachers, and the rest generally have the potential to achieve greatness. But when you have a few students trying to ruin it for everyone else, it can be a challenge. I try to weed out most of that kind, but a lot of times even the teachers are afraid to tell me what's happening in their classrooms."

"A lot of people live in fear these days. The world has become a crazy place. It's not unusual for us to have gunshot victims under the age of fifteen, or kids coding after using intense drugs."

"You and I both have a lot going on. It can be depressing."

Jemistry pushed play on the remote. "Let's chill, watch this, and talk later."

"Okay."

She propped her back up on some pillows and then pulled me between her legs. I could smell the sweetness of her pussy and feel my dick instantly become hard.

"I know you said that you were only going to massage me tonight, but, baby, I may need to take it a little bit further than that."

146

She giggled. "How much further?"

"I'm sure you know what I'm talking about."

Jemistry started massaging my shoulders and her hands were magical. She often gave me full-body massages. What I loved about them was that it was obvious that she truly enjoyed doing it. She wasn't doing it for show, or because they talk about all of that in romance novels. She told me once that her love language was physical touch. So I always tried to make sure that I held her hand, hugged her, or spooned with her in bed as much as possible. She said that it made her feel safe and that she slept better that way.

"Yeah, I get your drift," she said, "and after this movie, I'm going to put it on you."

I grinned as the opening credits started. "You'd better."

The movie was cool. Made me think about a lot of things regarding life — past and future. Finally getting some kind of closure with Estella earlier had left me with a sense of relief. Even though I never did anything intentionally to harm her, and even though people grieve the loss of children in different ways, I could have treated her better and could have been more understanding.

Jemistry had yet to tell me that she loved me, but there was no need for her to ever speak the words if she didn't want to. It was obvious that she loved me. A lot of people say it and act like anything but. My baby girl was there for me, had entrusted me with her heart, and things were going well.

She was in the shower about midnight when I joined her. She loved for me to wash her hair and I enjoyed doing it. She was much shorter than me and her caramel complexion complemented my deep choco-late one. What I loved most about her were her eyes. They were brown but they had this sparkle deep inside them that actually made them seem like they were twinkling some-times. She had a small gap in her front teeth, which turned me on, and her skin was smooth all over. She didn't have a single scar on her.

She told me once that she used to have a lot of bruises from being beaten, but had used vitamin E capsules, popped open and spread over her skin, to get rid of any vis-ible trace of them. I only wished that I could get my hands on even one of the men who had laid a finger on her. Sick motherfuck-ers.

She put a sliver of soap in her mouth, got down on her knees, and started sucking my dick. She'd grown used to the size and even though there was no way that she'd ever be able to take me entirely into her mouth, she had figured out a way to make it seem like she had it totally engulfed.

I was about to come when I pulled away. "No, not yet. Stand up."

Jemistry stood and took the soap out of her mouth. "Did you like that, baby?"

"You know I did. You're so creative."

"Freaky and creative. Don't you forget it."

We both laughed.

"I can be a little creative myself," I said.

"Oh yeah? So what are you going to do to me?"

"Turn around."

She turned toward the wall.

"Assume the position."

She spread her palms on the tile wall and spread her legs as far as she could in the space.

I stuck the tip of my finger in her anus and she twitched.

"I need to make sure you don't have any contraband in your ass." I spread her cheeks and pushed my index finger in farther. "Hmm, not too sure. I may need to do some further exploration."

"Are you serious?" Jemistry asked, looking over her shoulder. "I'm not sure if I can handle all of that in my ass!"

"I agree. I don't think you can either."

I'd actually never had anal sex. It never seemed like a mandatory thing to me. I loved pussy. But I did want to see what would happen if I played with Jemistry's ass.

I slipped two more fingers into her ass.

"What are you doing?" she asked.

"Being freaky and creative."

I bent my knees and placed the head of my dick at the rim of her pussy and started fucking her. Her pussy gripped around my dick as if it was milking it. Again, that is what I adored about her. Her desire for me was real, not fake, and she wanted me as much as I wanted her.

After a couple of minutes of going to town on her pussy, I started moving my fingers in and out of her ass at a rapid speed. The effect was immediate. Jemistry spurted pussy juice all over my dick and then screamed out in pleasure.

"Shit!" she exclaimed. "Oh my beejeezus!"

She tried to get out of the shower but I held her in place.

"Hold still," I whispered in her ear. "I haven't come yet. You know it feels good."

"Yes, it feels *real* good."

"I want you to cream all over my dick

again. I'm not taking it out until you cream again."

I kept plummeting my dick in and out of her pussy until we both climaxed together.

After that, we lay in bed and stared each other in the eyes until we both dozed off.

I fell asleep with the vision of Jemistry in my mind and in my heart.

Chapter Fourteen

"I was born with an enormous need for affection, and a terrible need to give it."
— Audrey Hepburn

"Man, your game ain't shit!" Floyd was talking mad shit as usual. "For someone so damn tall, you shoot like a ten-year-old."

"Whatever, man. I always beat you, and I'm going to beat your ass again today."

We were playing basketball, one-on-one, in his driveway. He lived out in Largo with his wife and four kids. We worked together at Sibley. Floyd was a cardiologist.

"That's an urban legend. You've never beat me."

I had the ball after Floyd had barely managed to make a layup with his five-eight frame. Midget!

I looked around. "No one else is out here so not sure who you expect to hear that lie. I'm up five points right now. Yet you call my game shit?"

"I'm fucking with you, man. It's all about knocking down some stress."

"Damn right!" I bounced the ball twice and made what would have been a three-pointer on a professional court. "Kind of like I just knocked that ball into the basket without you even touching it, huh?"

"Whatever, punk!"

We both chuckled as Floyd attempted to catch his breath.

"Let's take a break and get some of Courtney's lemonade."

"Ooh, I love your wife's lemonade," I replied. "Besides, you look like you're about to have a coronary. Not a good look for a cardiologist."

Floyd threw the ball at my chest and we headed into the house.

We ended up in Floyd's man cave watching sports highlights on ESPN.

His wife, Courtney, had come in from shopping with the kids. She came downstairs to speak and then vanished somewhere else in their spacious home.

"Why'd Courtney evaporate so fast?" I asked him.

"This is called a *man cave* for a reason, Tevin. No women allowed unless they're dropping off a twelve-pack of beer or some sandwiches."

I pushed the button to lift the foot portion of the recliner that I was sitting on. "It's good to see that you have such a high respect for women."

"Hey, I respect my wife and part of that respect is because she knows how to stay in her lane."

"Her lane? Isn't she in the lane right beside you? Your equal?"

"She's right behind me in the lane. I'm the man, which means that what I say goes."

"You're straight tripping. That is that old-fashioned mentality. Chicks aren't playing that today."

Floyd muted the television and stared at me. "Old-fashioned, my ass. It's biblical. Eve was made from Adam's rib. Point-blank, period."

We had already switched from lemonade to beer. Neither one of us felt like going back outside to finish the game. I was going to win regardless.

"Point-blank, but no period. While I totally agree that back in the day men ruled the world, you have to admit that a lot of our brethren have surrendered that kind of thinking and are trying to live off women instead. How can they be considered the head of anyone's household if they aren't paying any bills?"

"I'll give you that, but that's not what's happening up in here. I pay *all* the bills and Courtney stays home and raises the kids."

"Doesn't she have a degree in psychology from Hampton? Didn't she minor in business management?"

"Yes, but the only business she's managing for the next decade, at least, is the business of running this household and letting me take over once I enter my kingdom."

I shrugged. "Different strokes for different folks. If she likes it, I love it."

"Not only does she like it, she wants it this way." He turned the volume up a little so he could hear something the sportscaster was saying. Then he turned it back down. "Courtney went to college but never truly aspired to be anything more than a housewife. Her mother wanted her to become a psychiatrist, but her father sent her to Hampton to find a husband." He ran his fingers over his chest and patted his abs. "And she found the bomb diggity."

Floyd was the kind of doctor who thought he was the shit; you couldn't tell him anything. And as much as he sat there bragging about being such a great husband, I knew he had fucked at least a half-dozen

155

nurses at that hospital. He gave "making rounds" an entirely new meaning.

"Are you still messing with that nurse from the burn unit?" I asked him, trying to knock him down a peg or two. "The married one?"

"Depends on how you define 'messing with.' She loves to give head, so I lend her mine a few times a week. I wouldn't actually fuck her with someone else's dick."

"But why do you find it necessary to even do all that? I'm sure Courtney hooks you up. I know you, and there's no way you would've ever married a woman who didn't give blow jobs."

"And you are absolutely correct with that statement. However, women suck dick differently and there's nothing wrong with variety. It's what makes life interesting. You can't tell me that every single woman who's ever gone down on you had the same skills, any more than you can say that they all had the same pussy."

I couldn't argue with that and admitted it. "True enough, but I'm not married like you are. When I was, I never cheated on Estella, and I'm not going to cheat on Jemistry."

"What do you want? The male-saint-of-the-year award?" Floyd sighed and took a swig of beer. "Besides, I would never say never if I were you. There's always, always someone who could come along and make you eat those words . . . along with her pussy."

"Not in my case. The same nurses throwing cooch at you throw it at me and I deflect all of them like flies."

"Damn, now why would you call fine women flies?"

"You know what I mean. I'm not crazy enough to jeopardize my career over casual sex, and you need to stop before it all catches up with you."

Floyd waved me off. "Every chick I've fooled around with on the job has done a bunch of dudes. They all know what time it is. Long hours, a bunch of stressful shit always going on, and people dying all around us. Sometimes we all need to escape for a few minutes and there's no better way to relax outside of fucking. That shit's better than popping five Valiums."

"Sex is cool, but making love is where it's at. You're too old to still be trying to nail random broads."

"So you say!"

"Not to mention that you're married with four damn kids."

"Wow!" Floyd looked at me like he was shocked. "You mean to tell me that I have a wife and kids? I never knew that."

I threw my beer cap at him. "Okay, I'll drop it, but all I'm saying is that if I'm hearing about all of your extracurricular activities at work, other people know. I'm not one to gossip, so it's getting around. They're going to nickname you Water Cooler Dick in a month or two if you don't quit."

"I hear you. I do need to slow down. The shit's getting old."

"It's not only old, it's dangerous. All it takes is one doctor going home and blabbing to his wife during pillow talk, and her being one of Courtney's buddies, and it's a wrap. Courtney's cool and while she probably expects you're doing some dirt, if she finds out any facts, she'll take your ass to the cleaners. Not to mention putting foot to ass."

"She's not putting any foot to anyone's ass, but I get your drift. It's not worth it."

Floyd turned the television back up and we sat there watching it for a few minutes while we finished our beers.

"Speaking of pillow talk," Floyd said out of the blue. "When am I going to meet Jemistry? She's all you ever talk about."

"I'm not letting you around my girl; you might try to talk her out of her panties."

"Man, that hurts. I'd never do that to you."

Floyd really had a painful expression on his face.

"I'm only kidding. Relax. Sure, you can meet her. Why don't we plan to take Courtney and Jemistry out to dinner next weekend? Are you on call on Saturday?"

"No, I'm off. But Courtney already made me promise that we'd take the kids down to Williamsburg and stay at Great Wolf Lodge."

"Sounds like fun."

"Happy, happy, joy, joy," Floyd stated sarcastically. "I plan to catch me some serious Zs while they run around the indoor water park. I don't mind doing Busch Gardens, though. I need to keep my eyes on the kids in a crowded place like that."

"Isn't next weekend their season opening?"

"Yes, so it's going to be packed. Six Flags is damn near around the corner, but she wants to go more than three hours away. I don't get it."

"She can take the kids to Six Flags anytime. Go and make them all happy."

"I'm going. I'm going."

"There is something I want to run past you, Floyd," I said, my mood changing.

"Shoot."

"As you probably remember, I married Estella rather quickly. I'm not sure we knew enough about each other to make that move in that time frame. We loved each other, sure, but I'm not sure we knew enough about each other's capability to handle life."

"Man, you and Estella would still be married to this day if it weren't for . . . what happened."

"You can talk about the miscarriages. It's my reality. I had three children who never had a chance to experience a day of life, but I've finally accepted it. Matter of fact, I called Estella the other day and apologized."

Floyd sat up in his seat. "Apologized for what?"

"Not being as supportive as I could have been. Not understanding what she was really going through. I shouldn't have —"

"Tevin, I get it. Then again, I don't. You dealt with the loss the best way that you could and you were there for her. She shut you out. I remember. I was there. I was the one you talked to because she wouldn't even discuss it. Sure, it was probably harder on her. It wasn't that you couldn't get her pregnant. It was because she couldn't carry to term.

"We're both doctors so you and I both

know that everyone's body is not the same. It never weakened your love for her. It simply got to the point where the pain of looking at each other was too much. You'd work overtime and sleep in your office at the hospital to avoid going home. That was no way to live. Let that go."

"I have let it go. We've been divorced for years. She told me she's engaged and thinking about adoption."

Floyd stared at me. "And how do you feel about that?"

"I'm happy for her." He eyed me suspiciously. "I am. I did love Estella, but if I'm being honest with myself, I never loved her as much as I love Jemistry."

"Wow! I have got to meet this chick who has you all sappy and shit."

I chuckled. "She's a remarkable woman."

"Well, we can't do dinner next weekend but what about Wednesday night?"

"I'm cool for that day and I'll check with her."

"Let me guess. You brought up what happened with Estella because you're ready to propose to Jemistry?"

"Something like that, but I'm afraid it might run her away. Jemistry's not that trusting."

"So why be with a chick who doesn't trust you?"

"I never said she didn't trust me. It's only that she trusted the men in her past who hurt and abused her. She doesn't know whether I'm a lunatic or not. You know that's not the case, but she doesn't."

"I feel you. That's what happens when a lot of the men out there do trifling shit and then make women bitter for the next man."

I could not believe Floyd had the nerve to say that when he was cheating on Courtney on the regular, like it was his part-time career. I decided not to bring it up again. If he wanted to believe that he was dropping nuggets of wisdom, so be it.

I settled in, opened another beer, and started watching ESPN. Even though I believed that Jemistry loved me, and it showed in her actions, she still had yet to admit it. Part of me had to wonder if I was imagining that she felt the same way for me as I felt for her.

CHAPTER FIFTEEN

"Immature love says 'I love you because I need you.' Mature love says 'I need you because I love you.' "
— Erich Fromm

It was Memorial Day Weekend and Jemistry was floating on cloud nine since school was about to let out. She was also a bit over-whelmed with trying to get everything done. Medgar Evers had had their graduation the weekend before. More than six hundred graduates. It was a big-ass school. Jemistry had to stand onstage for all that time. Her principal's speech was astounding and motivational. She told everyone that it was crucial not to allow dream stealers and reality stealers prevent them from going after their goals. She spoke nothing but the truth.

She also told them that it was important for them to determine whether they wanted a steady paycheck from working forty hours a week, fifty weeks a year, or whether they wanted to be an entrepreneur and get paid based on their own efforts. She explained that neither one of those choices was any better than the other. It was whatever each person felt comfortable with. Her main concern was that they do something after making it through high school. Work, college, the military, something other than simply giving up like so many do.

After the graduation, I had gone out with her to celebrate with a few of the kids and their families. One of the parents had rented out the ballroom at the Renaissance Hotel on K Street. We had a great time chilling with them all. The food was good, the music was on point, but I must admit that the way the teenagers were dancing — in front of their parents no less — threw me for a loop.

They were doing something called the Red Nose, where girls spread their legs apart, and then shake their asses up on the boys like red nose pit bulls, and some other freaky shit that I had never seen. The parents joined in when they started doing the Wobble, a line dance. Jemistry even got out on the floor on that one. She couldn't act too loose around the students or parents. She told me once that with everything going viral, it was important not to get caught up in some foolishness. Not as a principal. I didn't need that as a highly respected surgeon either.

Earlier in the week, we had had dinner with Floyd and Courtney at Art and Soul on Capitol Hill. The two women hit it off well and exchanged numbers, making plans to do a spa day together in the near future.

Floyd pulled me aside when we were waiting for the valets to retrieve our cars after dinner and said, "None of my business during pillow talk, man. Looks like our women are about to become chummy and I don't need any drama."

I whispered to him, "Maybe you should tame it down like you said you would. I'm still hearing about your dirt, Water Cooler Dick. Something about a threesome in a maintenance supply closet last week?"

Floyd smirked. "I couldn't turn that one down. Two hyperactive nursing assistants at once? It was out of this world."

I shook my head as they pulled up with my Benz. Jemistry was hugging Courtney a few yards away. "Okay, I keep warning you, but you're going to have to learn the hard way. You can come stay with me when your wife kicks you out."

Floyd chuckled. "Not going to happen."

"Famous last words."

I decided to get into my car and mind my business. It didn't sit well with me, though. Throughout dinner Courtney had sung Floyd's praises. She really believed that he was faithful, or at least she was very good at making it seem like she believed it.

I glanced over at Jemistry in the passenger seat; she was catching up with her emails on her iPhone. Even under the streetlights, her exquisiteness blew me away. There was no way that I would ever betray her trust like that.

"It has been years since I've been on an island!" Jemistry was excited as we walked along the beach at the Ritz-Carlton in the Cayman Islands. The water was a clear green and even though there was a good crowd, we were completely caught up in each other.

"Yeah, me as well."

She jumped onto my back and wrapped her legs around my waist and her arms around my neck. "Thanks for suggesting this. I needed to get away, even for a few days."

She started sucking on my earlobe.

"Keep that up and I might drop you right here and make love to you on the sand."

166

"That's not exactly a way to get me to stop. I wouldn't mind if you did."

"Later on tonight, and I'm down. I'm not trying to get locked up over here."

Jemistry laughed. "So does that mean that I can't use the handcuffs that I brought along in my suitcase to chain you to the bed?"

"No, you can do that within the next fifteen minutes."

"Well, shit." She jumped down off my back. "In that case, I'll race you back to the room."

Jemistry took off running. I decided to give her a head start; her legs were so much shorter than mine. When she was about twenty yards away, I took off after her and still beat her to the elevator.

"Baby, I thought you were joking about the handcuffs." I squirmed as Jemistry was in the bathroom of our suite, singing "Do Me Baby" by Prince.

I was nude and freshly showered and she came out in one of the plush white robes the hotel provided, left open so I could see all of her sexiness.

"Here we are, in this big old empty room." She straddled my waist and gazed into my eyes. "Staring each other down."

She checked to make sure that the hand-cuffs were still secure. I could smell her bath gel, which smelled like the ocean. "You want me just as much as I want you. Let's stop fooling around."

I licked my lips as she took off the robe and totally exposed her breasts. Her nipples were hard and standing at attention. So was my dick.

She had ordered room service earlier and had requested a bottle of honey to use with her pot of tea. She reached over to get it off the rolling table, where the remnants of my steak dinner and her seafood dinner remained.

Jemistry started drizzling honey on her breasts until she had used up half the bottle. Then she rubbed it all over them and her midriff while my dick grew harder — if that were even humanly possible — by the second underneath her.

"You're not allergic to honey, are you?" she asked.

"If I was, this would be a fine time to ask me."

We both laughed.

"I'm not allergic; what I am is horny. You going to let me suck it all off?"

"Only if you answer my trivia questions correctly."

I took my eyes off her tits and looked into her eyes. "Are you serious?"

"Very. Don't pout. There are only a few of them."

"I'm not trying to take an exam, but if that's the only way you'll let me make love to you, shoot."

"What's my middle name?"

I grinned. "Easy one. Your middle name is Alicia."

"Correct."

Jemistry held out her left tit for me to suckle on. Right when I was about to try to choke on it, she pulled it away.

"Next question."

I sighed. "This is killing me!"

"What was the name of my first dog?"

It was almost impossible to think with all of the blood rushing to my dick. I remembered us discussing it. Shit! It was a German shepherd.

"Durango!" I shouted out.

She started grinding on my dick but didn't put it inside her. "Correct again. Damn, it turns me on that you remember so much about me."

"Climb on my dick."

"No, I'm not ready for your tree stump yet."

"Well, it's damn sure ready for you."

"That's obvious."

Jemistry reached behind her and started playing with my balls.

"I'll make this the last question."

"Baby, as much as I'm enjoying your game, I really need you to climb on my dick."

"First of all, I'm running this." Jemistry suddenly tried to sound militant. Loved it! "I'm going to climb on what I want to climb on when I want to climb on it." She grabbed me roughly by my chin. "You understand?"

"Since I'm handcuffed to the bed, this is your show. Ask the next question."

"Do you really, really, really love me, Tevin?"

"That would be a resounding yes."

I gazed into her eyes.

"You really, really, really, really love me?"

"You can add *really* on there a hundred times and my answer will still be yes, Jemistry. I fell in love with you at first sight."

I was hoping she was going to finally say that she loved me as well, but she didn't. Again, as long as I sensed it, I was going to roll with it and hope for the best.

When she just continued to stare at me, I said, "I'm glad you decided to give me a chance to love you the way that you deserve to be loved."

"I'm glad that I decided to do that, too."

Jemistry bent over me and slipped her tongue into my mouth. I gladly accepted it. Even though we kissed all the time, it was different. It was more intense and filled with more emotions.

Our kiss lasted a good five minutes. It was intense. She reached beneath herself, put my dick inside her, and started gyrating on it slowly.

She broke the kiss and whispered, "I wish you could stay inside me forever."

She grabbed my cuffed wrists for support and started riding me like there was no tomorrow, all the while allowing me access to her tits so I could suck them. She started speaking in tongues, *literally.* I had never heard any shit like that before. I had no idea that she even did that.

It was alarming and arousing at the same time. She let go of my wrists, grabbed her own breasts, and started motorboating them across my face. I licked and sucked, and licked and sucked, all the while we fucked. This woman had my nose wide open and that wasn't about to change . . . ever.

Later on that night, we went out on the beach with a couple of large towels, found a secluded spot, and made love again.

171

The next morning I told Jemistry to rest while I took a run on the sand. But I really needed to take care of some business . . . and I did.

CHAPTER SIXTEEN

"Where there is love there is life."
— Mahatma Gandhi

School was finally out for Jemistry and I decided to surprise her by cooking her dinner at her place. I had been over there several times to spend the night, but we rarely chilled there. She had a roommate and I didn't so it made sense to spend the majority of our time at my place. I'd given her a key within two months of dating. My mind was already made up that I didn't plan to see anyone else.

When we were flying back from the Caymans, I'd brought up the option of her actually moving in with me. She said that she didn't want to leave Winsome hanging like that. Even though their lease was month-to-month, she explained that Winsome did not have the income to cover the rent on her own. I asked if there was someone else they knew who might room with her, but she knew of no one offhand. Everyone was already settled in someplace else. But if things went my way, eventually Winsome would have to find someone else to room with.

I decided to bring that up when I showed up at their place that afternoon. Jemistry was not home yet. They were having an end-of-year faculty party in the teachers' lounge and she didn't anticipate arriving home until after six. My day had been light — no surgeries — so I was able to get out of the hospital by two and head over there, stopping at Whole Foods on the way to pick up everything that I needed to prepare dinner.

"Damn, that smells good!" Winsome walked into the kitchen right as I was putting the Chilean sea bass on the indoor grill. "What all are you making?"

"I'm grilling some fish, making some jasmine rice, some baby bok choy with sweet peppers, and garlic sourdough bread. Then I'm finishing it with a crème brûlée."

"Jemistry wasn't joking. You can really cook."

"I'm a master in the kitchen. You're welcome to a plate when it's done. There's plenty."

"Even if there wasn't plenty, I was going

to get some. I've been known to eat off Jemistry's plate. There's no shame in my game."

I chuckled as I turned to face her. "Can you hand me that fresh rosemary over there?"

Winsome picked up the bunch of rosemary and brought it to me.

"Thanks," I said as she handed it to me.

"You're welcome."

She sat down at the kitchen table. "I guess you and Jemistry will be spending a lot more time together since she's out for the summer."

"She'll definitely have more free time, but hospitals never shut down. I do plan to take a couple of weeks' vacation time so we can get away. She wants to go to Italy to take cooking lessons." I started breaking up the rosemary and sticking sprigs into the fish. "As you can imagine, I'm as excited as she is about that."

"Well, Jemistry definitely could benefit from cooking lessons, but don't tell her I said that. She's sensitive about her cooking."

"Don't I know it!" I paused for a few seconds and then went and sat across from Winsome at the table. "Since you brought up the topic, I do want to spend as much time with Jemistry as possible. It would be perfect if she could move in with me."

It was like all of the air was suddenly sucked out of the room, like a scene from the movie *Backdraft.* The look on Winsome's face told me that it was about to come back in and combust into flames.

"Move in with you?!" Winsome practically shouted. "But what about me?"

"Winsome, did you honestly think that you and Jemistry would be roommates until the end of days? We're in love and she's over my place at least four nights a week as it is."

"And she's here three nights a week," Winsome said in defiance. "Ya'll haven't been dating long enough to move in together. And when did she say she loved you? She never told me that."

Those words stung. She realized that if Jemistry was ready to admit to being in love, she would have told her about it. I refused to pay homage to her negative thoughts, though.

"Says who? You? You can't determine a timeline for our relationship." I crossed my arms in front of me. This was not going to be easy. "If the two of us feel like we're ready to take that step, no one has the right to judge us . . . even you. We're in love," I embellished by speaking for both of us, "and once we get married, she's going to have to move out any—"

"Get married? Jemistry hasn't said anything to me about a damn wedding, and trust, I'd be the first to know!"

"Actually, you'd be at least the third to know because the two people in the actual relationship, the two people who will be in the actual marriage, would have to know first."

I was hoping my point was delivered. When she rolled her eyes, I decided to clarify further.

"Winsome, Jemistry adores you. She talks about you all the time. She respects and admires a lot of your qualities, but there are some things that make her . . . uneasy."

"What things?" Winsome spat out the words. "Oh, let me guess. You have a problem with my sexuality."

"I don't, and don't even go there. What I do have a problem with is you bringing a bunch of strangers up in here while my baby is around. If you want to risk your life over casual sex with the masses, that's on you. But it only takes one person to be certifiably crazy before a tragedy happens. I don't want Jemistry to end up on *The First 48* or one of those other shows because you can't control your behavior."

"How dare you?!" Winsome jumped up

from the table and placed her palms on the surface. "If you weren't a fucking rosewood tree, I'd smack the shit out of you!"

"If it makes you feel better, smack me, but I'm not taking back what I said. And I'm definitely not going to hit you back. Not in my nature." I stood up to check on the fish. "I haven't officially asked my baby to marry me yet, but I'm sure she is anticipating it. I've been waiting for the right moment. Who knows? That right moment might come tonight."

Winsome stormed out of the kitchen, went into her bedroom, and slammed the door closed behind her.

I made sure the fish wasn't burning, flipped it over, and then reached into my pocket to retrieve the velvet ring box. I opened it and peeped the six-carat De Beers Signature collection platinum-banded ring that I'd purchased while we were in the Caymans. It was tricky trying to declare it at customs without Jemistry seeing it.

Yeah, tonight is the night! I hope she says yes!

Jemistry had called to tell me that she was running even later. Dinner was done so I decided to go into her room and watch the evening news until she got there. Somehow

I dozed off. I must have been more tired than I'd thought and the newscaster's voice might as well have been singing a lullaby. I was out like a light.

I was still completely out of it when I felt Jemistry unzipping my pants and pulling my dick out.

"Ooh, baby," I whispered. "You're home."

I loved it when Jemistry woke me up with her amazing head game.

"So now you want to have an end-of-the-year party with me? Do your thing, baby."

She didn't respond. She just took the tip of my dick into her mouth and went to work.

It didn't take me long to snap out of it, open my eyes, and push Winsome off of me, and completely off the bed.

I jumped up as she climbed up off the floor. "What the fuck?!"

Winsome laughed. "I was only trying to give you what you wanted."

"I don't want you!" I stared at her in disgust as I tried frantically to put my dick back in my pants. "You're fucking crazy!"

"That's a big-ass dick you've got there." Winsome bit her bottom lip. "Now I see why Jemistry's so sprung. I should've known when she gave up both of her fuck buddies so fast. They'd been taking turns banging her pussy out for years."

"You're a dirty bitch!"

"It's the truth. I bet you thought she was some kind of innocent and virginal chick when you met her, didn't you? She had your ass fooled and she has your ass fooled now."

"She told me about her past and what she was doing when we met. There's nothing you can say or do that will keep me from loving her."

We both heard the key in the lock at the same time. I tried desperately to beat Winsome to the door but, by the time I got there, Jemistry was standing in the hallway and saw both of us come out of her room. There was no way that we could hide the expressions on our faces.

Winsome walked past Jemistry and said, "I was keeping that dick warm for you until you got home. He's like a fucking python."

Jemistry glared at Winsome as she disappeared out of sight and then turned her look of utter disappointment toward me.

"Baby, I promise you, this is not what you think."

"Not what I think?" She pointed in the direction that Winsome had gone. "I come home, catch the two of you rushing out of my bedroom, your belt unbuckled and your pants unzipped, and it's not what I think?

It's exactly what the fuck I think!"

I tried to move toward her and take her into my arms. She pushed me away.

"Don't even *think* about touching me! I trusted you. It took me years to let the walls of my fortress come down, and you do this to me. You're like all the rest of them."

"No, I'm not. I promise you that —"

"Stop saying *promise*!" Jemistry screamed. "It's a lie! Everything you ever told me was a lie!"

"Baby, when you said you were running late, I went to lie down." I pointed to her bedroom. "I woke up with my dick in your roommate's mouth and *immediately* pushed her off me."

"You are so full of shit! How did she manage to get your dick out of your pants and into her mouth without you noticing?"

"I thought it was you. My eyes were closed, but the second she started . . . when she put it in her mouth, I could tell the difference."

"I don't believe a word coming out of your mouth. You need to get the fuck out."

"I'm not leaving until we get this straight . . . until you understand what happened. Ask her what happened. Can you at least do that?"

"I don't even want to look at that bitch in

this moment! She's —"

Winsome must have been hanging on to every word. She yelled, "Don't call me a damn bitch because your man wanted some of this!"

I couldn't believe that things were going down like that. I couldn't believe that the love of my life was about to reject me for something that I didn't do. How could a life already so fucked-up and plagued with disappointment take another fucking blow?

Jemistry went around the corner and I followed her. Before I knew it, she was on top of Winsome on the floor, pounding her fists into her face. Winsome was screaming for dear life and trying to protect her head.

I pulled Jemistry off her. "Baby, stop! It's not worth going to jail!"

"You filthy bitch!" Jemistry screamed, and started trying to kick Winsome as she got up off the floor. "It's not enough for you to fuck every Tom, Thomasina, Dick, Daisy, Harry, and Henrietta! Now you want to fuck my man!"

Winsome wiped the blood coming out of the right side of her lip. "Actually, your man came onto me."

"That's a fucking lie!" I said. "You came in there when I was asleep and tricked me. Admit it."

"I ain't admitting shit because it didn't go down that way!"

I was still holding on to Jemistry from behind. She grabbed at my wrists to try to free herself. "Let me go, Tevin!"

"Only if you promise you won't attack her again. I don't give a fuck about her, but I won't let anything happen to you."

Jemistry started breathing heavily; she was in a blind rage.

"No, I'm not letting you go. I'm taking you out of here before you end up hurt, or in jail. You're a principal. Think about it."

Jemistry started to calm down some. One thing was for sure: She didn't want to jeopardize her career. She had worked too hard for it.

"Let me go. I'm going to leave, and so are you."

I released. "Good, we can go back to my place. You don't ever have to come back here. I'll get all of your things by tomorrow and —"

"I'm not leaving any of my shit here, and I'm not going to your place." She glared at Winsome. "As a matter of fact, you get the fuck out."

"I'm not going anywhere!" Winsome proclaimed. "Ain't no man coming between

183

us! He needs to get the fuck out so we can talk!"

"Winsome, I swear on every grave of every dead relative that I have, if you don't get the fuck out of here within the next two minutes, I'm going to beat the living daylights out of you."

"Jemistry, this is silly. Where am I supposed to go?"

"I don't give a damn. Out of all the people you're fucking, at least one of them should have a sofa for you to crash on. Or you can just get in their bed and spread your legs like you always do. Tell them that you'll fuck for three hots and a cot."

"Are you really going to put me out of here?" Winsome asked.

"Are you really going to wait around and find out if I'll maim you?"

Winsome went into her bedroom.

I tried to reason with Jemistry. "All of this started because I discussed moving in together earlier and she flipped."

Jemistry turned and looked me in the eyes. "I can't deal with this right now. I need time."

"But —"

"I'll be back tomorrow morning." Winsome had put on a pair of tennis shoes and grabbed her purse. "By then, everything should be back to normal."

"Back to normal? How about you kiss my entire ass? Let's get something straight right now. We're no longer going to be room-mates. I decided to share a home with a friend, not a backstabbing whore."

Winsome stood there, tapping her right foot, and staring up at the ceiling.

"I'm not sure what happened between the two of you, but it's clear as a damn bell that it shouldn't have ever happened. You're so hurt and lonely that you want me to wallow in the shit pool of pity with you. Well, I'm not doing it another day."

"You do realize that I could call the police because you assaulted me, right?" Winsome asked and then smirked. "My face tells the story."

"Yeah, you can call the police and by the time they get here, there'll be bruises all over your body. If I'm getting locked up, I'm going to make it worth my time."

The smirk quickly disappeared from Win-some's face. Both she and I realized that what Jemistry had said made a lot of sense. That damn Virgo was analyzing and plot-ting. If she was going to get arrested, she was going to cause more damage on her way there. I couldn't argue with that logic.

Winsome didn't say another word. She

left out and slammed the front door.

Jemistry turned toward me. "Your turn."

"I love you. You know that I love you."

She went over and opened the door. "Please leave."

"Not until we talk."

"Look, Tevin, I'm not going to be the typical scorned woman, call the police, lie about you doing something to me, and then put you into the system with a restraining order. So many women do that, that when women really are in danger, people tend not to believe them.

"But I'm also not prepared to listen to any more of your lies tonight. It's too painful. If you truly give even an inkling of a damn about me, you'll leave. You'll leave right now and let me start to begin healing.

"The good part — if there is a good part in this cesspool of pure fuckery — is that I'm out of school for the summer. I'm going to deal with getting Winsome the hell up out of here for good. I'm going to drown my sorrows with peanut butter cups and butter pecan ice cream. I'm going to try to understand why my judgment in men is so poor yet again."

"There's nothing wrong with your judgment, baby. Not this time. I promise you that —"

"There goes that word again. *Promise!* Blah, blah, blah."

I realized that I was fighting a losing battle.

I walked toward the door and paused in front of her. She looked away from me. "You're not even going to look at me?"

"No, it's too hurtful."

I did as Jemistry wished and left. When I got into my car, I saw Winsome across the parking lot in her Toyota Camry, going off into her cell phone. *Bitch!*

How could planning a romantic dinner and a proposal turn into such a horror story? Someone was playing a sick joke on me!

CHAPTER SEVENTEEN

"Hate is easy. Love takes courage."
— Unknown

Many claim that there is life after death. I guess there is some truth to that because the biggest part of me died that night in Jemistry's apartment when she dismissed me from her life. My heart failed . . . it flatlined. I was like a zombie from *The Walking Dead* TV series. Sure, I was a functioning zombie, walking among a sea of functioning alcoholics, functioning gamblers, and functioning drug addicts. I went through the motions every day, even managed to stay on top of my game in the operating room, but once I left the hospital, all I did was go home, sit in the dark, and sink into a state of depression until the next morning.

I tried to call Jemistry but she blocked my numbers. She also blocked my email addresses. I staked out her parking lot a few times, but I never saw her enter or leave. Her car was never in the lot, which made me wonder if she had moved after all, or had left town.

After everything in her painful past that she had told me about, the last thing that I wanted on my conscience was her thinking that I was the kind of man who would do anything to disrespect or hurt her. Yet, that's exactly what she thought. In her mind, I was a liar and a cheater, one who would sink so low as to do something sexual with her own roommate.

To make matters worse, she had also lost her faith in her best friend that day. Even I was shocked that Winsome would do such a thing, especially considering I barely knew her. Whether Jemistry believed that I came on to her or she came on to me, either way, the blow had to feel just as bad.

Floyd showed up at my house two Fridays later, with a pizza and a bottle of Crown Royal. When I opened the door and saw him standing there, my heart sank. I had hoped that it was Jemistry.

"Don't look so happy to see me," he said as he brushed past me and entered.

"Floyd, I appreciate you coming by, but I wouldn't be much company right now."

"So we'll eat all of these carbs and get

drunk and pass out in silence. I know you're off for the weekend, as am I, so it's all good." He put the pizza down on the coffee table. "I can camp out for a couple of days, if you want. Courtney's used to my long hours."

"What part of me wanting to be alone don't you get?" I asked sarcastically.

"What part of 'I'm no longer going to sit back and watch you sink into a state of depression' don't you get?"

I sighed and plopped down on the sofa. "What amazes me is the irony of it all."

"What irony?"

"I warn you that you're going to lose Courtney when she catches you cheating, and I lose Jemistry instead, even though I wasn't cheating."

Floyd shook his head and opened the pizza box. "See, sometimes it pays to do the wrong thing. Courtney's at home vacuuming and doing laundry after an afternoon of getting a pedicure, a manicure, and a facial that I footed the bill for. If and when I go home, she'll be in bed freshly showered and ready to please her husband in every way imaginable."

"It still doesn't justify what you're doing."

"No, there is no justification for what I'm doing. I'm a dog and there's no doubt about it. I even know what kind of dog I am. I looked it up."

I couldn't help but ask. "Looked what up?"

"I went on the Internet and researched the traits of different breeds of dogs."

"Are you for real?" I sighed. "You have too much spare time on your hands."

"I don't have any spare time on my hands, but I wanted to know. Think about it. From childhood, both of us have heard about all men being dogs. Hell, chicks started calling me a dog before I even caught a good whiff of a pussy."

I chuckled. "That's true. Girls in middle school were calling us all dogs."

"Exactly. So I decided to finally investigate and see what the hell they were talking about. Most dogs are loyal, sit up underneath their owners, protect them, and will even lay down their lives for the people who feed them. Yet, we're called dogs like it's a bad thing. If you ask me, dogs get a really bad rap."

"Like I said, you have too much time on your hands."

Floyd grabbed a slice of pizza. He was the only man that I knew who liked pineapple on pizza. That always seemed like a female thing. One day I had asked him about it and he said that he ate a lot of fruit to counteract the other ingredients so his ejaculate wouldn't taste fucked up when chicks sucked his dick. Couldn't argue with that rationale.

"So what breed are you?"

"I'm proud to say that I'm an Alaskan Malamute." He pointed at the pizza. "You're not hungry?"

"Floyd, you know I'm not into pineapple on pizza. You should've brought me a meat lover's. That's my shit."

"Well, you can pick the pineapple off, but I suggest you eat it, and you already know why."

"I'm not having sex with anyone right now. I don't want anyone but the one I can't have." I paused. "I must be bored to ask this. What are the traits of an Alaskan Malamute? Never heard of it."

"Good question. And dig this. Alaskan Malamutes have natural hunting instincts. They're independent, resourceful, and highly intelligent. They're difficult to train but if an owner understands and keeps them motivated, a successful situation is possible. They rarely bark, but when they do, it comes out as more of a *woo-woo* than a bark."

"You're crazy, man!" I chuckled. "How

many breeds did you have to go through to find that one?"

"It only took me about fifteen minutes to define my character traits. Don't you think they fit me?"

"I have no fucking idea!"

"Well, let's break it down. I definitely have hunting skills. I can smell desperate pussy from a mile away. I'm independent and resourceful. I'm a wealthy doctor. I'm definitely hard to train. You're always saying how I don't let Courtney run all over me."

"I never suggested that you let her run all over you. I suggested that you allow her to walk beside you."

"Yeah, whatever. As long as Courtney keeps me motivated, the next trait on the list, our marriage will be successful. And I don't exactly *woo-woo* when I bust a nut, but it's definitely not a bark."

I nodded my head. "Like I said, you're crazy!"

"I'm not crazy. I'm the shit and so is my dick."

"Keep your dick out of this conversation. If I take mine out, this entire room will go dark."

Floyd and I joked around for most of the night. I even ended up eating some pizza —

after picking the pineapple off. We downed the entire bottle of Crown Royal. There was no way that I was letting him drive intoxicated. I sent Courtney a text from my phone — so she would know that he was really with me — and included a photo of him passed out drunk on my sofa. It was a "proof of fidelity" shot since so many men would lie and say that they were with a friend when they were out trolling for pussy. This was one time when Floyd was where he claimed he would be.

A lot of women did the same thing, though. One time, one of the nurses at Sibley asked me for hotel recommendations out in Northern Virginia. When I asked her why she was trying to pay for a hotel so close to DC, she said that she needed to get lost for the weekend because her best friend was going out of town to cheat on her husband and told him that they were vacationing together.

I couldn't decide whether it made her a good friend or a bad friend to agree to go hide out in a hotel. She said that her friend was going to foot the bill for the room, including room service, through her business account. That was an attempt to make it sound more kosher.

At the end of the day, I couldn't think

badly of her. She wasn't cheating on her man and she was only trying to be supportive of a friend. Besides, I couldn't talk since Floyd was cheating and I was smiling in Courtney's face every time I saw her.

Still, it was getting to the point where women would soon not be able to talk a bunch of shit about men. They were on the brink of being at least as trifling as we were. But I couldn't really blame them. A lot of them were simply adapting to the environment around them. They had developed an "if you can't beat them, join them" mentality. The only problem was that it meant the imminent demise of the nuclear family and it meant becoming bitter, and thus even more conniving. We were in serious trouble, though. Women used both sides of their brains while we used half of our brains and our dicks to guide us.

I couldn't stand the thought of Jemistry back up on that stage at The Carolina Kitchen on poetry night, reciting a poem that had something to do with me and her hatred toward me. I had to keep looking for her. I had to make things right.

CHAPTER EIGHTEEN

"When I say I love you, please believe it's true. When I say forever, know I'll never leave you. When I say good-bye, promise me you won't cry. Cause the day I'll be saying that would be the day I die."
— Unknown

For the next week and a half, every day when I left work, or all day if I was off, I sat out in Jemistry's parking lot waiting for her to go in or come out. No sign of her and no sign of Winsome. I knocked several times as well — no answer. So then I resorted to becoming a slipshod private detective and knocked on a few of her neighbors' doors to ask if anyone had seen her. One elderly woman said that she *thought* she had seen Jemistry putting some trash in the outdoor dumpster "a week or so ago."

I was so serious about it that I would bring something to eat and drink with me and make sure that I had plenty of gas to run my air-conditioning in the car as long as possible. It was extremely hot that summer and the humidity was high. One thing that I did notice was that, outside of parents or nannies bringing young infants and toddlers out to the play area, there were hardly any children between the ages of five and twelve outdoors doing *anything.* And if they were out there, it was because their younger siblings were on the playground. The younger kids would play under the watchful eyes of the parents and the older ones always had some kind of electronic gadget bolted to their hands. Either a handheld videogame system, a cell phone, or a tablet. It was preposterous and made me see firsthand why so many kids were overweight.

Sucking up a bunch of unhealthy calories from sodas and juices. Eating a bunch of fast food or processed, microwavable foods at home. Being too sedentary and not being forced to exercise. Sure, there were parents who still insisted that their kids play sports, but letting them sit on their asses was quickly becoming "the new normal."

When I was a child, my parents made my sisters and me stay outside all day on the weekends, and for at least two hours after we completed our homework and dinner during the week. They didn't care what we did, as long as it was some kind of activity. My sisters did a lot of Double Dutch, Hopscotch, and and-patting games. Or they played Mother, May I?, Red Light/Green Light, or Simon Says. My friends and I either skateboarded, rode our bicycles up, down, and around the block, or played stickball. We found something to do because there weren't any other options. Nowadays, kids were playing high-tech video games, ruining their eyesight, encouraging migraines in the near future from looking at screens so long. They didn't even know about the majority of the things we used to do outside.

I was sitting there shaking my head and running all of those thoughts through my mind when I heard a tap on my driver's side window. I looked up to see a Metropolitan Police officer standing there, with the billy club that he had used to hit the window in one hand and his other hand on the latch of his gun holster. I never even saw him pull up in his cruiser, I was so busy daydreaming.

I nervously rolled down my window. "Good afternoon, officer."

"Sir, may I ask what business you have here?"

I shrugged. "I'm waiting for a friend to get home."

"A friend? What's your friend's name?"

I thought about it for a second. I didn't want to bring any more drama into Jemistry's life. For all I knew, she could have called them.

"Why does it matter? I'm not bothering anyone, but I'll leave immediately if you want."

"License and registration."

"Oh, wow, do we really have to go there?"

"Sir, I'm not going to ask you again. There have been several complaints by residents stating that you are out here every day sitting in your vehicle for long periods of time. Why would you wait for days on end for your *friend* to return home?"

I carefully took my wallet out of my back pocket and reached over to my glove compartment to get my registration. He bent down to watch my every move. I was a big dude and there were a lot of trigger-happy cops in DC. I could see the newspaper headline in my head: PROMINENT VASCULAR SURGEON FROM SIBLEY MEMORIAL SHOT DEAD BY METROPOLITAN POLICE.

"Here you go," I said as I handed him the items. "Do you mind if I'm honest with you?"

He glared at me and practically snarled. "That would be your best bet right now."

"You look to be about the same age as me, so maybe you can relate to what I'm going through. I'm not a pedophile or a rapist; I have a clean record; and I've never committed a criminal act in my entire life. All that I am is a brother in love with a woman who doesn't want anything to do with me. I've been sitting out here hoping for an opportunity to apologize yet again for something I never did."

I could tell that I had sparked his interest. "What do you mean?"

I sighed. "She and I were dating. I promised her that I would never hurt her. I came over here one night about a month ago to cook her a romantic dinner after work. Her roommate got upset when I told her that I planned to ask my girl to move in with me and get married. I fell asleep. When I woke up, the roommate was giving me head. I pushed her off and got out my girl's room right as she was walking in the front door. She jumped to conclusions, the roommate lied like a professional actress, and my girl kicked me out.

"All I want is a chance to see if she's cooled off enough to discuss it and hear me out. She's been hurt time and time again in the past and, even if she never takes me back, I need her to know that I didn't betray her like every other man before me."

"You couldn't even make that shit up," the officer said with a smirk.

"I'm not making it up. I love her, but I'm willing to let her go. And after what just happened here today, I'm prepared to finally do that." I looked at the building. "I'm not even sure she still lives here. I guess that I was holding out false hope. I haven't seen her, her car, or even the roommate or her car. I don't know what's going on."

He handed my license and registration back. "I've been where you are. I'm a good man myself. Not flawless, but a good man. It took me forever to get my wife over her trust issues and insecurities."

"Well, it didn't take me forever, but her river of pain runs deep. I wanted to be the one to put the smile back on her face. And I accomplished that for a short period of time."

We both fell silent for a few seconds.

"If I let you slide, you promise not to come back around here?" he asked.

"I promise. It's over and the last thing that I wanted was to upset the neighbors. I never considered that, but I'm sure it definitely looked strange . . . me being out here all the time. It's good to know that people actually call in and report stuff like that."

"Yeah, it's a mixture and varies by neighborhood. Some neighbors are paranoid and will call if they see a person they don't recognize walk by their house on the sidewalk. Others will watch someone get gunned down in front of them, not call, and then play dumb when we get there."

I nodded my head. "I can imagine."

"Take it easy, brother."

He started to walk away back to his cruiser.

"Thanks for giving me a break."

He turned toward me as he opened his door and put his right foot inside the car. "Women won't cut us a break. Sometimes we have to help each other out."

He got in and started up his engine. I pulled away and he followed behind me to the next corner and hooked a right.

The hospital was having a Fourth of July staff picnic. They did it yearly because, unlike most companies, hospitals never close on holidays. In fact, those are usually the busiest days. While people are supposed to be celebrating and relaxing, they end up doing some of the most life-threatening things. Alcohol leads to a lot of madness on the

Fourth. Putting too much lighter fluid on the grill and cooking part of yourself instead of just the meat. Shooting off illegal fireworks because you want to be the life of the party and blowing off a hand or finger, or taking out someone's eye. Drunk driving while you're cookout hopping. Getting angry over some bullshit and trying to kill someone who was one of your favorite people before the day started. It was a madhouse.

Since most of the staff had to work, or at least be on call, the picnic was held on the grounds under a big tent. We were able to invite people if we wanted. I would have invited Jemistry, if she were still with me. I started not to even go out there, but, sans a couple of assists in operating room C earlier that morning, I was sitting in my office twiddling my thumbs and catching up on news on the Internet.

Floyd barged into my office without knocking. "Get your ass out of that chair. You're going out to the picnic with me."

"Maybe I'm crazy, but that sounded like an order to me," I stated with much sarcasm. "Who do you think I am? Courtney?"

"Whatever, man. Let's roll out there and get something to eat. I heard they have some apple cobbler this year that is a must-have."

"Man, I'm already eating myself half to death. Women aren't the only ones who turn to comfort foods after a breakup."

"Then that cobbler is shouting out your name. This weekend, we'll hit the court so I can beat your ass in some b-ball."

"I swear, Denial is more than a river in Egypt. You're straight up hallucinating. You sure you're not hitting up the narcotics cabinets on the low?"

We both chuckled as I got up and traded my white coat for my black pinstripe suit coat.

"Tevin, what the hell? You need to leave that jacket off. You'll detonate out there in that heat."

Floyd had a point. He had on a shirt, no tie, and had the first two buttons undone. It had to be at least ninety degrees outside and the tent might or might not make it worse.

I took my jacket off. "Cool. Let's roll."

I paused at the door. "Aren't Courtney and the kids coming?"

Floyd slapped me lightly on the back and guided me out. "Now you're the one hallucinating. I can't let my wife be around all of these women enrolled in the 'dick-share' program with me."

I shook my head without responding as

we headed for the elevators.

The apple cobbler was indeed off the hook. They had Upper Crust do the catering. The sister, Karen Black Wright, who owned it, had a great reputation in the area and I'd always wanted to try out her food. Sibley went all out. In addition to hamburgers, hot dogs, and the regular Fourth of July food staples, they had grilled chicken, lamb chops, ribs, pulled pork, and all the fixings. For a second, I was predicting having to waddle back up to my office.

"You look stuffed," a female voice from behind me said.

"Oh, man, that's an understatement," I replied.

She walked around and took the seat next to me at the table, without even asking if it was vacant. Floyd was off someplace doing God knew what with God knew whom. I had not seen him after the first ten or fifteen minutes of coming down there.

She held out her hand to shake mine. "I'm Magdalena Chavez."

"Tevin Harris," I said, accepting her hand.

"Are you a doctor here, or in the administration? I've never seen you around."

"Actually, I'm a vascular surgeon." I looked at her. She was definitely an attractive Latina. Long, black silky hair, a smooth, olive complexion, great teeth, banging body. But not for me because she wasn't Jemistry. "What about you? You work here?"

"Oh, no, I'm with Lincoln Pharmaceuticals. I'm here quite often though, but most of the drugs I deal with are for the oncology unit."

"Gotcha. That's why we've never crossed paths."

She eyed me seductively for a few seconds. "I'm not usually this forward, but I have to ask. Are you single?"

"Technically, yes, but I'm taking a hiatus from dating."

"Damn shame. And why is that?"

"Hope. Very likely false hope that the woman I want to marry will come back to me."

Magdalena giggled uncomfortably. "Well, where the hell did she go?"

"Good question. I can't find her. She's never at her place and she's off work for the summer so I can't stake out her office."

"Wow, you'd actually do a stakeout?"

I smirked. "Been there, done that. Got the T-shirt."

"You must really love her."

"More than I love my next breath. She's

everything to me, but I'm trying to face facts."

"So what happened?"

I started playing with the remnants of the cobbler on my paper saucer with a plastic spoon. "It doesn't matter." I paused and glanced at her. "Besides, we just met. I don't want to burden you with my issues. This is a Fourth of July celebration. An *extrava-ganza.*"

Magdalena scanned the tent. While there were a lot of people there, most were talking about the latest articles in medical journals, bragging about their skills in an attempt to see who was the smartest doctor on staff, or stuffing food in their mouths.

"I wouldn't go so far as to call it an extravaganza. It actually kind of sucks," she said.

"I'd have to agree."

"Do you want to go for a walk?"

I shook my head vehemently. "No, no thank you."

"It's only a walk. Seems like you could walk off some of those calories so you won't fall asleep at your desk."

"Listen, Magdalena. You seem like a lovely woman, but I don't want to waste your time. I'm not in the right place to even engage in any type of romantic conversation, and I'm a grown man. I can tell when a woman is coming on to me."

"Well, you can't blame a girl for trying," she said as she got up from the table. She reached into her purse and pulled out her business card, then laid it in front of me. "Let me know if you change your mind. We can grab a quick bite, even here in the cafeteria, if you want. I'm usually around on Tuesdays and Thursdays."

I didn't respond as she walked off and Floyd appeared out of nowhere behind me, grabbing onto my shoulders. "Damn, who was that?"

I stood up and gathered my trash. "A pharmaceutical rep. I'm surprised you haven't picked her up already."

"You and me both, but there's always time. Did she give you her number?"

"Yes, but I'm not giving it to you." I tucked her card in my shirt pocket. "You're not going to call that woman and harass her out of the blue."

"Then you definitely need to be hitting that!"

Floyd was too loud and I gazed around to see if anyone had heard him. "Damn, do you have to be so loud?" I noticed that he appeared disheveled. "Where have you been?"

He chuckled. "Let's just say that screwing in a helicopter isn't easy."

"You didn't?!" I exclaimed.

"Hey, it's not like anyone is being airlifted at the moment."

"How did you even get access to one of the helicopters?"

"Haven't you seen the female pilot that started a few months ago?"

I shook my head. Floyd was a maniac. He had zero respect for his wife.

"Floyd, you need to slow your roll. I keep telling you that. You're married and acting more single than any single man I know. And doing all of that at work will cost you in the long run. One of these women is going to expect you to leave Courtney for her and the proverbial skeleton is going to fall out of the closet."

"Stop trying to speak that shit into reality."

I waved him off. "I'm going back up to my office. Do you."

Floyd started talking to a group of candy stripers as I walked off. He was going to have to face the music sooner or later. He realized that, but, like a lot of men, decided to go for broke if it was all eventually going to backfire anyway. Courtney was a great woman and she didn't deserve that kind of treatment. No woman did.

Chapter Nineteen

"The most sincere feelings are the ones hardest to be expressed by words."
— Unknown

"Dad!"

I was shocked to come home one evening and discover my father sitting on my front stoop, sipping on some Gatorade.

He stood up and gave me a hug. There was a rental car parked in my driveway.

"When did you get in?" I asked, shocked because he had never alerted me that he was coming.

"I had to fly in for a conference in New York and thought I'd stop by here for a few days to spend some time with my one and only son."

I was excited to see him. "I'm glad you're here. Come on in."

I unlocked the door and we went inside.

"Do you want me to grab your luggage?"

"I'll get it later." He went into my living room and walked around, checking everything out. "So how are things going?"

"Things are good," I lied. "Working hard, as usual; taking after you."

He sat down in the armchair and I sat on the sofa. "Have you eaten?" he asked. "We could go out. My treat."

"I had a sandwich a couple of hours ago, but if you're hungry, we can either go out or order in." Daddy was staring at me like he was trying to read me. I didn't like it. "Why are you looking at me like that?"

"I've always been honest with you, so I'll come right out with it. Alexis told your mother about you getting dumped; your mother called me, and told me that I needed to come check on you since she knew you'd never discuss it with her."

"Wow, Alexis has a big mouth. I should've known."

"Don't put this off on Alexis. She's only being a concerned sister."

"So they called you all the way in Sweden to tell you that my woman walked out on me, and you came here? Daddy, I'm a grown-ass man."

"Tevin, I do have a conference to attend in New York. They're paying me ten grand to give a thirty-minute speech. But I came back stateside a couple of days early to check on you. Grown-ass man or not, you're my legacy and any man worth his weight in pride makes sure that his legacy remains in a good place."

My father had a way of making the most ridiculous things sound profound. I had to give it to him.

"Well, I appreciate you loving me . . . and I've never doubted your love for me. But there's really nothing you can do. She's gone."

"What did you do to her?"

I was stunned. "Why is it always assumed that the man has to be the one to mess up a relationship?"

"Maybe it has something to do with that being the case at least eight out of ten times, possibly nine."

"Like you messed up with Mom?"

My parents' divorce continued to be a touchy subject, regardless of how many years had elapsed.

"Yes, exactly like how I messed up with your mother." He sighed and took a guzzle of Gatorade. "I was young, dumb, and full of cum. I was reckless and thought that the world belonged to me. I believed that as long as I took care of things on the home front, everything would be fine. But your mother wasn't having that shit . . . not at all."

"Oh, I remember how she went off on you when she found out about your affair. That fight was legendary. The difference between you and me is that I was framed. I never touched Jemistry's roommate, but it didn't matter."

"Tevin, rarely does it matter what's actual or factual when it comes to women and how they think. All that matters is what they perceive."

"I see that now."

"You're still young, though. You'll snap back and find someone else."

"But I don't want anyone else."

I untied my Kenneth Cole shoes and kicked them off. My feet were killing me.

"Tell me about Jemistry. What made her so special to you?"

"What good will it do for me to tell you all the reasons why I love a woman that I can never have?"

Daddy shrugged. "Okay, then. Tell me how you plan to move forward. You have to do that, you know. Just like you had to move on after what happened with Estella."

I leaned forward and buried my face in my hands, took a deep breath, and then looked at Daddy. "I need time to get over this. I'm not ready to date again yet. I'd only be using another woman to fill a void, and that's not fair."

"It's only unfair when the woman doesn't recognize what you're doing. Look at me. I haven't committed to another woman since your mother, but I damn sure haven't been celibate either."

"I've been there, Dad. After Estella and I divorced, I had plenty of lovers. Even had one a few months before I met Jemistry. I'm not trying to go back to that. That's like eating a fast-food burger instead of an aged rib-eye steak."

"Well, the point is that a man's got to eat. If you don't get back out there and get laid, it'll only make things worse. The best way to get over a woman is by taking another woman to bed . . . at least one. And that's a known fact."

I smirked. "It's not a known fact. It's the typical musings of men who want to have an excuse to have sex with a lot of women."

"Call it what you want, but if you're coming home alone every night, or trying to find extra work to do at the hospital so you don't have to come home at all, you're going to drive yourself crazy."

Damn, he's reading me like a book!

"Break bread with another woman. Go

see a movie with one. Let one come over and sit here and talk. See what happens. You'll eventually find some kind of connection with another woman as you did with Jemistry. If not that kind, just screw her and relax."

I shook my head. "Daddy, I realize that you're only trying to help. But is there something wrong with me desiring to be with one woman for the rest of my life? I'm not in my twenties and I've already been through one failed marriage. I made a commitment to settle down then. Why wouldn't I be ready to make a commitment now?"

My father stood and came to sit down beside me. "I understand everything that you're saying. When you and Estella lost those babies, the entire family went through the pain with you. When your marriage fell apart, same thing. And right now, we're all in the trenches with you again." He placed his hand on my knee. "But, son, you can't make someone be with you, and you can't waste your life away waiting on a woman who has moved on to come back. How do you know she hasn't found a new man?"

"For all that I know, she has. Then again, I know Jemistry. She hasn't gotten involved with anyone else. I'm sure she's back behind her steel bars, even more bitter toward men than she was before. The sad part is that it's all my fault."

"It's not your fault, Tevin."

"If she believes it's my fault, then it's my fault."

"She's probably at least having sex with another man by now."

The mere thought of someone else touching Jemistry made me angry. Daddy could tell that he shouldn't have said that.

"Not that I know enough about her to say all of that," he added.

I sat there in silence for a moment. Daddy got up and went to the restroom. When he returned, he didn't bother to sit back down.

"Get up. Let's go. I'm hungry and I already peeped your fridge. Nothing interesting. I want some seafood. Let's go to Mo's in Baltimore."

"Baltimore?"

"Yes, Baltimore. You act like it's a road trip. We'll be there in forty minutes. Besides, I'm driving. Let's go."

I put my shoes back on, got up, and followed him out to his rental car.

Daddy and I had a great three days together before he had to leave for New York. He managed to keep my mind off Jemistry for most of the time. We hung out every night at various restaurants, played golf on my day off, and he even chilled around my office while I was at work. Most of the people in my department were picking his brain about various techniques or new technology. My father was no joke when it came to surgery. And the fact that he had been hired by a hospital in Sweden gave him great credibility in the field. That's why they were paying him to speak at a conference.

I ran into Magdalena in the hallway, which was strange considering that I never had before and I was located nowhere near the oncology unit three levels below. She was determined to try me.

Daddy spotted her talking to me and drilled me with twenty questions afterward. He tried to insist that I take her out; I told him that I would think about it. The one thing that I could not deny is that staying busy outside of work was helping to keep my mind off my heartache. Working overtime didn't always do it because the fact that it was all about avoidance was always there. Spending time doing other things meant that I was somewhat moving on with my life.

Once Daddy left, I invited Floyd to go out bowling. I hadn't picked up a bowling ball in more than a decade. From the looks of it, neither had he. While I'm sure that he partially showed up at Lucky Strike in Gallery Place because he wanted to hang out, I'm sure trying to see what kind of women congregated there was also a part of his plan. He left there with seven phone numbers locked in his phone under male names or initials. I left there with two but never planned to utilize either of them. The women were attractive but desperate — exactly how Floyd preferred them — and I was not ready to toss my dick around to the masses simply to be doing something.

I decided that I might actually ask Magdalena out for dinner . . . once. It was going on nine weeks since I'd heard from Jemistry. Frankly, I was beginning to be upset with her. If she ever truly loved me, she at least owed me some type of closure. Blocking me from communication was rather childish. If she didn't want to be bothered with me, I had finally come to the point of acceptance. It was time to claim my life back.

Chapter Twenty

"Love is most weak when there is more doubt than there is trust but love is most strong when you learn to trust even with all the doubts."

— Unknown

I asked Magdalena to meet me at the Capitol City Brewing Company on New York Avenue. We got settled into a booth and ordered some Southwest Keg Rolls for an appetizer, and an order of the Brew House Ribs to share as an entrée. The meal was really enough for at least three adults so we were definitely about to throw down.

"I can't believe you actually asked me out." Magdalena beamed from across the table.

I chuckled. "You make it sound like you won the lottery or something."

"In a sense, that's what it seems like. I'm sure you realize that there are very few eligible, successful bachelors around here."

"So I keep hearing."

"It's the truth. I've been single for almost five years."

"Wow, really?" I was shocked. "That has to be by choice. You're a career-driven, attractive woman who interacts with people on a daily basis. I could see if you were teleworking or something, but you're always out and about."

"Out and about, and down and out." She sighed and took a sip of her wine. "Most men out here want to play games. They only want to get women in bed, take them for a test drive, and then toss them out the window."

I could tell that she was damaged goods like so many women and wanted to make some things clear upfront.

"Let me be straight with you. Rather, let me be straight with you *again,* like I was the day we met at the Fourth of July picnic. I'm not looking to get involved right now. I went through a nasty breakup less than three months ago, and I haven't gotten over it. I haven't gotten over her."

"Tevin, I feel you. I'm not trying to pressure you into anything. All I'm saying is that if we hit it off, you might change your mind."

I stared into her eyes and my eyes dropped down to the cleavage she was showing in her black dress. My body was betraying me — in particular my dick — and I had almost become immune to jacking off.

"See, that's the entire point. Maybe this wasn't a good idea after all. You said a moment ago that most men are after sex. What I'm saying to you is that, if anything were to develop between us, all that I have to offer is sex. I can't fall in love with you or anyone else because I'm still in love with my ex."

"Sex can change things."

"Not for me it can't. I've been having sex my entire life, with all kinds of beautiful women. And out of all the women that I've bedded, only two made me want to make a commitment — my ex-wife and my recent ex-girlfriend."

"Damn, that's cold!" She started pouting. "Talk about fucking with a chica's self-esteem."

"I'm not trying to do that, and you shouldn't take it personally. That's the point. It's not about who you are; it's about you not being her. I don't believe that women are interchangeable like a lot of my friends do. I have these various . . . compartments, for lack of a better word. Compartments where I place people, in reference to my life, and they very rarely switch over into another one. I've ended up dating some women who started out as platonic friends, and it never worked for me.

"Even though I cared for them as human beings, that initial chemistry wasn't there, and it's something that can't be faked or fabricated later on."

"So you're trying to say you don't feel any chemistry with me?" she asked defiantly as the waitress set the Keg Rolls on the table and walked off.

"I don't feel like I have to have you, in every way imaginable, no. You're nice, pretty, aggressive. You seem like a cool person, but can I envision us being together around the clock, waking up together, or dying together? No, and I'm only being honest."

"I see."

I hated it when I said a bunch of words and the other person merely said, "I see."

"Magdalena, if you want me to pay for your dinner and leave, I will do that. I don't want to offend you."

"Why did you even ask me out?"

"Good question, and I'll try to answer. For me, part of it was the fact that you kept asking me to ask you out. The other part is that I realize that sitting at home sulking is not going to change my situation. My baby is out of my life and it's difficult for me to cope with. I don't expect you to understand but —"

"Actually, I do understand how you feel. What you're feeling is what most of us women feel after being dumped, except it happens to us time and time again. I have to admit that I appreciate your honesty, so allow me to be honest with you, Dr. Tevin Harris. I want you to take me to bed tonight. No strings attached. No expectations — unrealistic or otherwise. Just two people sharing a couple of hours of intimacy so that tomorrow doesn't seem as dismal as it did today."

I sat there, staring at her with my dick rock hard in my pants. Maybe the touch of another woman would start to make me feel something again, instead of feeling like a dead man walking. Maybe shutting out the rest of the world and relieving myself inside of her would ease a little bit of my pain.

"So, what's it going to be?" Magdalena asked, finishing off her glass of wine.

We ended up back at her place, a studio in an expensive condo building not far from the restaurant. It amazed me how people would pay thousands for a small space to be in a certain area of town when they could purchase a house for the same amount less than two miles away. But she was single and it made sense to her, so I rolled with it.

The sex was there but it was nothing memorable. I didn't do much to her but she licked all over my chest, then my dick, and waited for me to pound the bottom out of her pussy. I went through the motions until I exploded inside the condom, spent a few minutes making small talk, and then told her that I needed to leave because I had an early surgery in the morning.

After all of that effort that she put forth, I'm sure that sex with me was a letdown. Not because of the size of my dick. She oohed and aahed over that like every other woman. But because I wasn't all over her like she was the most exquisite thing on the planet. However, she had asked for it: a couple of hours to knock the edge off. So we knocked off some edges and went our separate ways. It would undoubtedly be awkward if we crossed paths at Sibley, but I had a feeling she would be avoiding my floor from then on out.

Chapter Twenty-One

"If I could give you one thing in life, I would give you the ability to see yourself through my eyes. Only then would you realize how special you are to me."
— Unknown

I decided to spend a few days in Florida with my mother and my sister, Alexis. I moped around most of the time, but the change of scenery helped a little. Mom didn't drill me with questions about Jemistry. She'd already sent Daddy on that mission and I was positive that he'd reported back to her. It was obvious that my parents still loved each other but my father had fucked up and there was no turning back from that. I hadn't fucked up and there was no turning back for me either.

When I landed back at Baltimore–Washington International Thurgood Marshall Airport, I was waiting curbside to catch the shuttle bus to the long-term parking lot when I smelled her. I could never forget her smell. I turned around and Jemistry was standing behind me, staring at me. She had on a flowing sundress made up of a kaleidoscope of colors and a pair of sandals. Her nails and toes were painted a pastel blue and she had auburn highlights in her hair. She had a tan and it was obvious she was returning from a trip herself. She had a suitcase on wheels and a large tote on her shoulder. Sunglasses shielded her eyes, but she was definitely looking at me.

I could barely breathe.

"Good afternoon, Tevin," she said. "It's been a while."

"Yes, it's been months," I replied. "I've been looking for you. I've been to your place. I called DC Public Schools, but they wouldn't help me and since school was closed, I couldn't show up at your job."

"What did you go through all of that for?"

Was she seriously asking me that?

"Jemistry, I love you. I'd walk over burning coals, or fight a shark for you."

"Or fuck my roommate!"

I took two steps closer to her and she didn't move away.

"Baby, I've had a long time to look at this from your perspective and I understand that you're going to believe what you want to believe. And if you don't want anything to do with me, I'll accept that. I have accepted it, but only because I had no choice.

"But I want you to know something, and you can take it or leave it for what it's worth. The only fear that I have in this world is losing you forever. I'm not afraid of dying, but I'm afraid to live without you. Nothing else matters to me. I'm just going through life on autopilot right now."

"Yeah, well, that makes two of us," she replied and switched her tote to the other arm.

"You need me to carry that for you?"

"No, I'm fine."

We stood there in silence. My shuttle pulled up and I pretended like I didn't even see it while other people boarded.

"Weren't you waiting on that bus?" Jemistry asked and pointed.

"I'm not walking away from you. Not again. I should've let you call the police on me that night and waited for them to drag me out of there. If it gave me five or ten more minutes with you, it would've been worth it. But I'm not ever walking away from you again. You're going to have to walk away from me."

Jemistry turned her back to me and took

a few steps. My heart sank. I wanted to cry out to her, but what else was there to say? I'd already told her that I hadn't betrayed her. I'd already professed my undying love for her. I'd already told her that I'd rather die than be without her.

I turned around and faced the curb and started wiping away the tears falling down my face. Seconds seemed like hours. A few people started looking at me, but I didn't care, and I couldn't help it. What I felt was real and, contrary to what many believe, a real man will cry over his emotions.

Then I felt her hand on my back, and smelled her perfume. "Tevin? Tevin?"

I turned and looked down at her. She had removed her sunglasses and I was staring into her beautiful eyes. "I want to believe you, I do. It's just that the last thing that I expected was to come home that day and —"

"Baby, think about it. Do you honestly believe that I would make plans to cook you a romantic dinner, and then try to fuck your roommate when you could show up at any minute? Even if I was the biggest man whore on the planet, which I'm not, I'm not that damn stupid."

She bit her bottom lip and continued to gaze at me.

"You said yourself that Winsome was promiscuous and you also know that she didn't want you to move in with me. We'd talked about that; we'd discussed it.

"That day, when I was grilling the fish, I told Winsome that I wanted us to make it official. Not only had I planned to ask you to move in, I was going to propose."

"Propose?"

"Yes, propose. I bought you a ring when we were in the Caymans. That day that I said I was going out for a run. Instead, I went into town and purchased a ring. A ring that I still have to this day because I've never given up hope on us. I've tried to accept losing you, but that's an impossible concept to me."

"I . . ."

"Jemistry, all I want you to do is analyze this, and I know for a fact that you have before. It's in your nature. Even though it may seem easier to believe that I'm the typical man who would think with his dick, you know that I'm not that man. I'm your man.

"Which one of us had more to gain by you walking in on us that day? Winsome or me?"

"Winsome got kicked out!"

"Yes, but she went out with a bang. She wanted to see you hurt because she was trying to be selfish and controlling. She couldn't stand to see you be happy. She couldn't stomach the thought of you finding true love with anyone. It had nothing to even do with me. It had everything to do with her being jealous of you.

"You weren't throwing pity parties with her all the time anymore. You weren't telling every man in the world to kiss your ass. You weren't spending as much time at home, and how dare you actually consider moving out and making her become self-sufficient or find another roommate. That was the ultimate straw to her.

"She didn't have that shit planned, but she was quick on the draw, and it worked. It worked like a motherfucking charm. She played on your history of getting rid of men and she knew exactly what trigger to push to make you eject me out of your life.

"But I'm always going to love you, whether you love me back or not. You can't tell me that I can't love you . . . no one can. I'll go to my grave loving you, no matter what."

Jemistry looked like she was about to cry, but she fought it. She did a better job than me.

"My car is in the daily lot," she finally said. "I'll leave here and drive directly to your house. I'll meet you there . . . so we can talk."

I was scared to let her out of my sight. "You promise?"

"I promise." She pushed her suitcase toward me. "Here, take my suitcase so you'll know I'm serious."

I picked up her bag as she started backing away, still maintaining eye contact. "We should talk. There's a lot that I need to tell you as well."

I grinned, an authentic grin for the first time in months. "If you beat me there, your key still works."

She smiled, turned from me, and started walking to her car as the next shuttle bus pulled up and I climbed onboard.

■ ■ ■ ■

JEMISTRY

■ ■ ■ ■

CHAPTER TWENTY-TWO

"Love is not about how much you say
'I love you,' but about how much you
prove that it's true."

— Unknown

Tevin beat me to his house, even though he had to catch the shuttle to long-term parking first. I wasn't the least bit surprised. My emotions were all over the place as I got out of my SUV and walked up to his door. It would have been easier to continue to be away from him and go on with my life, but I had spent a few days on the beach in St. Thomas trying to decide what made sense and what didn't with regards to what went down.

He was correct in his assumption that I had analyzed the entire situation over and over. He was also correct that I had ascertained that Winsome had been the aggressor and that he had not come there intentionally to be with her in an intimate way. What confused me was the guilty look on his face when I caught them both coming out of the bedroom. What had actually happened? Did they have intercourse? And if so, how could she have forced him to do it?

I had kicked Winsome out and had her taken off the lease. Then, since it was a month-to-month anyway, I moved and sublet a place for a few months from a friend from college in Northeast. She had to go to Japan on business for the summer so it worked out for both of us. Her place was furnished so I had put the majority of my things into storage. I didn't want any of those memories at my old place. I didn't want to come home to that every day.

At some point, I did plan to finally have it out with Winsome, but first I had to figure out what to do about Tevin.

He had the door open by the time I got to the front steps. He was smiling from ear-to-ear.

Damn, he's so fine!

"Come in, baby," he said, moving aside so I could enter. "I was down in Florida visiting Mom and Alexis so I don't have that much in the fridge, but I can throw something together from the freezer if you're hungry. Or I can order in."

"I'm not hungry," I replied. "I ate on the plane."

He cleared his throat as I stood in front of his sofa. "Where were you coming from?"

"Saint Thomas. I needed to get away for a few days. I haven't taken a vacation all summer."

"Oh, did you go alone?"

"That's none —" I had to attempt to maintain some composure. "Yes, I went alone."

I sat down on the sofa and he sat in the armchair.

"Well, you look great. Nice and tanned."

Instead of saying "thanks," I said, "The only reason that I came over here is because we have to discuss something of great importance."

"Everything that comes out of your mouth is important to me."

Tevin always tripped me up by being so damn attentive. I wasn't used to it.

"Before I tell you what I need to say, I need you to tell me what really happened between you and Winsome that day."

"Wow, that's all I've ever wanted . . . a chance to explain. That day you wouldn't —"

I held up my palm. "Today is a new day . . . a different day."

He sighed and said, "I cooked dinner. You called and said that you were running late. I fell asleep. I heard you, or who I thought was you, come into the room. She undid my pants. Within five seconds of her putting me in her mouth, I realized it wasn't you. I jumped up and started cursing her out, while she implied that I had acted like I wanted her.

"She got angry. I got angrier. We heard your key in the lock. What can I say? I panicked. I tried to make it out of the room before you came in the front door but she halfway blocked me long enough to make it seem like we were coming out of there after fucking.

"I don't want Winsome. You should know better. Not only do I not want Winsome, I don't want anyone else but you."

Tevin got up and said, "I'll be right back."

While he dashed up the steps two at a time, I looked around the room. I had missed being at his house, lying in his arms, being the object of his desire. My past insecurities were telling me not to let my guard down again. But he seemed sincere and I wouldn't put anything past Winsome. She was lonely and, in many ways, wanted me to always be lonely with her. As long as I was in the mode of not wanting a real relationship, it worked out in her favor.

Tevin reappeared with a velvet box, dropped down on his knees, popped it open, and asked me, "Jemistry, will you marry me?"

The rock was huge. I had always imagined a man proposing to me and thought the ring would be nice, but nothing like the engagement ring in that box.

I shut it slowly and closed his palm around it.

"I'm not ready to have that discussion yet."

The painful expression on his face hit me in the pit of my stomach.

"I understand. You're right." He stood up and set back down in the armchair. "Baby steps. All that matters is that you're here. That we're in the same room, breathing the same oxygen. If that's all I get for today, I can accept that."

"I have another question," I said. After he just stared at me, I asked, "Have you been seeing someone new?"

"No, I'm not seeing anyone. Who am I going to see?"

I shrugged. "I don't know but you're a man and men have needs."

"So do women. Does that mean you've been seeing someone?"

I smirked. "You should know better."

"Jemistry, when we met, you were having casual sex with two men. You told me that yourself. So why does my question sound crazy to you?"

He placed his left hand over his mouth for a few seconds.

"Okay, I'm not going to risk anything coming out later."

This bastard just lied to me!

"I had sex one time with this woman who sells pharmaceuticals at the hospital . . . but not in my unit."

"You had sex but you're not seeing her?"

"Not at all. In fact, I made it painfully clear that I was not interested in any kind of relationship with her or anyone else. That I was trying to heal and accept losing you. She kept coming on to me so I eventually caved. We went out to dinner and then we went back to her place and had the worst sex ever. I didn't do anything to her . . . if you know what I mean. I used a condom, it was over and done with, and I left. Haven't spoken to her since."

It could have been a lot worse. I honestly had expected Tevin to go out and bed a lot of women, or hop into a rebound relationship.

"And that's all you need to tell me?" I

asked, crossing my arms.

"That's it. I pro—" He caught himself before he used the word *promise.* "I assure you that I have nothing else to tell you. Outside of that, I've been miserable. I felt like I'd been robbed, or prosecuted for a crime that I never committed."

Tevin eased over onto the sofa next to me and took my hand. "I realize that I just said that all I needed was to be in the same room with you, but I need you. I need to be inside of you. I need to caress you, and taste you, and make love to you."

Shit! Time to come clean!

"Tevin, if we hadn't run into each other at the airport, I would've contacted you within the next few days anyway."

He seemed surprised. "Really?"

"It would've been mandatory." I paused and took in a deep breath. "There was no way that I could've continued to hide it from you."

"Hide what? Your emotions?"

"No. Our baby."

Tevin's mouth fell open, and then his eyes fell to my stomach, which was covered by the loose sundress I was wearing. He reached out and touched it. I wasn't show-ing in a major way but, as my lover, he knew

241

that there was more there than there used to be.

Finally, he spoke. "How many months?"

"I'm about eighteen weeks."

"What . . . did . . . are you okay?"

"I'm fine. And the baby's fine. I don't want you to panic."

"I'll try not to. It's just that . . ."

"I understand. There's no indication that I won't be able to carry the baby to term. I realize that you're concerned about a miscarriage." I ran my hand across his face. "Even though things fell apart between us, I'm sure you know that there was no way that I would ever, or could ever, abort your child."

He got down on the floor and laid his head on my stomach. "I know you wouldn't."

"This child was conceived out of love, and I couldn't have picked a better father for my child. As loving as you are toward me, this baby is in for a lifetime of attention from both of us."

He glanced up at me. "Please don't make my child be born out of wedlock. It would be different if we were casual, or it was a one-night stand, but your ring is right there on the coffee table and I didn't want to marry you because of the baby. I asked you before I even knew you were pregnant."

"Tevin, we need to get used to each other again. We need to talk and do things and feel comfortable around each other again."

"You don't feel comfortable with me, Jemistry?"

"I'm not sure. I think so, but it's been months. And it's really not so much about you as it is about me. I still have some unresolved issues from my past and before I commit to marriage, I need to work them out."

"We can do premarital counseling!"

"Yes, we should definitely consider that, if and when we officially become engaged."

Tevin looked like he had been slapped. "If and when?"

"If it were an automatic yes, then I would just say yes, baby."

He moved his head up from my stomach to my mouth and started kissing me. I was a goner and we both knew it. The fact of the matter was that I was in love with him and could no longer run from it. It would have been insane for me not to love him. I was going to have to let go of the past and make a sincere attempt at happiness . . . for me, for him, and for our unborn child.

CHAPTER TWENTY-THREE

Tevin ran me a bath in his step-down garden tub. Then he sat beside me and washed me all over in the most tender way. His eyes were glued to the baby bump on my stomach the majority of the time. He turned on Marsha Ambrosius's *Late Nights & Early Mornings* CD to help me relax. Her music is like being serenaded by a songbird.

"When's your next doctor's appointment?"

"On Tuesday."

"I'm going."

I giggled. "You didn't even ask me the time. What if you have to work, or have a scheduled surgery?"

"I'm going to take off work and if there is a surgery scheduled, we'll rearrange your appointment so I can be there."

"Tevin, it's not that serious. It's only a routine prenatal checkup. Why don't you wait until I get a sonogram next month? I heard that's when the excitement begins."

"The excitement began for me the second you told me that you're carrying my seed. They listen to the baby's heartbeat and check your vitals and everything, right?"

"Yes, but you can do that right in your bedroom, can't you?" I splashed some water at him. "After all, you are a doctor."

We both laughed. "True enough. I'm going to do that, too."

"I bet you will."

"But I'm still going Tuesday. I want to make sure."

"Everything is fine. I feel fine."

He started caressing one of my breasts that were both fuller since becoming pregnant. "Yes, you do feel fine."

"I want you to make love to me tonight, Tevin. I want us to try to rebuild what we had."

"We will, and sooner or later, hopefully sooner, you'll agree to be my wife." He started washing my back with a towel. "I meant what I said. I want us to be married when our child is born."

"I realize you meant it, but you do know that a lot of people have kids prior to marriage, and a lot of them never get married at all. It's the new trend."

"Yeah, well, fuck that. Trend or not, I was

raised to be married to the mother of my children. It's crazy to me that people will commit to making children together but won't commit to each other in the truest sense of the word."

"It's become the norm now. I'd guess that half of the mothers of the kids at Medgar Evers have never been married."

"But I bet they're telling their kids not to have sex outside of marriage, let alone not to have kids," Tevin said. "I'm not sure why they would be surprised when it happens, if they provided the blueprint for doing it."

"Well, a lot of parents are single because they got divorced."

"I get that and you're preaching to the choir. That happened with my own parents."

"I know."

The conversation was not going well. Tevin had a point. I was willing to carry his baby because I believed that he would be a great father but I hesitated to marry him. But I was no dummy either. Men could be amazing fathers and be horrific mates, or vice versa. They could be terrific mates, but fail at fatherhood altogether.

The CD switched to the next song: "Chasing Clouds."

I stood to get out of the tub. Tevin received me into a towel and dried me off from head to toe. I had almost forgotten how tender he could be with me.

He sat on the edge of the tub so that his head was level with my chest and then started gingerly sucking on my left breast. It was tender because my hormones were out of whack and it was a little painful. But I liked the feeling just as I always did in the couple of days leading up to my period every month.

One thing was for sure. I didn't miss my periods. Hated them. Men had no idea how disgusting and traumatic menstrual cycles were for women. And we had to go through that shit every month.

I palmed the back of his head and pulled him closer to me. He sucked harder and I moaned. He reached between my legs and started fingering my pussy. I spread my legs wider so he could stick a couple more inside of me. I started gyrating my pussy on his fingers as I swayed to the slow rhythm of the song.

Tevin stopped sucking my breast for a moment. "I've missed you, baby."

I kissed the top of his head as he wrapped his arms around my waist and buried his face in my chest. "I've missed you, too, my love."

I lifted his head and gazed into his eyes.

"You are my love, Tevin. I realize that now. I love you and even though I need some more time before I can take it to the level of marriage, what I feel for you is real."

"You have no idea how long I've waited to hear you say that, Jemistry. But I'm glad you waited . . . until you were sure."

"Well, I'm definitely sure. I love you."

"I love you, too."

I buried my tongue in his mouth. His was thick, sweet, and we explored the caverns of each other's souls.

We continued the kiss as he lifted me up and carried me to bed.

He laid me down on a pile of pillows and ate my pussy until I came all over his tongue. My senses seemed heightened because of the pregnancy. It must have been the hormones but all I know is that I could barely take the sensation. A couple of times I tried to pull away from him but he pulled me right back so he could get what he wanted. Once I climaxed for the third or fourth time — I lost count — he was ready to have intercourse.

He seemed nervous about getting on top of me so I got on top of him in a reverse cowgirl position and rode him as he grabbed my breasts from behind.

"I'm not ever letting you go, Jemistry.

Never again," he whispered.

"You never have to worry about it. Never again."

We both came and I curled up into his arms and fell asleep.

The next morning, Tevin was in the kitchen bright and early cooking breakfast. The man really knew how to throw down. Turkey bacon, egg whites with spinach and fresh garlic, grits, and buttermilk biscuits.

He had the morning news on and, as usual, it was nothing but bad news. The world was truly going to shit. Parents killing their own kids, men killing their pregnant wives, child molesters raping kids in school classrooms, school shootings at least monthly, and drugs like meth and bath salts turning people into animals.

"Do you mind if I turn this off?" I asked, pointing at the TV as I entered. They were showing a story about a teenaged girl who stabbed her mother to death in the shower because she had placed her on punishment for missing curfew. "After such a relaxing and *stimulating* night, I don't want to wake up to this."

"Sure, turn it off. Change the channel. Whatever you want," Tevin replied as he started plating the meal. "The last thing I want is for you to get upset, not while you're carrying our baby."

I chuckled. "Well, then I need to take the year off from school. There will be drama in my life between now and when I go into labor. I just don't want to hear it this morning."

Instead of turning it off, I opted to tune into *Jerry Springer.* There were two women on there fighting over the same man.

Tevin smirked as he set my plate in front of me.

"What?"

He shrugged. "You said you don't want to watch any drama but then you turn to a talk show?"

"This isn't drama to me," I replied. "It's funny. The people on these shows want their *segment* of fame, not even fifteen minutes. Anyone with common sense wouldn't go on one if a producer called them up and said they were invited to be a guest."

Tevin sat beside me and started digging into his plate. I got up to get two glasses and to grab some orange juice from the fridge. It was packed with food.

"I thought you said that you were low on groceries, since you were in Florida."

"I was," he said. "I went to Whole Foods at six AM."

250

"Wow, I was really knocked out. I didn't even hear you leave out or come back in." I sat back down at the table and poured both of us some juice. "The island must've worn me out."

Tevin rubbed my thigh. "Don't give Saint Thomas credit for the magic that only my dick can do."

We both laughed.

"I kind of recall being on top last night and putting in most of the work," I stated jokingly. "But your dick was my sleeping pill last night. I haven't had my medication in a hot minute."

"So when are you moving in?"

I almost choked on my juice. "Moving in?"

Tevin stopped eating and stared at me. "Jemistry, I can understand if you're not ready to get married yet. And honestly, I don't want to go to the justice of the peace. I want a big wedding. You deserve that. But I'm drawing the line at us living separately while you're pregnant. Anything could happen and I need to be there in case it does."

"Tevin, I still have to go to work and so do you. You make it sound like you're going to be on watch around the clock."

"I may not be able to do that but I can damn sure be around you as much as possible, and that means you moving in here."

251

"I told you yesterday, I'm subletting from Tiana for the next month. I promised her that I would rent her place for three months, and I plan to keep my word."

"So pay the rent. Better yet, I'll pay her the rent and you can still move in here." He paused. "Where's your stuff?"

"In Public Storage on Bladensburg Road."

"Then we need to figure out what furniture we want to keep of mine and what we want to keep of yours. I'm not emotionally attached to any of my furniture so I'll defer those choices to you. The only thing I care about is you being here."

"How can you make those kinds of decisions off the cuff and act like I don't have any say in the matter?" I was getting irritated but tried to remain cognizant of the fact that my hormones were changing. "I'm used to being independent. It's been a long time since I was under the same roof with a man."

"I'm not *a man.* I'm *your man,* and the father of *our child.*"

It was obvious that he was letting his feelings enter into the discussion.

"How about a compromise?" I said. "I'll stay here most of the time but still keep Tiana's place for the next month or so, in case something hap—"

"In case something *what*? Happens to break us up again? Jemistry, why all the negativity and assumptions? It is possible for two people to make a life work together. Granted, we live in a different time than even our parents but it doesn't mean that everyone is incapable of having a functional situation. Nothing's going to happen."

"I get what you're saying but we just got back together last night."

"You keep making it sound like we've been apart for a decade. Neither one of us has changed that drastically since the beginning of June. And we love each other. That's all that matters."

He pushed his plate away. I felt bad since he had gone through all of the trouble to go shopping at sunrise and come back and cook. Then I made that comment about not wanting to see drama on television and we were outdoing everyone on it.

"Tevin, okay. I'll move in."

He eyed me sideways. "Now you're only trying to satiate me."

"Isn't that what you wanted? For me to cave? So I've caved. I'm moving in." I picked up his fork, scooped up some of the egg whites, and held it up to his mouth. "Open wide."

He ate it and laughed. "Don't treat me

like an infant!"

"I'm practicing." I picked up some more food and pretended the fork was an airplane then started making engine noises. "Come on, Poor Little Tink-Tink, one more bite."

He almost choked on the food from laughing at me.

"I have to get to work," he said. "I have a consult in an hour."

"That's cool. I'm having lunch with Courtney today anyway."

Tevin had stood and was halfway to the kitchen entryway when he stopped and turned to look at me. "Courtney who?"

I giggled. "Courtney as in Floyd's wife."

"I didn't realize that the two of you were still communicating. She hasn't said anything to me, and neither has Floyd."

"Yes, we are. We've been hanging out quite often. She's my new BFF."

"What's a BFF?"

"Best friend forever, silly."

"Forgive me. I don't hang out with fourteen-to-eighteen-year-olds like you do at school." He seemed hesitant. "Does Floyd know that the two of you have been spending time together?"

I laughed. "You make it sound like we're screwing each other. *Spending time?*" I finished off my juice. "I guess he knows but

I honestly haven't seen him. We usually meet up. Sometimes with the kids and sometimes without them.

"After this huge breakfast, I may have to push lunch back an hour so I can get a nap in. Since I'm pregnant, I can throw down every few hours though. I hope you don't dump me if I put on too much weight."

Tevin waved me off. "Never going to happen. But let me ask you one more thing. Does Courtney know that you're pregnant with my child?"

I wasn't sure how to respond to that question. Lying would have been easiest because the truth would only lead to Tevin not trusting Courtney — and Floyd. Courtney had sworn Floyd to secrecy, making him promise not to divulge anything to Tevin. He had confronted me about it and I begged him not to say anything to Tevin.

"Well," he stated impatiently. "Does she know?"

I stared up into his eyes.

"Never mind," he added. "I get the picture."

Tevin walked out and while I felt some kind of relief, the words unspoken were enough to make him recognize the truth. He was far from stupid.

CHAPTER TWENTY-FOUR

"It's not about who hurt you and broke
you down. It's about who was always
there and made you smile again."
— Unknown

"Girl, you look fabulous pregnant!" Courtney gave me a hug and then we headed into
DC Coast for lunch. "Have you eaten here
before? I heard it's ridiculously good!"

"Courtney, I'm only a few months. I'm
sure that I'll be waddling in a couple of
months and that shit is not cute."

"Jemistry, you're glowing. I've had four
babies and each time I looked like all the
blood was drained from my body by the end
of the first trimester. Pregnancy has always
been rough on me."

"Hell, this is no walk in the park for me
either."

We gave our name for the reservation and
were seated.

"Lots to choose from on the menu," I said as I started checking out the selections. Like most pregnant women, my cravings changed from day to day. "Did you eat a lot of pickles and ice cream when you were pregnant? I always thought that was a myth but I love the combination and I've always hated pickles."

"What about ice cream?" Courtney asked as she used her knife as a mirror to make sure she didn't have any lipstick on her teeth.

"I've always been down with ice cream, even though I'm lactose-intolerant."

"Aw, that's the worst. But I feel you. I eat mushrooms and tomatoes like they are going out of style and neither one agree with me. I spend half the night on the toilet after I indulge."

I made my selections. "I'm going to do the Heirloom Beet Carpaccio for starters, and then try out the Pan Roasted Arctic Char with squash and eggplant, and some spinach with garlic and chili."

"Hmm, you're going to need some acid reflux medicine after all of that. I'm keeping it simple since I don't know what half the shit is that you just named."

We both giggled.

"I'm going to try the chicken Caesar

salad, and the crab cakes."

"Chicken!" I exclaimed. "You could cook that at home."

"Exactly!"

Courtney was looking for the waitress so we could place our order. I decided that then was as good a time as any to say what needed to be said.

"I have some good news and some bad news. Which one do you want to hear first?"

"I despise it when people give me that kind of choice. It's a fucked-up situation either way."

"How so?"

"If I tell you that I want to hear the bad news first, then I'll be too upset to appreciate the good news. If I tell you to hit me with the good first, once you tell me the bad, the good becomes quickly overshadowed."

"You do have a point."

Courtney shrugged. "So you choose and I'll deal with it. It's either a win-lose or a lose-win."

"Tevin and I ran into each other at BWI yesterday when I was coming back from Saint Thomas."

"Hmm, I planned to ask you about your trip, but this is definitely going to be juicier." She took a sip of her water as the waitress approached. After we ordered, she said, "You ran into each other and then what?"

"He was standing there waiting for the parking shuttle and he didn't see me at first. I hesitated about saying anything, but he must've sensed me somehow. Next thing I knew, he was turning around and staring at me."

"And then what happened?"

"He was happy to see me. Told me all about how he'd been searching for me and staking out my old place. How he'd called the school system but they told him to beat it.

"Tevin told me how much he loved me and begged for another chance." I paused for a few seconds. "I took running into him as a sign. I'd come to the conclusion on my trip that I had to tell him about the pregnancy. It wasn't fair to continue keeping him in the dark."

"That's what I've been trying to get through your thick head all along."

"Yes, you have, and you were right." I started smiling. "He's so excited about the baby. But I can tell that he's going to drive me insane with worry."

"Jemistry, you're going to have to be patient with Tevin. He's been through a lot. Estella's three miscarriages took a toll on him. It took him years to snap back from that. It was tragic."

"I realize that."

The waitress brought Courtney's Caesar salad and my beet whatever it was.

"I'm doing the most. I've never tasted a beet in my life."

"Well, it certainly looks delightful."

"I'll let you know." I took a bite and debated on my opinion. "It's different but good. Want to try some?"

"No, I'm going to play it safe with my salad."

"Yeah, it's damn-near impossible to fuck up a Caesar salad."

We both chuckled.

"How well did you know Estella?" I asked Courtney. "Did you hang out, like the two of us do?"

"No, not really. Estella was kind of a homebody. When I met her, she'd already had one miscarriage, but I'd known Tevin for a few years prior to that. He and Floyd didn't start doing things together outside of work for a while. Now you can't keep them apart."

"So back to my news. We met up at his house, talked things through, and I've decided to try again . . . to give us another chance. I even told Tevin that I'm in love with him. I had to admit it to myself first."

Courtney almost choked on a piece of lettuce, and then drank some water to get it down. "That's wonderful! And it's about damn time you came to that conclusion. A blind person could have seen that you're in love." She glanced out the window at an ambulance passing by with its sirens blasting. "I keep telling you that Tevin's not the type to cheat. He's always been like some mythical creature from an old fable. They don't make men like him anymore."

"Please, Courtney, Floyd worships you from what I've seen."

"Floyd is definitely there for me. He's a great provider and he adores the kids. But . . ."

"But nothing. The two of you are doing it. You have what most couples yearn for — a happy marriage."

Courtney seemed like she wasn't too sure about what I'd said.

"It is a happy marriage, isn't it?" I asked.

"I presume that it is."

"Presume?"

"We've had our issues. Nothing major."

"Everyone has issues. Think about it. It's not easy allowing another person to be a part of your world *all the time.* It's been years since I've been serious, until Tevin, and it is definitely a challenge. You have to get used to each other's ways and temperament. Habits, both good and bad. Trigger points and trying to prevent pressing buttons that don't need to be pushed."

"Sounds like you know what you're getting yourself into. You and Tevin will be fine. I'm glad he won't be moping around like a lovesick puppy anymore."

"My hormones are wilding out. Floyd might have to take Tevin out somewhere to relieve some adrenaline at least once a week until I have this baby."

"What about a wedding?" I looked at Courtney with surprise. "Oh, come on. Tevin's not going to let you have that child without being married. I know that for a fact. Besides, he told Floyd he bought a ring and had planned to propose when all of that bullshit went down with your roommate."

"He did, and I couldn't believe that he snuck behind my back and purchased it when we were in the Caymans. Slick ass!"

We got our main courses and ordered some iced tea with lemon. Again, Courtney's crab cakes looked like, well, crab cakes, and my entrée looked *thought provoking.* I had no idea what Char was when I ordered it but assumed it was fish. It was and it was actually good.

"I'm normally a creature of habit but I'm going to start being more daring with trying different things from now on."

"Do you, baby girl. I'm sticking to what works for me." Courtney wiped her mouth with her napkin. "So when do I need a dress for the wedding? Hopefully a bridesmaid dress. Hint. Hint."

I sighed. "I suggested that we wait on the marriage. Just for a little while. But he convinced me to move in with him. That's easy since I'm subletting anyway. I'm going to pay Tiana for an additional month regardless."

"But are you going to be married by the time the bundle of joy arrives?"

"If Tevin has anything to say about it, yes. I'm not even sure why I'm putting it off. I should at least wear the engagement ring."

"Damn right! You should've worn it today so I could see it. I'm sure it is sick."

"Sick? Yeah, it's stunning!"

"Well, you should've worn it today so I could be stunned!"

We laughed and kept eating.

Once we ordered desserts, Courtney asked the question that I hoped she'd forgotten all about.

"You haven't told me the bad news yet. What is it?"

I wiped my mouth, sighed, and put my cloth napkin back across my lap. "While I didn't flat-out confess to it, Tevin asked if you and Floyd knew about my pregnancy. He had no idea that you and I were even talking on the regular. When I mentioned that I was having lunch with you, he nearly lost it."

Courtney seemed irritated.

"Aren't you going to respond?" I asked.

She shook her head. "See, this is why I wanted you to tell him from jump. Trust and believe, there will be drama."

"Let's hope not."

"Oh, it's about to go down. Floyd and Tevin are a lot alike but they're also very distinctive when it comes to their emotions."

"What do you mean by that?"

"They're both type A personalities."

"Which means what?"

Courtney put her napkin on the table after finishing a massive slice of strawberry cheesecake. "I'm stuffed and I'm tapping out."

"As much as I pride myself on knowing it all, what makes our men type A personalities?"

"They're both ambitious overachievers, organized, proactive, impatient, good at managing their time, and they prefer people to get straight to the point."

I laughed. "I can see that in both of them."

"Indeed, but that's where they part ways."

"Uh-oh, not the parting of the ways," I joked.

"Tevin is an idealist and Floyd is a protector. Well, in essence, they are both those things but there is always a dominant personality."

"You're too smart to be a stay-at-home mother. I keep telling you that."

Courtney had a degree in psychology from American University but had chosen to raise the kids while Floyd worked. Still, I was often amazed at how she would go from talking about swimming lessons and day camp to really deep shit.

"One day, I'll go out into the world and make my own millions. Right now, my life is all about making sure my kids make honor roll, have dinner on the table, and that they feel loved."

"Well, I can't give up my career, but I will take maternity leave."

"And no one is suggesting that you should."

I had to admit that I felt some kind of way about the way the conversation was headed. While I could understand women making the decision not to work to stay home with their children, it was not for me. I had struggled too hard to get where I was and it was more important for me to allow my child to see me become successful.

"I realize that you're not suggesting it. In many ways, I admire the fact that you're there with the kids all the time. You've had a husband from day one while I was somewhere being mistreated, beaten, or humiliated. I had to learn to fend for myself."

"The past is the past, Jemistry. I really pray that you can let all of that go. Tevin has a lot of values and I don't believe that he'll relinquish them for any reason. If he didn't think that he could be the man you deserve, he'd walk away first.

"When you broke up with him, he was devastated . . . beyond devastated. He would try to hide it around me, when he was coming over and heading down into Floyd's *so-called* man cave. But he couldn't mask his pain. I've seen it before, and not to compare apples to oranges, but he took losing you at least as hard as he took losing Estella."

"Speaking of Estella, do you think Tevin's still in love with her? Be honest."

Courtney stared at me from across the table.

"Seriously! Tell me what you think!"

266

"Okay, I'll tell you what I think. Sure, I think he still cares for her. Tevin's not the type to marry someone he doesn't truly love. There's probably something still there, but it's not what it once was. If she was in some kind of dire situation, I'm sure he'd try to help her, but he's a doctor. He'd do that for a stranger on the street, or on the operating table, so one would expect him to be there for those who matter to him.

"But he's very loyal, and extremely honest. He's not going to do anything to hurt you, Jemistry. He deserves a chance at happiness, and so do you."

After we paid and left DC Coast, Courtney and I decided to hit up a few boutiques to look for maternity clothes. I couldn't believe that I was about to have a baby. Then I felt the fetus kick for the first time.

CHAPTER TWENTY-FIVE

"True love doesn't have a happy ending
because true love has no ending."
— Unknown

The first day of each school year could always be either exciting in a positive way, or straight up ridiculous in a negative way. It really depended on the attitudes of both the students and the faculty. The incoming freshmen were nervous no matter how you sliced it. Even the ones who thought they were the shit and had huge egos because they were the most popular in elementary school and middle school got a reality check — fast, quick, and in a hurry. The ones who had always been shy, afraid of their own shadow, or bullied had it the worst since they expect more of the same treatment.

High school is a totally different experience, though. It is an opportunity to "reinvent" yourself. Even if the ones who made your life a nightmare were in some of your classes, the student body was at least three times larger than middle school since several fed into Medgar Evers. The ones considered weak in eighth grade could become student body president within two years; the ones that were most popular could end up being bullied and find themselves outcasts within mere months.

A lot of the weight on how a student flourished or fell off the cliff rested on their parents' shoulders. Despite societal views, and seeing so much negativity on the Internet and in the media about wayward youths, most parents still wanted the best for their children. They wanted their children to surpass anything that they had ever accomplished. They wanted to try to ensure that their children had a good education and were established in financially stable careers before they had to leave this earth and their offspring behind. Most worked hard to provide for their families and struggled every day to make sure that their children did not have to endure the same struggles. Most of them. And those were the parents who came to PTA meetings, and made sure their kids participated in organized sports and various academic clubs. The ones who sent their kids on college tours, were proactive in trying to seek out financial aid and scholarships for them to get a higher education. The ones that burned the midnight oil to help them complete science fair projects and homework on time, and drilled them on test material until they had everything memorized. The ones that would hire tutors that they may not have been able to afford if they saw their children slipping in any given subject.

Then there were the parents that I called "the others." The ones that I never blamed for their actions because I realized that a lot of it stemmed from deep issues, dark secrets, and generational curses. Those parents also believed that they were doing the right thing . . . most of the time. If they had to beg, barter, and steal to survive because their parents begged, bartered, and stole, that was all that they knew. If they grew up watching their parents, aunts, and uncles strung out on drugs or alcohol, and skating through life by the skin of their teeth, many believed that was all life had to offer them. Sure, they heard stories about and saw successful people in the media, or worked for some, but they never believed they could achieve success like that.

I considered a great portion of my responsibility trying to make those children "see" that they could achieve greatness. To present them with case studies of famous people — inventors, doctors, lawyers, politicians, celebrities, professional athletes — who grew up in conditions at least as bad as them, and not only survived but thrived.

I arrived an hour before school opened to get settled in my office. There were already some kids standing around anxiously, even though the doors were still locked. In DC, children who lived within a mile radius of the school were required to walk, be dropped off by a parent, or take public transportation. No school buses unless it was a greater distance. While I could see the health benefits of making them walk — that was the only exercise many of them would get because they had no choice — I took issue with their safety being placed at risk. Many walked alone. And in the winter months, since DC rarely closed down the schools in inclement weather, we always ended up with children sick and missing a lot of days that could have been avoided by keeping the schools closed for one day. It made no sense but if we took too many snow days, it meant extending the school year.

I was gathering a crate of paperwork out

of my hatch when I spotted Winsome approaching me from across the parking lot.

Great! Just what the fuck I need this morning!

She didn't even say hello first. "Jemistry, we need to talk. We've gotta hash this out."

I closed the back of my SUV. "I can't believe you showed up on my first day of school. You know this is one of my most hectic days."

"What I know is this is the one place I could find you this morning since you've been avoiding me for months."

"I haven't been avoiding you. I don't want to be bothered with you at all. *Avoiding* implies that at some point I plan to deal with you again. That shit's not happening."

We stood there looking each other in the face. Then Winsome squinted. "You're pregnant!"

I wondered how she knew that. I had on a loose dress; I wasn't trying to announce my pregnancy right off the break to anyone at the school. Not even Lilibeth.

"You're tripping. I'm not pregnant."

"I can see it in your face. It's not fatter or anything, but you have that glow."

"I went to Saint Thomas for a few days. It's a tan."

Winsome stood there and started tapping

her foot on the concrete. "Humph, you can't fool me. I've seen your ass when you've come back from vacation before and I've had enough chicks in my family and friends who've had babies to tell a pregnancy glow."

I was in a panic. Not because I cared about Winsome figuring it out, but I wondered if other people at school would figure it out. My faculty was comprised of people who had at least one child, if not several. And Lilibeth had grandchildren.

"How many months are you?" Winsome asked, snapping me out of my trance.

"None of your business," I replied, walking past her. "I don't have time for this. I have more than two thousand students to get situated and organized. I need to finish writing my back-to-school speech."

"I'm sure you finished writing that a month ago." Winsome smirked. She was right. I would never wait until the last minute for something like that. "You look good, girl. So I take it that you and Tevin are back together. He is the father, right?"

That does it!

"I don't have whore tendencies like you!"

Winsome sucked her teeth. "Wow! You just gonna stand there and call me a whore. So that's where we are now!"

273

I sat the crate down on the ground. "No one told your ass to come here, to my place of employment, trying to start some kind of spectacle with me. You already know. I don't do theatrical performances.

"And that's why we are nowhere now. I didn't come for you; you came for me. Now you can turn your scandalous, stank ass around and go crawl back into the cave you came out of."

"Jemistry, I swear. If you weren't pregnant, I'd —"

"Tell you what. Meet me here on the first day of school next year. Same place, same time, and we can go out in the woods behind the school and fight until I knock your fucking block off."

Winsome was obviously shocked. Truth be told, I was shocking myself by talking and acting that way.

"You think resorting to violence is the answer?" I asked her. "That says a lot about your character, or lack thereof. Grown women discuss matters. Little girls throw punches. But if you want to go there, like I said, next year, and we can make it happen."

She was about to say something, opened her mouth, and then shut it again while she thought of a comeback and digested my words.

Meanwhile, I attempted to regain my composure. People were starting to stare at us, sensing that something was wrong. The last thing I needed was to end up on some YouTube video and end up losing my job. Winsome wasn't worth it.

"Winsome, this is exactly why we can't be friends." I waved my left hand up and to the side. "There's nothing left. You went too far. I did nothing but support you, love you like a sister, and even paid your bills when that bullshit job you were doing fell off. I bet you're somewhere mooching off some-one else right now."

She dropped her eyes, letting me know that I was on point.

"We're too damn old . . . you're too damn old to still be trying to figure out what direc-tion you want to take with your life. You've had twenty different jobs since I've known you, none of them with any chance for progression. You've been crawling your way through life instead of getting your ass up and running.

"I'm sick of it. What you did to Tevin was the final act of a tragic Shakespearean play."

Winsome glared at me. "What I did to him?"

"Oh, please!" I exclaimed in disgust. "Even now, you're prepared to still stand there and lie to my face. I admit that you had me there for a hot minute. Hell, months even. You made me break off the first real thing with the first real man that I've had in years, over your weak-ass self-esteem."

"How dare you?"

"No, how the fuck dare you?" I retorted. "You've been riding the fence your entire damn life. Not sure what you want to do for a living. Not sure what you want to study in school. Not sure whether you want to settle down with a man or a woman. Not sure about jack shit.

"And then you wonder why no one has ever loved you, or even tried to love you."

Winsome started trembling. If I weren't pregnant, she actually may have jumped me she was so mad.

"Damn, Jemistry. Why not just whip out a switchblade and carve my ass up? Better yet, a machete and chop my head off?"

"I'm trying to tell you the truth . . . for once. People have always sugarcoated shit for you, including me. In many ways, I've been your crutch — something that's supposed to be a temporary easement so that strength can be regained in a limb."

"You're not my crutch. I've always taken

276

care of myself."

"Again, you're standing there lying." I looked around the parking lot. People were walking into the building and waving at me, but no one was currently within earshot. "And for whose benefit? You and I both know that's not true.

"It was a bad idea for you to come here, Winsome. I don't hate you. I'm done with you. I'm done allowing you to bring havoc and chaos into my life. There was a time when I needed that. I craved it like a crack junkie craves a pipe. We were perfect for each other. Two hurt people, living together, wallowing in pity together, and licking each other's wounds.

"But I'm in love now. I'm in love with a man who genuinely loves me back, and I'm not risking my last shot . . . my one shot at happiness for you or anyone else."

Winsome started walking backward toward her car. "I hate you."

"I'm going to pretend like you really don't mean that, but if you do, I accept that. If having you hate me means having Tevin love me for the remainder of my natural life, I'll accept that."

"I can't believe you're choosing him over me."

"Winsome, you're my friend. You were

277

never my woman." I paused, picked my crate back up, and then added, "I hope that you find love one day, but that's never going to happen until you're receptive to it. Trust me, I speak from experience.

"I wasted so many years trying to deflect men that it made it impossible for any man to get through my barrier. I finally decided that I don't want to die with a lot of regrets. I want to grow old with someone. I want to die in someone's arms, or have them die in mine and know that I am there for them, or better yet, die in each other's arms."

"So that's it? You're casting me completely out of your life? After I came here to work things out?"

"This can't be worked out. Working this out would mean crawling back down in that hole with you and burying my face in the sand, and I'm not doing it. Working this out would mean going home to Tevin tonight and disrespecting him by telling him that I'm dealing with you again. I can't do that."

I anticipated Winsome saying something else sarcastic, going the hell off, or at least saying something deep and reflective . . . in an attempt to get in the proverbial last word. Instead, she just turned and walked away in silence.

I yelled after her. "You need to go talk to

someone, Winsome! Please go talk to some-one!"

By the time I got to the front steps of the school, she was peeling out of the parking lot. One of the male students offered to carry the crate inside for me.

I looked at him and forced a smile. "Thanks, and welcome to Medgar Evers. What's your name and what grade are you in?"

CHAPTER TWENTY-SIX

"Love doesn't make the world go 'round.
Love is what makes the ride worthwhile."
— Unknown

Tevin met me at my OB/GYN's office for my prenatal checkup after school. He was excited and asked a thousand questions even though he was a doctor himself. You would've thought he was back in medical school and that I was a test subject with an assigned number like E-105.

After Dr. Horton assured him that both the baby and I were fine, he calmed down a little. I made an appointment for four weeks later and Tevin walked me to the parking garage. He had found street parking.

He suddenly seemed quiet. A few moments earlier, no one could shut his ass up.

"What's wrong with you?" I asked him, locking my left arm into his right. "Dr. Horton said everything's great."

"And that's fantastic. I can't wait until the next visit so we can see the sonogram."

"I meant to ask you about that. Do you think we should find out the sex?"

"That's up to you, baby."

"Well, don't you want to know whether we're having a boy or a girl?"

"All I really care about is the baby being healthy, having ten fingers and toes, and coming home with us." He stopped walking and turned toward me, then took my hands. "Coming home to his or her *married* parents."

I blinked twice and then sucked in a breath.

"Jemistry, come on. This is ridiculous. We love each other and we're bringing a life into the world together. Let's get married. I have no intention of ever getting a divorce."

"I'm sure you didn't have any intention the first time."

I regretted the words the second they left my lips.

"I didn't mean it li—"

Tevin grinned and kissed me on the forehead, then whispered, "It's okay. It's the truth. And no, I can't promise you that nothing will ever happen to break us up, but what I can say is that you'd have to leave me." He gazed into my eyes. "I'm a man of my word. I didn't file for divorce the first time and I won't do it this time."

"I understand."

"Do you really? I want you to realize that when I marry you, and I will, the vows will mean everything to me, and I won't default on them. I won't turn my back on you . . . ever."

I started walking again to avoid eye contact. I couldn't possibly tell Tevin what was actually on my mind. I wanted to wait until I got past my second trimester before we got married. Even though I would be showing, I didn't want to run the risk of having a miscarriage and having Tevin relive his nightmare all over again by being in a marriage with a woman who couldn't give him a child. Despite what the tests said, and what my doctor said, I'd never carried a child to term . . . but I had aborted one.

Back when I was with Wesley, in the darkest of my days of abuse, I got pregnant. I was on birth control pills, just as I was on birth control when I got pregnant with Tevin's child. What can I say? The method worked for the majority of the time with the handful of men that I had ever allowed to enter me without a condom. It's true that women need to seriously consider the men they are sleeping with as father material, in case something happens.

We walked the rest of the way to my truck in silence. I used the key fob to unlock it, open the door, and tossed my purse onto the passenger seat.

I turned to give Tevin a hug. "I'll see you at home."

He gave me a half-hug back. "You never answered my question."

"What question?"

"Do you understand what kind of man I am?"

"Yes, I do. I understand. I appreciate. I love you for it."

"Then pick a date. A date for us to either go to the justice of the peace, plan a small backyard wedding, get married at a church, or a date to take off to an island or go to Vegas so that you can become Mrs. Tevin Harris."

I needed a glass of wine but that wasn't happening. I wouldn't even touch a soda while I was pregnant, much less alcohol.

"Go back to the hospital. We'll discuss it tonight."

"Speaking of the hospital, Floyd's been hiding out for the past couple of days."

I played dumb. "Really? Maybe he's just busy, or maybe he took a couple of days off."

"No, he's around. I hear them paging him and his car is in the lot. He's the only doctor there with a Bentley. Every time they call him over the intercom, I'm hemmed up but I'm going to catch up to him sooner or later."

I decided continuing to play dumb was my best bet.

"Oh, okay. Well, I'm sure he's fine."

"For now."

Tevin had an angry expression on his face. *No more playing dumb!*

I sighed and leaned against the back door. "Tevin, I asked Floyd not to mention my pregnancy to you. He never wanted to go along with it. In fact, he pleaded with me to tell you. I told him that I needed time to tell you in my own way. I didn't want him delivering that kind of news when we weren't even speaking."

"Floyd is supposed to be my best friend," he stated vehemently.

"And he is your best friend." I ran my fingers over Tevin's chest. "Think about it. If he'd told you and I wasn't prepared to even face you, what would you have done?"

He sighed. "It's not only about the pregnancy. Floyd sat there and listened to me for months, describing how I would go sit outside of your old place and wait for you.

He knew that I was about to go crazy with worry and his ass knew how to contact you all along. That's unforgivable!"

"No, it's not unforgivable. He only did what I asked so if you must take it out on someone, take it out on me."

Tevin frowned. "I'm not taking anything out on you. I love you."

"And Floyd loves you. Don't try to punish him or confront him about any of this. He's avoiding you because he feels bad. I told Courtney at lunch the other day that you'd figured it out, about them knowing. I'm sure she related that to him."

Tevin smirked. "I'm sure she did."

"Floyd's a good man. You need to cut him a break. He was only trying to do the best for all involved." I wrapped my arms around his waist and laid my head on his chest. "Besides, what does it matter now? We're back together, you know about the baby, and everything's all good."

Tevin's heart felt like it was about to jump out of his chest. "Floyd's not the saint you and Courtney believe him to be."

I giggled, let him go, and started to climb into the driver's seat. "I never said Floyd was a saint. But he is a good man and he loves his wife and kids. And he loves you. So go kiss and make up."

"I'm not kissing his ass." Tevin finally laughed. "But I am going to make sure I see him today, tomorrow at the latest."

"I'm going to stop by Eatonville and pick up dinner. You want some of that gumbo you like?"

"Yes, get some gumbo and grab some of those corn muffins while you're at it."

"Bye, baby."

Tevin leaned in and kissed me gently on the lips.

"Now go lay one of those on Floyd," I joked as I put on my seat belt.

"Shit! There's not a snowball's chance in hell of that happening."

We both laughed as he shut my door and watched me start the engine and pull away. He seemed like he was in a better mood. I hoped that Tevin would let the entire thing with Floyd go. He had been stuck between a rock and a hard place, and made the only choice that made sense at the time. That's all any of us can ever do.

CHAPTER TWENTY-SEVEN

"You don't mean anything to me. You
mean everything to me."
— Unknown

When Tevin got back that night he had
indeed tracked Floyd down at Sibley. It did
not go well.

"That motherfucker!"

I was sitting on the sofa with my feet up
when he stormed into the living room and
threw his keys on the coffee table.

He collapsed into the armchair as I stood
up and walked behind him to start massaging his shoulders. It was obvious that he
was talking about Floyd.

His muscles were tensed up like bricks.

"Baby, you need to calm down before you
have a stroke or something."

He sounded like he was hissing but didn't
respond.

"I hope you didn't get into a loud confrontation in front of people at the hospital."

He shook his head. "No, I finally told his punk ass to meet me at the bar down the street so we could talk about the situation like men."

I sighed. "Sounds like you wanted to have some kind of gladiator fight."

"I should've whipped his ass."

I stopped massaging him and walked around the chair to look down on him. "Tevin, I already told you that Floyd only did what he thought was best. He honored my request and I appreciate that."

Tevin glared at me. "You do realize that I can never trust him. I should've never trusted him in the first place. Any man who fucks half of the women at work and then smiles up in his wife's face is a damn good liar. I should call Courtney and rat his ass out."

It was not the norm for someone to render me speechless but that was exactly what happened when Tevin blurted that out about Floyd.

He stared at me. I stared at him. We both knew the situation that we now faced. It was unwritten man code and woman code that once either knew that one of their friends or relatives had a cheating spouse or mate, the man should feel obligated to tell the other man and the woman should be obligated to tell the other woman. It was so obvious that I decided to call him on it.

"So, you're going to put that burden on me?"

Tevin lowered his eyes.

I went and sat back down on the sofa.

For a few moments, we sat in silence.

Tevin finally spoke. "I'm sorry, Jemistry. I didn't mean to put Floyd's business out there but I was pissed."

"You do realize that you just told me that Floyd is a man whore? And that now I can either betray my friend by allowing her to believe that her husband is faithful, or I can conspire against her, hope she never finds out the truth another way, and that she never asks me if I already knew."

"Kind of like you enlisting Floyd to conspire with you against me, huh?"

We were about to have a serious argument and we both recognized that. He was not ready to drop it.

"For the last time, Tevin. I asked Floyd and Courtney to give me time, and allow me the opportunity to tell you when I was ready. There was never a single moment in time when you wouldn't have known about our child. Abortion never crossed my mind, and I would never have raised your child without you playing a significant role in their upbringing.

"You're one of the most loving men — persons — that I've ever met and my child is blessed to have you as their father. Even if we never got back together, it was a given that you would be ever-present."

Tevin sat up on the edge of the armchair and reached for me. I scooted over on the sofa so he couldn't.

"No, let me finish my thought. On the flip side, what you told me is completely different. Are you going to sit here and say that, sans you spilling the proverbial beans, that Floyd was eventually going to tell Courtney that he's fucking around on her?"

Tevin sighed. "No, I guess not."

"Exactly!" I paused. "How long has he been cheating and with how many women?"

"Why would you want to know all that? Isn't that making it worse?" he asked and sat back, settling into the cushions. "That'll only give you more information you have to cover up."

"I don't have to cover up a damn thing. I'm not sure why you would think that I would."

He went into a panic and loosened his tie. "It's not our place to interfere in their marriage, Jemistry."

"How long and how many? You said that you'd never lie to me. Like a bad defense attorney, you've introduced this evidence into the mix, so now you have to give me full disclosure."

"Are you serious?"

"Yes. Tevin, here's your chance to prove that you're not a liar. I should be upset about the fact that you've been cosigning on his behavior and then going over to their house and smiling all up in Courtney's face. That says a lot about you, and it's nothing nice."

Tevin practically catapulted out of the chair then. "Hold up!" He started pacing the floor with an attitude. "I hope you're not trying to imply that I'm the navigator of Floyd's dick!"

"That's not what I'm implying at all. What I am saying is that you always pride yourself on what you will or will not do to a woman — me in particular — and yet you've been *apparently* idly sitting by while Floyd not only dicks down various women but risks the health of his wife in the process."

I stood up as well. "All this shit being spread around today and he's fucking random broads? He could bring anything home to her and you think that's cool?"

"Hell no, I don't think it's cool! I'm the

one who's been telling Floyd he needs to stop before the shit catches up to him. I've warned him over and over that he needs to grow the fuck up and do the right thing."

"And what did he say?"

Tevin crossed his arms in defiance. "As of late, all he was doing was boasting about the fact that you dumped me over something that I never did, and that he was doing him and that Courtney worships the ground he walks on regardless."

"That's because Courtney doesn't know he's a filthy, mangled mutt!"

"Actually, according to him, he's an Alaskan Malamute."

"An Alaskan what?"

Tevin walked over to me and took me in his arms. "I don't want us to fight about this. What they're doing has nothing to do with us."

"They're our friends," I reminded him.

"Yes, but they're grown friends and we have to stay out of it."

I looked up at him. "Are you asking me not to tell?"

"I'm asking you to really think about what doing that will accomplish. As of today, I'm not even feeling Floyd like that. We may eventually be able to be friends again, now that I've calmed down and can see it from another perspective. But even if we do start hanging out again, you telling Courtney will only make matters ten times worse.

"If she's content, let the woman be happy. They have four kids. If she divorces him, it'll affect them in the long run."

"And if he gives her HIV, or some lunatic broad shows up on their doorstep to confront her because he refuses to leave her and attacks her, how will that affect the children?"

Tevin chuckled. "You and your imagination. It's not going to go that far. The STD concern is valid, and I would hope Floyd's not irresponsible enough to fuck women raw. But as far as him lying and telling a chick that he's in love or leaving his wife, he's definitely not that reckless.

"I don't know all of his comings and goings but the ones from work that I know about are only interested in getting fucked."

I pushed him away from me.

How the fuck do you know all that?

"How do you know that's what they want? Have they come on to you?"

"Jemistry, I'm a young, successful, black surgeon in the DMV. Women try to get my attention. You know that. But you didn't have to do that, because I tried to get your attention, and since the night we met, you're all I ever think about."

I tried to fight it, but I blushed.

"All I want you to concentrate on, baby, is feeding my baby, loving me, and deciding which bedroom you want to turn into the nursery. That's all you need to be concerned about. Why bring any unnecessary drama into our lives? We've had enough of it while we're trying to establish our future."

I had to give it to him. He did make a valid argument. Telling Courtney about Floyd cheating would be the equivalent of throwing an alligator into a swimming pool full of people.

"Let me tell you something about Floyd," Tevin continued. "Not in his defense but to explain a little bit about his crazy behavior."

"There is no defense or legit excuse for him cheating."

"I agree. All I'm saying is that I recognized something about him a long time ago. We all have flaws but one of Floyd's biggest ones is being born with such a ridiculous ego. He thinks so highly of himself, which makes it both a blessing and a curse. He's successful because he always knew he would be, and no one would've been able to convince him otherwise, even if they'd had the audacity to try.

"He takes care of himself physically because he believes that he's godlike material. So he'll never succumb to any kind of addiction. Not alcohol, not drugs, and not —"

"Pussy?" I asked sarcastically.

"No, definitely not that." Tevin sighed. "Floyd's wilding out because he believes that's what men are supposed to do. He grew up in a family where he was told that's what men do. His father and uncles told him that he was supposed to get a wife, buy a house, father some children, and always have some backup action."

"So what you're trying to say is that Floyd is a victim of circumstance?" I laughed. "You can miss me with all of that! He's a typical man!"

"That's the point. In his world, he's only being typical."

"And is that typical in your world, Tevin?"

"Jemistry, you have a lot of trust issues. I get that. And what happened with Winsome's crazy ass didn't help, but I'm not fucking around on you. I can't make you believe it, but I hope that I'm not going to have to go through this kind of speculation on the regular. I want us to have a long, peaceful life together. That's it. That's all."

I decided to lighten up the mood.

"You know, being pregnant has heightened my senses." I pointed to my vagina. "Especially down there."

"What do you mean, especially down there?"

"I've been playing with myself a lot more lately."

Tevin chuckled. "You don't need to play with yourself. You have me."

I pouted. "Why can't I have the best of both worlds?"

He doesn't get it!

"I was thinking. Maybe we could make love with a device inside of me."

"A device? You want me to share you with a big-ass vibrator or dildo?"

"First off, I have not seen a vibrator or dildo that can give your elephantine dick a run for its money."

We both laughed.

"I'm talking about a bullet. I'll stick it in, turn it on, and then you can bang my pussy out while it turns us both out."

Tevin looked appalled. "I'm not using a sex toy!"

"Why not?"

"Because . . . because I love you."

I giggled. "You have completely lost me." I waved my hand toward the ceiling. "That went way over my head."

"Let me school you on something about men, baby. All that freaky shit in the bedroom is cool. Food play, role-play, whips, chains, blindfolds, all kinds of shit. But to ask a man to share you with a sex toy steps over the line. Men will do that with women they are just fucking. It is what it is, but when a man loves a woman, he wants to feel like he can satisfy her all by himself.

"Asking me to be up inside of you with a bullet is like asking me to be up in you with another man's dick."

I fell out laughing. "You are completely shot out. That is the craziest thing that I've ever heard."

"It's crazy to you because you're a female. What if I asked you to let me put a female blow-up doll next to us in bed so I could go back and forth between the two of you? Or even if I pulled out of you and started jacking myself off? How would that make you feel?"

I stood there pondering what he had just said. He may have been onto something.

"I see your reasoning, kind of. However, women are supposed to use sex toys."

"Says who?" Tevin stared at me. "Exactly. Women making excuses for using a bunch of sex toys and saying that they're for variety is like men saying that they go out and fuck other women for variety. Those are merely attempts to justify wanting to do what you want to do regardless."

Again, he had a point. I had never thought of it that way. Men did often claim that they cheated because their wives or girlfriends weren't giving them what they needed at home. A lot of women cheated as well, but Tevin's theory about sex toys being a substitute for a man's dick was valid. Then again, a lot of women weren't getting any dick on the regular. They still needed to relieve some stress.

"I see where you're coming from but, on the real, a lot of women get used to utilizing toys during dick droughts. When they get a man, they still use them because they're a part of their lifestyle at that point. It's part of their routine, like getting a manicure and pedicure every other weekend, or getting their hair done every week, or working out at the gym three days a week. At least they're not fucking someone else."

Tevin took me into his arms and slobbered me down. I felt his dick harden against my midriff.

I pulled away. "What's gotten into you?"

"Hell, all this talk about fucking, inanimate objects inside your pussy . . . inside *my* pussy. Of course, I'm horny now." He pecked me on the lips. "Aren't you?"

I grinned and started taking off my

clothes. "Baby, I was born horny."

I turned, ran toward the foyer and up the steps. "Last one to the bedroom has to perform oral sex first!"

Tevin was rushing behind me and then slowed down. "Well, shit, let me take my time. I'm starving!"

Chapter Twenty-Eight

"Being deeply loved by someone gives you strength, while loving someone deeply gives you courage."

— Lao Tzu

It was my birthday. September eighteenth. Tevin planned to take me out to dinner later that night, but we were doing something a little different. He had paid about four hundred dollars to sign us up for a couples cooking class at CulinAerie on Fourteenth Street in downtown DC. I was excited. We were going to make some surf and turf and then eat what we had prepared. It was great to have a man who loved to cook. An added bonus.

It was the third Wednesday of the month and, as usual, both the students and faculty were complaining about it being "Hump Day." I had always wondered if the "Hump Day" phenomenon was as bad in other cities or whether it was because Washington, DC had so many federal government workers. To me, Wednesdays were simply another day of the week. Maybe it was because I enjoyed my job. If I were doing something I despised, I probably would have been doing a weekend countdown as well. Maybe that was the defining factor. People only worried about celebrating or dreading Wednesdays — depending on whether they were a glass half-full or a glass half-empty type of person — when they didn't feel happy in their careers.

I was delighted to be a principal. Ever since I was a child, I had always wanted to be an educator. I had taught English after getting my master's, and then moved my way up the food chain until the superintendent took a liking to me, and made me an assistant principal first. In 2010, he had promoted me to principal when the previous principal at Medgar Evers retired after nearly forty years of service.

We had a guest speaker that day. A former student, Lee Ricci, who had recently registered the patent for a new digital platform that had quite a buzz surrounding it. Many experts predicted that it would one day rival Google or Internet Explorer. He was major and everyone was very proud of him. He was under twenty-five and on track to become a billionaire by the time he hit thirty.

He gave an amazing and motivational speech, followed by greeting students individually in the auditorium. The baby was kicking inside of me like crazy. While uncomfortable, I loved it all the same. The experience of carrying a fetus in my belly was one that I could not describe before I actually went through it. I was getting more and more nervous, and overwhelmed with the thought of being responsible for the life of another human being . . . forever.

"Mr. Ricci, that was phenomenal!" I told him as I walked him out of the chaos toward the flight of stairs leading down to my office. "We are so proud of you here at Medgar Evers. You're one of our most accomplished alumni."

"People can say what they want about DC Public Schools," he replied. "I was given a great education and I want to make sure that youth understand that it is up to them to use the opportunities presented to them instead of wasting them."

I nodded my head as I felt the little one kicking inside my belly. "As you can imagine, every day is a challenge when it comes to trying to keep thousands of students under control and interested in school."

"I can do more than imagine it. I remember it."

We both laughed.

"Add on all the new technology and distractions, and I'm sure you have to keep things creative," he added.

"Indeed. It's hard to compete with iPhones, Androids, and tablets. And threatening to confiscate them does very little. The kids are not going to leave them at home and when they're bored in class, the temptation to log on to something can be overwhelming.

"Are the classrooms here equipped with the latest computerized learning gadgets?"

"Is that a trick question?" I giggled. "We barely have up-to-date textbooks."

"Well, I'd like to donate whatever you need."

I was stunned. "Are you serious?"

"Yes, very. It's the least I can do."

"Thank you so much. I can't believe you'd —"

That's when it happened. I felt a sharp pain in the left side of my back as two male students pushed past us on the steps. Next thing I knew, I was losing my footing and falling.

Mr. Ricci tried to grab me but he couldn't

hold on to my arm.

I toppled down the flight of steps, hit my head, and passed out as I heard several people yelling out my name and saw Mr. Ricci and Lilibeth running toward me.

I woke up in the hospital under what seemed like ten-thousand-watt light bulbs on the ceiling. As my eyes adjusted, I could feel the IV needle in my arm and was grateful that I wasn't dead. The bars were raised on the sides of the bed so I wouldn't topple out and I heard Lilibeth whispering to someone in the distance.

My mouth was extremely dry and I was sore all over.

You fell down a flight of fucking steps! I reminded myself.

The baby!

My left arm, the one without the IV, instinctively dropped to my stomach. I still had a little pouch there but I panicked. I didn't feel the baby moving.

I attempted to speak but nothing came out, so I rattled one of the bed rails to get someone's attention.

Lilibeth and a nurse appeared in my range of view within seconds.

"She's awake!" Lilibeth exclaimed, and then leaned over me, staring into my eyes.

"Jemistry, can you hear me?"

I nodded and held my hand up to point at my throat.

The nurse said, "She has cotton mouth. Let me go get her some ice water. I'll be right back and I'll alert Dr. Horton that she's awake."

The nurse left the room and I realized that I was at Providence Hospital where Dr. Horton practiced. Thank goodness the school was in the correct zone for the ambulance and that Lilibeth remembered his name from making my appointments with him over the years, prior to my pregnancy. I had been making the prenatal ones myself over the summer months.

I had confided in her about my pregnancy the week before. She giggled and said that she had already suspected. Her exact words were: "I know more about your mannerisms and eating habits than you probably know about yourself. You've been having me order some interesting food choices for your lunches since school started back up. Plus, you have that glow."

Everyone kept talking about the "pregnancy glow." I couldn't see it.

I was quite sure that I was not glowing at the moment. I clamped my eyes shut and said a silent prayer to God not to take my child away from me. Not to take another child away from Tevin.

"The two students that knocked you down need to be expelled," Lilibeth said. "That was inexcusable."

I shook my head and tried to get the word *accident* out of my windpipe. It came out as something unrecognizable.

The nurse returned with a pitcher full of ice water. "Dr. Horton has been paged. He'll be here in less than five minutes."

She poured some water into a plastic cup and then raised the bed so I was sitting up enough to drink. There was an excruciating pain in my lower back.

Once the water hit the back of my throat, I coughed but it felt like I could function again.

I cleared my throat. "It was an accident, Lilibeth. Donald and Leon didn't mean to push me down the stairs. There was a lot going on today and they were simply trying to make it to their next class on time. We should have delayed the fourth-period bell."

Lilibeth took a seat in the chair beside the bed. "Leave it to you to try to make excuses for those kids, even today. You're always looking out for them."

"That's my job. And they're both good kids. Good grades, honor-roll students. I'm not about to expel them and ruin their chances at making it because of an accident. Accidents happen all the time."

I really wanted to ask Lilibeth if they had said anything to her about the baby, but I was too afraid. From the expression on her face, it didn't appear that they had delivered such distressing news to her. She was not good at hiding her emotions. I knew that from experience.

The nurse was jotting my vitals down on my chart and had broken out a thermometer to take my temperature. Before she could stick it in, I asked Lilibeth, "Has anyone called Tevin?"

While the thermometer was in my mouth, she responded, "Yes. I did. He was in surgery but they said that they'd give him the message the second he was done. I asked them to disrupt but —"

The nurse removed the thermometer in time for me to interrupt her. "No, they can't bother him while he's in surgery. It'll be fine. He'll be here."

Dr. Horton entered the room and smiled at me. I felt a sense of relief. My baby was alive!

Two hours later, Tevin came bolting through the door of my hospital room.

Before he could even say anything, I assured him, "The baby's fine."

He came over and laid his head on my stomach and embraced me, kissed my stomach, and then moved up and kissed my forehead.

"It's okay, baby," I said, caressing the back of his head. "I fell but everything's all right."

He stood and walked to the end of the bed, grabbed my chart and started flipping through it, his eyes speed-reading the pages. He had yet to say a single word.

"Dr. Horton said that I was lucky. He's going to have to monitor things and wants me to start coming in to see him weekly, at least for the next month or so." His silence was beginning to frighten me. "Tevin, did you hear what I said? Tevin?"

He looked up from the chart. "Sorry, sweetheart. I'm a little overwhelmed at the moment." He set the chart down. "Everything looks good. They did a sonogram?"

"Two of them. One when I was still knocked out and another one when I was awake." I paused to consider whether or not I should elaborate. I decided he needed to know everything. "At first I didn't feel the baby kicking, but the little sucker is moving around now."

"I'll ask them to see the film."

"Yes, you can do that. But there is something you should know before you see it."

He came over and took my hand into his. "What? Is something wrong with the baby?"

"No, he's fine."

"That's good because . . . He?"

"Yes, *he.* Even though we'd decided not to find out, it was kind of obvious this time around. Little Man looks like he's going to be hung like his father."

Tevin chuckled. "You could see his dick?"

"Oh yeah, couldn't miss it this time. Congratulations, Tevin Harris, *Senior.*"

"We're going to name him after me?"

I shrugged. "I assumed that is what you'd want. Don't you?"

"I'm not sure. I kind of want him to have his own identity. But then again, it would be great to have my name carry on."

I brought his hand to my lips and kissed it. "It's a great name. He has a lot to live up to. I say we go for it. No point in breaking out baby name books or doing Internet searches when the perfect name already exists for him."

Tevin grinned from ear-to-ear. "Did they say how long you have to stay in here?"

"At least until tomorrow morning. I'm glad that I didn't break anything. My ankle's going to be sore for a few days, and my lower back. All in all, I took that flight of steps like a trooper."

Tevin frowned, probably envisioning the horrific fall in his mind. "So what exactly happened?"

"We had a guest speaker today, a former student. I was walking him downstairs from the auditorium and he was telling me that he plans to donate what amounts to a few million dollars' worth of electronics and software to the school. I must've gotten too engrossed in the conversation and I slipped."

There was no way that I was going to tell Tevin that two students had accidentally caused my fall. He wouldn't have seen anything but blood.

"You have to be more careful, baby," was all that he said. "I'm just glad that you and the baby are okay."

"I know that you were petrified when they told you. I hope you didn't drive recklessly on the way over here."

"Floyd drove me. He's downstairs parking and calling Courtney to meet him over here."

It was my turn to frown. "Great!"

Tevin sighed. "Please try to be nice to him. It's not the time."

"There's never *a time* to call someone on

their bullshit. When Courtney gets here, it's going to take every ounce of self-control that I possess not to say anything. I haven't spoken to her since you told me that Floyd is a whore."

"I haven't told him that I let that slip. We need to get through this without drama. If you feel like you have to tell Courtney about his dirt, can we at least wait until we get home?"

"Yeah, you're right. The day has been long enough already."

Tevin wiped his right eye. "I was so scared. I don't think that I can handle losing another child."

"God's will and mercy shall prevail. Today, He spoke and gave us His blessings."

Tevin grinned and kissed me lightly on the lips. "I agree."

CHAPTER TWENTY-NINE

"Every love story is beautiful,
but ours is my favorite."
— Unknown

I was on medical leave for a few weeks, against my will. I was never one to sit around doing nothing and the boredom was killing me. As much as I was accustomed to watching daytime TV shows that were recorded on my DVR, watching them in real time irritated me for some reason. It meant that I had to sit through the commercials instead of skipping them and, for some reason, I hated that. Even when I was out of school for the summer, I rarely sat around during the day. I played the shows in the evening or late night when I was falling asleep.

It was amusing to me that companies were still spending millions to produce commercials and purchase airtime on television shows. A lot of them were never actually watched. Either people skipped over them with their remote, flipped channels during the ads, or had their eyes glued to laptops, cell phones, or tablets, with their attention diverted until the show started back up. Even the online ads that were placed before videos and shows online rarely got any attention. Companies really needed to realize that they had to take to social networking to really get any attention. They had to engage the consumers in contests or do something so different, amusing, or shocking that everyone would share it on their pages or retweet it.

I did catch up on some reading while I was laid up. I read several novels by Allison Hobbs, Cairo, and William Fredrick Cooper, and a couple of self-help books. The greatest room in anyone's house is the room for improvement. But the books that I read the most of were parenting books. I definitely needed to know all about that. A mother? Wow! I was at the point in my life that I never thought it would happen for me. A mother and, if all went well, a wife.

I was still apprehensive about setting a wedding date. I had progressed somewhat by sporting the ring that Tevin had purchased me. I needed to go shopping to purchase him a wedding band at some point. I planned to get him one that matched the color tone of mine. My ankle was still sore so I tried to stay off my feet as much as possible. I was not in the best of shape since I got pregnant. I had not been going to the gym or doing any real form of exercise. I was becoming too lazy and complacent. As soon as I had Tevin Jr., I planned to reclaim my body and become fly all over again.

I was scanning the Internet one afternoon and ran across a blog written by a man. Rarely did I agree with much that men said about life. It was hard to relate, not being one. But this blog really caught my attention. It was written by a thirty-year-old man who had been with his wife since he was seventeen, and had been married to her for eight years. They had several children and he was under the impression that he might lose her.

He felt like he was not good enough for her, like she had outgrown him over the years. He had to admit that he might have tried to keep her pregnant in order to keep her in his life. *They had nine children.* But while she normally would get herself back together — losing weight, reading, perfecting her hair and makeup, dressing good, smelling good — he had always felt that it was for his benefit. He sensed something was different this time — like she was doing it for herself and that she would eventually leave him, even if it were not specifically for another man.

He said that if she were single and he met her now, she never would have given him the time of day. That she would only be interested in men who had themselves more together, men who were on her level both physically and financially. He was making excuses for why he had not achieved more.

Then it came down to the truth, slipped nonchalantly into the last paragraph. A couple of years before, he had cheated on her and she had forgiven him. That was what it came down to. It was different this time around after childbirth. He didn't think she had actually gotten over his shit and that caring so much for herself meant that she would likely feel like she deserved better than a man who would disrespect her like that.

He was definitely onto something. I immediately thought of Courtney and what she would do if she found out that Floyd was cheating on her. Even though Courtney had "elected" to be a stay-at-home mother and wife, she was brilliant and attractive and any man would be blessed to have her. She took care of herself — spiritually and physically — and her clothes, hair, and makeup were all always on point. Courtney was thebomb.com and she really did not deserve the shit that Floyd was doing to her.

Ever since Tevin had "slipped" and told me the truth, I had fought a never-ending war within myself over whether or not to tell her the truth. The way I looked at it, the outcome had a few possibilities. Courtney could tell Floyd to kiss her ass and file for divorce immediately. Courtney could decide to stay and suggest marital counseling. Courtney could pretend like it never happened and stay for her kids, but never trust Floyd again.

There was one other possibility. That Courtney could curse me out because she already knew, or at least suspected, that he had cheated once, or was a habitual cheater. I decided that I would try to feel her out before I said anything. Then again, I was not one to play games.

Shit! I wish he'd never told me!

It was one of those "your ears must've been burning" moments. As soon as I finished that thought, my cell phone started ringing. It was Courtney.

"Hey, girl," I said into the phone.

"What you know good?" she replied. "Just calling to check on you. See if you needed anything. The kids and I can drop by and bring you whatever you need. Or I can get a sitter and come keep you company for a while."

"Aw, you're so sweet, but I'm fine. Just watching a bunch of television, reading tons of stuff, and sleeping way too damn much."

"There's no such thing as sleeping too much when you're pregnant."

"What about eating too much? I am eating like ten men."

We both laughed.

"Girl, do you," Courtney said. "That's part of the joy of pregnancy. You have a valid excuse to go buck wild and throw down six times a day if you want."

"Yeah, but if I get too fat, Tevin is going to have to roll me out the door and to the hospital when I go into labor."

She giggled. "Talk about exaggerating. I bet you haven't put on ten pounds yet."

"Try twenty-six."

"Twenty-six? Must be all tits and ass because it's damn sure not in your stomach."

"You haven't seen me undressed. As soon as I get it back together, I'm going to have to do some serious shopping for maternity

317

clothes. Or borrow some of yours."

"Yes, yes. My shit is fly. I'll get some of it together and bring it over this weekend. I probably spent more on maternity clothes than my regular stuff."

"Well, it's hard to feel cute when you look like a whale. But I'm sure you have some awesome stuff. Would love to use some, if you don't mind."

"Of course I don't mind." She paused long enough to tell one of the kids to stop switching channels on the television remote. They were constantly fighting over the TV in the family room, even though all four of them had their own sets in their bedrooms. *Sibling rivalry* was more than just a passé term. "Tell you what. Why don't we all have dinner together on Friday? If you don't feel like going out, I can prepare something and bring it over."

"I don't want to put you out like that."

"Put me out? Girl, I cook at least five days a week for a gaggle of kids. Making dinner for you and Tevin and getting a break is exciting. We can all catch up."

When she said that, I closed my eyes and took in a deep breath.

Say something, Jemistry!

I tried to be creative right quick.

Feel her out!

"Can I ask you a question, Courtney?" I readjusted myself on the sofa to lie on my left side. "About marriage."

"Sure, shoot."

"Tevin's been married before but I haven't. I realize it's a huge commitment but what are the biggest differences between dating or living together and marriage? At least in your opinion."

She giggled. "That's a loaded question and it highly depends on the two people in the marriage, what their expectations are, and what kind of family background they had."

"I keep forgetting that you were a psych major. You're going deep."

"Okay, I'll try to tone it down." She chuckled. "All I'm saying is that everyone has different outlooks on what it means to make a commitment. And there are different reasons people get married in the first place.

"Some consider marriage to be a business arrangement. Two people with like-minded goals agree to build a life together of the three Ps."

"Three Ps?"

"Prosperity, procreation, and productivity."

"Like I said, deep."

"Others get married because they are so in love that they can't imagine ever living without each other. They want to grow old together, change each other's diapers and dentures, and be buried side by side.

"Then there are those who fall somewhere in the middle. Ones that get married because they believe it is expected of them, because all of their friends are doing it, and because they come from a situation where their parents have been married for decades."

"I see."

"Oh, and I cannot forget the females who get married just so they won't be alone. Those kind want their men to be a different set of three Ps. They want a priest, a provider, and a protector on twenty-four-hour duty."

"Yeah, I have quite a few friends who fall into that category. They are afraid to do anything by themselves." I sighed. "But I have to add that when you start adding women into the mix who are abused, get pregnant young, and are economically at a disadvantage, that leads to a lot of other reasons."

"True enough."

Tevin Jr. kicked and I felt like the wind was being knocked out of me. I gasped.

"Are you okay, Jemistry?" Courtney asked in a panic.

"I'm fine. The little one kicked. Might be upset about those enchiladas I ate for lunch."

"Yeah, those can cause some serious indigestion."

"What about women who share their husbands?" I blurted out. "I'm not talking about being polygamous and all that, but women who know their men are dicking other chicks down and don't say anything about it."

I could hear Courtney sucking her teeth through the phone. "Shit, that could never be me. I wish Floyd would step out on me. It'd be the official date of his death. I can tell you that much right now. I don't see how any woman would sit by and let a man disrespect her like that. I'm not having it. Fuck that!"

Whelp! That answers that question!

"Why'd you ask that?" she inquired. "I hope you don't think Tevin's cheating on you. It'll never happen. He's the most honest man I've ever met. He's a man of integrity and I know for a fact that he never cheated on Estella."

"I don't believe he ever cheated on her either."

"You need to let that shit that happened with your former roommate go."

"I have let it go. I trust Tevin. I was simply throwing out a topic out of boredom," I lied, trying not to make it seem like I was feeling her out. "Sitting here day after day is not my friend. When Tevin comes home every evening, I almost feel like he's coming back from a two-year deployment."

"Wow!"

"Yes, it's bad. Friday night sounds good, though. I should be okay to go out. Heaven knows that I need to get out of here. The weather's still nice. It's going to get cold soon."

"I know, right. *The Old Farmer's Almanac* is predicting another blizzard like we had at the beginning of 2010. Do you remember it?"

"Hell, who could forget Snowmageddon?"

We both chuckled.

"School was closed for ten days in a row. It was a mess," I added. "Next time they call for something like that, I'm catching the first thing smoking out of here for Florida or somewhere else warm."

"Well, you can pack the kids and me in your suitcases because we're leaving, too. Never again. I can see why our men have to stay, but we can jet. Schools are going to be closed regardless."

"Exactly!"

The doorbell rang. I couldn't imagine who it might be. Maybe a delivery.

"Courtney, let me holler at you later. There's someone at the door."

"No problem. See you on Friday, if I don't talk to you before then."

"For sure. Love you, sis."

"Love you, too."

CHAPTER THIRTY

"To love is to receive a glimpse of heaven."
— Karen Sunde

"Who is it?" I asked at the same time that I glanced through the peephole in the front door. Before she could answer, I took a step back. I recognized her from older photographs.

This cannot be happening!

"Jemistry, my name is Estella Harris," she said from the other side of the door.

I hesitated to open it. Then I decided that I was too damn old to be acting so damn immature.

I opened the door. "Tevin's not here right now."

"Actually, I came here to see you."

I looked at her like she was crazy. Her eyes dropped to my stomach and I felt guilty. Not sure why but I did.

"Do you mind if I come in?"

There was no win-win answer to that question. If I said that I didn't mind, I was going to have to hold a conversation with her that I had neither anticipated taking place nor wanted to have. If I said that I did mind, she would think that I was jealous of her and throwing shade. Part of me wanted to know what she wanted to say. The other part asked myself why would I give a damn what she wanted to say.

There was no reason for me to dislike her. She had never done anything to me and, as far as I knew, she had never done anything to Tevin either. Still, the mere thought that she was the woman that Tevin had once loved, and professed his love for like he was now doing with me, was unnerving. The fact that he had planted his seed in her numerous times was almost too much. Almost.

I moved aside. "Come in."

"Thank you."

Estella entered and walked into the living room as I shut the door.

I followed her and pointed to the sofa. "Please, have a seat."

She sat and scanned the room. "Lovely house. I've never actually been here before."

"Oh, I figured you had been." I sat in the armchair. "He's had this place for a while."

"I've had the address, to forward his mail and all, but no, I've never actually been here. He purchased this house after our divorce was . . ."

"Final," I said, finishing her sentence for her. "I don't mean to sound rude, but why exactly are you here?"

"Tevin called me last week."

"Oh?"

Yes, I'm jealous!

"It's not what you might imagine," she quickly stated, sensing that I was wondering what the fuck he'd called her for. "He called me to ask me for advice."

Are you for real?

"He wanted my help in trying to convince you to marry him."

I frowned. "Being that we've never met a day in our lives, what made him think that you could give him that type of advice?"

"I get what you're saying, but I also understood where he was coming from. Tevin doesn't have a lot of people to open up to. And let's face it, if he were to discuss his true feelings with most men, they'd call him a pussy or weak, and tell him to man up."

I nodded. She had a valid point. Men were taught to hide their emotions a lot and other men did tend to ridicule them for expressing themselves. It was part of the "man code" to act hard at all times, right along with never letting them see you cry, and if you are caught doing some shit you have no business doing, deny, deny, deny.

"Estella, I appreciate you coming over here, but I don't feel comfortable discussing my relationship with Tevin with you. You're his ex-wife and that means that, at some point, you were his world. I'm not trying to take your place but I don't want you interjecting your opinions either.

"There's no reason for us to get to know each other, hang out, or trade fairy tales. You're in his past and, from what he told me, you're engaged, maybe even married by now, and you've moved on. It would be different if the two of you had ki . . ."

Shit!

The expression on her face changed.

"I'm sorry. I wasn't trying to —"

"Understood, Jemistry. I get your point. If we had children together, you and I would have no other option but to get along. And you're right. I am his past and I have no intention of being in constant communication with Tevin, any more than he plans on doing that with me.

"We've only spoken twice in the past six months. Prior to that, I hadn't spoken to him in years."

"I see."

"We don't have to discuss your business. You can merely listen."

We stared at each other for a few moments. She was really an attractive and well-put-together woman, and she seemed genuine. Suddenly, sadness swept over me. I could see why Tevin had married her, and how they were a cute couple that had been ripped apart by tragedy after tragedy. But I had to admit that I was glad that their marriage did not last. If it had, Tevin and I would have never met.

"Sure, I'll hear you out," I said. "I'm sure you know more about the inner workings of Tevin's mind than most people, even me."

"Tevin loves you and it is quite upsetting to him for his son to be born out of wedlock. For a lot of men these days, they could not care less, but he's different. He has a core value system and this entire situation is going against it. I'm surprised he even agreed to live together prior to marriage."

"He insisted on it," I stated defensively. "I had my own place but he wanted me here with him. I explained to him that I wasn't ready for marriage."

I held out my hand so she could see the ring. She also had on one but I refused to ask if she was remarried yet. Then I recalled her saying that her name was Estella Harris at the door. She had not tied the knot yet.

"It doesn't mean that I don't plan on doing it. That's why I have this on. But I want to wait."

"Wait for?"

None of your damn business!

"I'm not trying to dredge up any painful memories for you, so I prefer to bypass that question, Estella."

She squinted, analyzing what I had said. I hated when people outthought a thinker like me.

"Let me take a shot in the dark," she said. "You're afraid you might lose the baby and you don't want Tevin to end up in another toxic marriage behind it?"

"Actually, I almost lost the baby already. I had an accident."

"He told me."

"But, yes, even prior to then, the thought definitely crossed my mind. I wanted to make it through my second trimester first. Is that a crime?"

"No, but I assume you're almost there."

"Almost."

"Then I guess you really didn't need me to come over here after all," she said and then grinned uncomfortably.

"You could've saved the trip."

We both sat there looking at each other.

"I'm sorry. I'm being rude," I stated after a pregnant pause. "Would you like something to drink?"

"No, but thank you," she said. "I have to say that I'm delighted Tevin found you. He deserves to be happy."

"So do you," I replied, shifting in my chair.

She stared at my stomach. "He told me that it's a boy."

"Yes. We plan to name him Tevin Junior."

"Of course. He deserves that, too. There are times when I wish that things could've been different. But I wasn't in a stable frame of mind after the miscarriages. I shut down. I became a phantom. Tevin was in a marriage by himself.

"He hung in there. He never would've left me on his own. We both realized that. It wasn't in his nature. So I filed for divorce and set him free.

"I've matured a lot now. The old me could've never sat here, across from you, the woman he loves now, pleading for you to marry him."

"We all evolve as we age," I replied. "The old me never would've answered the door if my man's ex-anything came knocking on it. But the *seasoned* me realizes that both

Tevin and I have a past. If he ran across one of the men that I used to be with, I'd hope that they could act like grown men and not boys.

"Tevin loves me and only me; I'm convinced of that. He will always carry feelings for you but they're not the same."

I couldn't believe that I was now preaching everything that Tevin had been trying to convince me of all along.

"No, they are not the same," Estella said. "I'm in love with another man, engaged to be married in a few months."

"Congratulations!"

"Thank you. I never thought I'd open up to someone else. I had to find a man who didn't want, nor expect me to bear, children." She lowered her eyes. "I never told Tevin this, and he still doesn't know. I had my tubes tied after my last miscarriage. I couldn't go through that again . . . not ever."

"I honestly don't blame you. You did what you felt you had to do . . . but he does know you tied your tubes."

Estella looked up at me, stunned. "But how?"

I shrugged. "I'm not sure but he definitely knows. He told me that you'd done it."

"I should've known that he'd figured it out." She sighed and then added, "That was one of the main reasons that I decided to divorce him. It was a lie, a deception, and I could not face him every day knowing what I had done. Nor could I confess what I had done . . . not back then."

"I understand."

"He already felt robbed. Telling him that I had removed any chance of him ever fathering a child with me would have killed him."

"Well, everything happens for a reason. We'll all be fine, and now you can stop worrying about deceiving him since he already knew. Life goes on and every day is a gift. Truly, it is."

Estella stood up, and so did I.

She gathered her purse and keys. "I'm glad that we could share this brief encounter together. Thank you for even letting me in the door."

"I'll tell Tevin that you came by," I said.

She was walking toward the foyer and froze, then turned back to me. "I'm not going to encourage or discourage you from telling him that I was here. He doesn't know. I took it upon myself to come and speak with you. He was only asking for advice, not for me to contact you."

I nodded. "I see."

"I wish the two of you nothing but a happy, long life together. And many, many more kids."

I giggled. "I don't know about all that. I'm not a spring chicken. This one pregnancy is a chore."

We walked to the front door together and I opened it.

She was about to walk out without saying anything.

"Estella, thanks for coming to see me. Even though my first inclination was to be upset about it, this has actually been . . . intriguing. Getting to meet you, even for a few moments, gives me a lot of insight into Tevin."

"Good. And I'm glad we met as well. It gives me peace to know that he's in such wonderful hands now."

I don't know what inspired me to do it, but I hugged her . . . tight. She hugged me back. When we let go of the embrace, she smiled and walked away to her car.

Chapter Thirty-One

"Everyone has their own reasons for waking up in the morning. Mine is you."
— Unknown

Geesh, I was horny all the time. Tevin was horny as well but being overly cautious when it came to having sex with me. It was driving me crazy. So I would take matters into my own hands. I decided not to mention Estella coming by. It would have solved nothing and he would have been worried about my feelings. I was actually cool with the entire thing, which shocked even me. In many ways, it had helped to solidify my decision to eventually get married.

Courtney and Floyd had joined us for dinner that Friday night at the Old Ebbitt Grill on Fifteenth Street, within walking distance of the White House. It was amazing how DC had gone through a massive gentrification. When I was a child, it was truly "the

Chocolate City." Now it was about fifty percent African-American, forty percent Caucasian, and the rest was made up of Hispanics, Asians, and others. Areas that used to be infamous for gang activity were now crowded with nightlife, new hangouts, and people out mingling way into the wee hours of the morning, without any fear for their safety. The reputation had changed for the better. It had evolved.

The world had evolved, though. We had our first African-American president in office. When it became clear that Senator Barack Obama had an actual chance of winning, I had rushed to have anything to do with his campaign. It was an exciting time and his wife, Michelle, was my idol. Everything about her was stylish, sophisticated, and she clearly was a unique, incredible woman.

President Obama had won his second term and it also made one thing clear. Even though he had won both elections by incredible, unquestionable margins, racism was still alive and well in the United States. In my opinion, no other POTUS had ever been disrespected or talked down upon in recent history as he was. At least, not to my recollection. But still, he stood strong, confident, and assured. A spectacular role model for young men of all races who ensured them that having the audacity to hope could actually pay off in the end. That was what I admired about him the most. He believed that he could do it and that was half the battle.

Since we were so close to the White House, we partially discussed that topic over dinner. Tevin was not big on talking politics but Floyd and I were, and Courtney was neutral.

"Hillary's going to win in twenty-sixteen," I said with much confidence.

"Hmm, I don't know about all of that," Floyd replied. "We don't need a woman running this country. Too much at stake."

"That's my male chauvinist husband," Courtney joked as she sliced into her rib eye with a steak knife.

"Floyd, you can miss me with all that," I said. "Let's have this same discussion after she wins."

"Biden will beat her in the primary," Floyd added. "And you can take that to the bank."

Tevin smirked. "We sure have a lot of fortune tellers at this table."

I tapped Tevin lightly on the arm and then picked up a forkful of my Trout Parmesan. "It's not being a seer, baby. It's common sense. It's Hillary all the way, boo."

"Women have a place in this world. That is it and that is all," Floyd stated with much sarcasm. "Accept your role and everything is all good."

He's getting on my last fucking nerve! Rat bastard!

I tensed up and Tevin must have felt it all through my body beside him. I really, *really* wanted to burst Floyd's bubble right there at the table. Call him out on his shit. Tevin must have sensed it. He changed the subject.

"Hey, you two," he said, addressing Floyd and Courtney. "Jemistry and I are thinking about spending New Year's Eve in New Orleans. You should join us."

Courtney looked concerned. "Jemistry, can you travel that far, with the pregnancy and all? When are you due again?"

"Close to Valentine's Day," I replied. "February seventeenth to be exact, but we all know that it's not going to go down like that."

Everyone at the table laughed.

"Oh no, little man is going to make his appearance when he is good and ready," Tevin said.

"But to answer your other question, Dr. Horton said that everything is fine with the baby, so I can fly." I reached over and took Tevin by the hand. "Besides, you know from experience, it pays to be married to a doctor so you always have emergency medical care."

"No doubt," she said.

Tevin pulled his hand away. "Yeah, it does pay to be *married* to a doctor."

I was stunned that he would come at me like that in front of them. "Tevin, please don't. Not tonight."

"Okay, whatever," he replied and took a sip of his Arnold Palmer.

"You really need to make my boy an honest man," Floyd interjected.

Nobody asked you shit! And you are far from honest!

"Let me put everyone out of their misery, speculation, and need to express opinions. I was hoping that the trip to New Orleans, which was *my suggestion,* could also serve as our honeymoon. I honestly had no idea that Tevin planned to invite you, but that's cool. The more the merrier."

Everyone fell silent.

I looked at Tevin. "Did you hear what I said? Can we get married in December and go on our honeymoon?"

Tevin grinned. "You already know my answer. I only wish we could do it sooner."

What the hell! Cave in and get it over with!

"Fine. I love you, I want to marry you, so you pick the date and I'm there."

Tevin stared at me. "Really?"

"Yes, so when?"

"It's Friday, we have to go apply for the license, it takes three days to process, and then we can pick it up." He paused to add dates up in his head. "How about next Saturday?"

I shrugged. "Works for me, on one condition."

Tevin leaned over and kissed me on the cheek. "Anything."

"That you get us a suite at the Mandarin Oriental that night to consummate our marriage."

"Done."

"And that you still take me to New Orleans for New Year's Eve."

"Done."

"And that you let me switch out that hideous blue paint you bought for TJ's nursery."

Courtney said, "Aw, you're calling him TJ already. Awesome!"

"Done," Tevin said, "but I thought you said on *one* condition?"

"I might as well go for broke," I said and laughed.

"Might as well," Floyd said and then rolled his eyes. Then he caught himself slipping and grinned. "That's great about the wedding. I'll put in tomorrow for the day off."

"Cool," I said, trying to suppress a frown. I was feeling some kind of way about Floyd.

"So, where are we doing this?" Courtney asked with excitement. "Is the justice of the peace even available on Saturdays?"

"I'm sure they are," I said, "but I'm gonna ask one of my coworker's husbands to do the honors. I'm glad that the two of you will be able to come." I looked at Tevin. "Do you want to invite your parents?"

"Of course. I'll see if either one of them can make it on such short notice."

I reminded him, "We could have waited so they could definitely make it."

"Nope." He shook his head. "Not waiting."

"Then let's do the damn thing."

When we got home that night, I couldn't go another minute without some sex. Tevin pulled the car into the garage since it was getting chilly outdoors. During the warmer months, we both had parked in the driveway. Now we were both utilizing bays in his three-car garage on the regular.

I went ahead inside. He was getting some bags out of the trunk. We had been shopping earlier that day for some things for TJ. I hoped that he planned to leave that hideous paint in the car. It was definitely going back. We had agreed on blue for the room — obvious choice — but the shade he had selected was bland and too dark. I desired something more vibrant. I also planned to hire the art teacher from school, Mr. Richie, to paint a colorful mural on the biggest wall. I was going to leave that wall white for now and let him come up with something creative. He had asked me what I had in mind and I told him that I was asking him because I wanted *his* imagination at work, not mine. He was scheduled to come by the next weekend. Now I had to reschedule. *I was getting married!*

By the time Tevin walked in from the garage, I was sitting in the kitchen, butt naked, with my right leg thrown up on the table, and two of the fingers from my left hand exploring my pussy.

"Oh damn," Tevin said, dropping the bags on the floor. "Excited much?"

"What can I say?" I replied. "You turn me on . . . so much. The thought of finally becoming Mrs. Tevin Harris has me all . . . hot and bothered."

"Baby, I don't want to hurt the baby."

I sighed. "Tevin, I've asked Dr. Horton several times if it was okay to have sex. We have months left until February, and I need you."

"And I'm not saying that I don't need you, baby. My thirst for you never ends."

"Then can you do me a favor and at least come drink at my fountain?"

I pulled my fingers out and sucked on them, one at a time.

"Um, you don't know what you're missing."

"Oh, I know it very well. I would know it anywhere." He chuckled and walked toward me. "That's my pussy."

"Damn right it's your pussy. And you need to stop neglecting it. It's going to get a complex. Pussies can have low self-esteem. We don't want to have to put her in therapy."

Tevin laughed and kneeled beside me. I took my leg off the table and placed it over his left shoulder.

He stared at my pussy like it was a rare diamond.

"God has made a lot of beautiful things in this world, but you are a masterpiece."

Whenever I was intimate with Tevin, he made me feel so unique and special. Other men in my past had never done that. Sure, they made me feel like they cared, but they never made me feel like I was one-of-a-kind. Tevin did that for me, and I loved him all the more for it.

"You make me feel so . . . exceptional," I said, running the fingers from my other hand through his hair. "You always make me feel so damn special."

He gazed up into my eyes. "That's because you are. You're everything to me, Jemistry. Everything. Sure, I'm passionate about my career. I've accomplished a lot in my lifetime and still have a long way to go, hopefully. But what good does it do a man to prosper if he loses his soul in the process. You are my soul."

Not sure how it happened but I was crying. He wiped my tears.

"I'm so glad that you decided to finally allow me the honor of becoming your husband."

"Tevin, I never had any doubts about marrying you. That's not what it was about. I just —"

He placed three fingers over my lips. "Shhhh, it doesn't matter whether you had any doubts or not. All that matters is that it's really happening." He moved his hands down over my stomach. "Everything is really happening. I've always wanted a family. A woman to come home to, a child to play with, and a legacy to leave behind."

I pulled Tevin's face to mine and kissed him intensely. We must have kissed for a good ten minutes. It had been a while since we had shared a kiss so full of unspoken words and feelings. I was still crying but it was all out of joy.

When we finished kissing, Tevin lowered his head and drank from my fountain.

■ ■ ■ ■

TEVIN

■ ■ ■ ■

CHAPTER THIRTY-TWO

"When we are in love, we seem to ourselves quite different than what we were before."
— Blaise Pascal

Even though I had been married before, taking Jemistry as my wife had an effect on me that was foreign to me. We got married at a small church in Northeast, DC, with about thirty people present. It could have been three, three hundred, three thousand, or just us and I would have been ecstatic.

Courtney and Floyd were there with their children, several of Jemistry's coworkers and their spouses, including Lilibeth and her husband, and both of my sisters came with their families and both of my parents. My father flew in from Sweden and I was not the least bit surprised.

It was interesting seeing my parents interact. Even though they discussed their offspring from time to time, they had not actually seen each other in several years. Daddy was happy for me but I could tell that he was also sad about ruining the one good thing he ever had: his connection with my mother.

What happened between them was the main reason why I would never, ever cheat on a woman. I watched the pain Mom had endured at the hands of my father and there was no way that I could ever do that to another individual, much less someone that I loved. Too many men did the exact opposite. They followed in their fathers' footsteps and made a mockery out of marriage. That could never, and would never, be me.

Jemistry walked down the aisle in a stunning, off-white, floor-length gown. Two of the students from the school choir — a male and a female — sang a duet for her entrance: "After All is Said and Done" by Marc Nelson and Beyoncé.

Both of us cried during the ceremony, along with everyone else, even Floyd. We had a reception on a chartered, private yacht and sailed up and down the Potomac River for three hours. It was an amazing day.

I got Jemistry the suite she'd requested at

the Mandarin Oriental Hotel — the Presidential Suite. The suite had three bedrooms and it was more than 3,500 square feet. No, we did not need all of that but Jemistry was worth every penny.

We actually made use of most of the rooms, though. We made love like we had never made love before. After speaking to Dr. Horton myself a few days earlier, he had not only assured me that it was fine for us to have sex, but he also told me that Jemistry was "sexually frustrated" and had asked him to call me to discuss, one medical professional to another. She tickled me.

Jemistry had gone on a web site and found all these animated sex positions with the female on top. She had sent me a text with the link and instructed me to "study up on them." I did and was ready to rock her world . . . gently.

I was not about to go for broke like most men claimed that they did on their wedding nights. It always tripped me out when my friends would brag about how they "tore the pussy up" instead of simply making love. They would share the intimate details and try to outdo each other. It was quite outlandish but not unexpected. Men loved to brag on their dicks, especially to other men.

Once women reached a certain age, or

status, it was a great *turn-off* for a man to brag on his sexual skills. Now if women were feeble-minded and going through a dick drought, it was a different story. Those were the kind of chicks Floyd preyed on.

I was so glad that Jemistry hadn't told Courtney about Floyd's wandering eyes, and dick. I had not brought it up to her again — I didn't want to press my luck — and things were getting back to normal between Floyd and me. I'd forgiven him for not telling me about Jemistry's pregnancy in the beginning. The main reason being that I was not quite sure what I would have done if the roles had been reversed. As much as I would have liked to think that I would've told him, I wasn't a hundred percent convinced of that.

Jemistry emerged from the master bathroom of the suite in a lavender satin gown, freshly bathed and smelling like the ocean. I loved the way she played around with using different scents for bathing. She had told me once that she tried to use scents that matched the mood and location, kind of like a florist who makes bouquets based on the occasion. Since we had a suite overlooking the Potomac, and had sailed the Potomac for the reception, I was feeling her flow.

"You look so beautiful," I told her. I had taken a shower in another bathroom and was only wearing a pair of black pajama pants tied with a string.

She giggled and ran her fingers through her hair in a seductive way. "That makes about the hundredth time you've told me that today."

"It's the truth."

I poured us two glasses of sparkling apple cider. Because of the pregnancy, we skipped the champagne.

She walked over to me and I handed her a glass. "For you, Mrs. Harris."

"I love the sound of that."

I leaned in for a quick kiss. "Get used to it. It's your name now."

"Forever."

"And a day."

We clinked our glasses together.

"To us," we said in unison, entwined our arms, and took long gulps.

Jemistry spilt a little on my chest when we were untangling our arms. "Let me get that," she said, and then licked the few drops off my chest.

Then she went lower, sitting down on the sofa, and unfastening my pants with her teeth.

She set her glass down on the coffee table,

pulled my pants down, grabbed my dick, and said, "Let me get this, too."

Jemistry had given me some off the chain head since we'd been together. She had never been able to take in all of my mass but she was definitely more into it and more comfortable with it. But I still wasn't prepared for what came next.

She started humming on the head of my penis, and whispering, "I want to recite something that I wrote for this special occasion." She held on tight to my dick and looked up at me. "I penned a poem for my dick."

"A poem?" I chuckled. "Let's hear it."

She stared at the head of my dick, at the eye, and started reciting an actual poem. I was blown away — no pun intended.

"I call this 'Glaze on my Doughnut.' You are the glaze on my doughnut. The milk to my shake. The shake to my bake. The twinkle in my eye. The blue in my sky. You are the peanut to my butter. The sweet in my dreams. The sprinkle on my sundae. The spring in my step and the jewel on my crown. You are the beat of my heart. The flip to my flop. The —"

I couldn't hold it in another second. I fell out laughing and took my dick out of her hand. "Baby?"

"Yeah?"

"Um, that shit doesn't rhyme."

She laughed and then swatted me on my dick. "Well, you get the point."

"Yes, you like this dick."

"I love this dick. So much so that I started to recite it at the wedding in front of everyone."

I chuckled. "Mom would have loved it."

Jemistry started sucking me off like she was starving and it took me less than three minutes to explode in her throat. I almost fainted.

"Damn, I'm going to have to take a break before I can do anything else. You drained me," I said.

"Nope, no damn breaks!"

She led me into the master bedroom and pushed me down on the bed on my back. Then she went over to her overnight bag, pulled something out, and put it behind her back.

"What's that?" I asked, sitting up on my elbows.

"You'll see. Close your eyes." I hesitated so she asked, "You don't trust me, Tevin? You married me but you don't trust me?"

"Of course I trust you."

I closed my eyes and waited to see what she was going to do next.

She started sucking my dick again gently, then took more and more of me into her mouth. Miraculously, I achieved another erection.

"Wow, I didn't think I could get hard again right now," I whispered. "Your lips are magic."

Then I felt something strange. Her mouth started contracting in and out on my dick but not like normal. I heard a buzzing noise, opened my eyes, and Jemistry had a vibrator on the side of her cheek, causing the sensation to ripple inside onto my dick.

"Damn, you're creative," I practically yelled. "Oh shit!"

By the time she was done with sucking my dick for the second round, she had my ass curled up in a fetal position behind that shit. She could've put the top-of-the-ladder porn stars to shame with that head game.

"Did you like that, baby?" she asked after I had come again.

"You see me laid up in bed like your little bitch, don't you?" I joked, all the while trying to catch my breath.

I'll be damned if Jemistry didn't act like a man on our wedding night and attempt to fuck me half to death. She had been serious about all of those sex positions. She went to work, and put me to work until I literally passed out about three AM.

We went to Sunday brunch at Georgia Brown's about noon and sat there like two lovesick puppies. The rest of the world ceased to exist. We fed each other and talked about our future. Both of us took guesses on how much TJ would weigh when he was born. Jemistry said nineteen inches long and six pounds eleven ounces. I asked her did she realize how damn big I was. I was thinking more like twenty-three inches long and at least ten pounds.

"The Devil is a liar!" Jemistry exclaimed. "I'm not giving birth to a toddler."

When I informed her that I had actually weighed closer to eleven pounds at birth, she looked like she wanted to pass the hell out.

"Get the fuck out of here!"

"No, I really did. You can call Mom and ask her if you don't believe me."

She shook her head in dismay. "If TJ is that big, I'd rather bypass even considering natural birth and go straight for the Caesarean section."

I chuckled. "No one's giving you a C-section that's not needed, baby."

"It *is* needed. I have to protect my pussy. Ten, eleven pounds, though? Um, no."

"Well, missy, it's not like you can control his size. Two things are for sure: He's coming and you're the only one who can push him out."

"Like I said, C-section all the way, Big Meech," she said and giggled. "Besides, if I push him out, his head might get all jacked up coming out of the birth canal. What if he wants to go bald one day, or ends up bald, and the shape of his head is deformed?"

"You're tripping, baby," I replied, scooping some eggs up off my plate. I was starved. "His head will be fine."

"I'm just saying. I've seen enough men with bald heads that look like a two-year-old's Play-Doh project gone bad."

"Here's what we'll do. At your appointment next week, we'll ask Dr. Horton to guesstimate his size and go from there."

Jemistry seemed please. "So you agree? If he's too big, I can get cut."

"No, I agree that we can ask and you're going to have to push his ass out, big head and all, unless there's a medical reason not to."

Jemistry realized that it was a touchy subject for me. It was. The thought of something actually going wrong during TJ's birth terrified me.

"Okay," she said. "I'm going to prepare

myself for the madness. The things us women have to go through."

I grinned. "We're already signed up for Lamaze classes. It'll be fine."

She rolled her eyes playfully. "So both of us going in there and taking fake breaths is going to do exactly what when the time comes? You're not seriously planning to sit beside me going through the motions and acting like you know exactly what I'm feeling, are you?"

I didn't respond. It was a crazy concept now that she put it that way.

"I sure hope not. I can see me losing it right then and there. If you or the male doctors start trying to tell me to 'just push' or 'relax,' I'm going in. Fair warning. I'll listen to advice from the women but you men don't know jack shit about labor. Hell, I don't know jack shit about it yet."

I changed the subject. "Are you sure you're ready to return to work?"

"Tevin, we have almost four months before I'm due. I'll be a freaking sociopath if I sit at home all that time. I'd rather watch paint dry than watch another episode of the shows that I've been watching."

"Baby, there are hundreds of cable channels."

"I know, and half the time I still can't find

anything interesting on. Crazy, isn't it?"

Again, she had a point. Outside of the few sports- and news-related shows that I watched, there wasn't much on that interested me either.

Jemistry pushed her plate away. "I'm tapping out."

I pushed mine away as well. "I'm tapping out, too."

"Just because it's a buffet, it doesn't mean that I have to pig out," she said.

"Agreed."

She eyed me with "that look." "You need to take your missus home and put me to bed."

I winked. "My pleasure."

When we got to our house, I carried Jemistry over the threshold. Then I did what she requested: put her back to bed and made love to her for the rest of the day.

I finally had it all, and I would do whatever it took to keep it.

CHAPTER THIRTY-THREE

"Love in its essence is spiritual fire."
— Lucius Annaeus Seneca

November 22nd, 2013, will forever go down on record as being one of the worst days in my life. I will never forget it. We'd been married a little over a month and we were looking forward to spending our first Thanksgiving together as husband and wife. We had decided that we would spend it alone together. The following year, we would have TJ there and would invite a lot of friends and relatives over.

Jemistry was decorating the house early for Christmas. She had enlisted me to put up a nine-foot tree in the living room for us to enjoy in the evenings, and another seven-foot one in the sunroom with lots of lights so that passersby would see it and hopefully be inspired. She had even almost completed all of her Christmas shopping, so she said.

Something told me that once Black Friday sales hit, she would hit the pavement as well with some of her friends. She was really in the spirit.

I could tell that she was glad that she had decided to go ahead and marry me. I was walking on air. Seriously, it seemed like my back had straightened and I was walking taller, like someone had snuck into my closet and put some lifts into the heels of all my shoes.

Being back at work had truly helped Jemistry out the most, though. I had never seen someone so committed to changing the lives of children. Her hormones were definitely throwing her for a loop and having to deal with the hectic schedule somehow managed to calm her down instead of overwhelm her. She wasn't the type of woman who appreciated being able to sit at home and chill. And I actually had never been attracted to that kind of woman. I wanted to be able to talk about each other's day at the dinner table every night. To be able to give each other career advice and cuddle when a rough day presented itself from time to time. Even if every day ended up being rough, we would be there for each other.

A lot of men — including "he who walked behind the rows and shall remain nameless"

— wanted to control their women economically. They wanted their women to have to rely on their income for everything from toothpaste and toilet paper to maintain their hygiene to lipstick and hairbrushes to maintain their looks. I really had nothing against that theory. No man could force a woman to sign up for that, after all. However, my mother had been a stay-at-home wife and I saw how it had affected her in the end.

Daddy had to pay her alimony and child support . . . for a while. Like most women who take the option of not pursuing a career or stacking their own savings, Mom assumed that Daddy would always take care of her. Once all of us — their offspring — were grown and the five years of alimony were up, Mom had found herself struggling financially. No money paid into social security. No pension plan or 401K. No stocks, no bonds, and no true net worth.

She had been given the family home in the divorce, but that was only because Dad didn't want to look bad in front of my sisters and me. He would've never misplaced us out of spite. He had nothing to be spiteful about, really. If not for his actions, there never would have been a divorce. I never blamed my mother for deciding that enough was enough. While my siblings and I surely were not privy to all of what occurred, we knew enough details to determine that Daddy was a disrespectful dog who couldn't control his dick.

Mom eventually sold the house after we were all grown. Her funds were low so she needed the equity. When she called to inform me that she planned to sell it, I immediately offered to cover all of the household bills and send her several thousand extra a month to live in the lifestyle she was accustomed to. She refused me and she refused both of my sisters who made similar offers. I will never forget her exact words to me: "Children are not supposed to take care of their parents. Your father and I did not put forth the effort to make you all successful, only for me to have to turn around and financially drain you. I love you, but I will not accept your money."

Mom also said that she would be lonely, living in a seven-bedroom mansion by herself. It was pointless. So she sold the house, moved into a condominium in New York City for several years, believing that being in "the city that never sleeps" would make her life exciting. She had several longtime friends there but all of them had lives of their own and she would often feel like the third wheel.

Eventually, she tapped out of the equity; a lot of it went toward purchasing the condo since the cost of living in New York was so high. Then she had to swallow her pride, call Alexis in Florida, and ask if she could move in. It was devastating to her to have to go there but, out of the three of us and where we were located, Florida made the most sense.

I sent Mom a few thousand dollars a month despite what she had initially said. I refused to see her worry about money; not the woman who had sacrificed all of her time for me as a child, the woman who made me study and complete my homework on time, the woman who fought for me to be valedictorian when my high school tried to rob me of it because another girl's relatives were "important people." While I credited my father for a lot — after all, I had followed in his footsteps and became a vascular surgeon — my mother was the glue that held our family together. Such was the case with many wives who, while married, often felt like single parents because their husbands were workaholics — or "playaholics."

Yes, women were amazing creatures. Women who did everything that they promised to do, who took their marriage vows seriously, and who took raising children even more seriously. And yet, that didn't prevent a lot of men from trying to self-destruct their family units during a divorce. A lot of men who found themselves no longer desired or tolerated by their wives straight up showed their asses. I had seen many male friends and associates do that over the years.

I bring all of this up for a good reason. November 22nd, 2013, was the day that all of the shit hit the fan in the marriage of my *former* best friend. And instead of blaming himself, he tried to blame all of his drama on me.

I had been out of the operating room less than ten minutes. I was in the waiting room on the sixth floor speaking with Mrs. Rosella McCoy, whose husband was in recovery after I had cleared up a clot in his leg.

"Is Michael going to be all right?" she asked, as if she was afraid to know the answer.

"The surgery went very well." I grinned at her. "He's in recovery now. You'll be able to see him in about an hour."

She sighed in relief and hugged me. I was still wearing my scrubs.

"Oh my God, thank you." She put her hands in front of her face, palms together as if she was praying, and then lowered them. "So, that's it? No more complications?"

I was always cautious not to mislead patients or their families. The fact of the matter was that something could always go wrong after surgery. A person could do anything, from suddenly bleeding profusely to suffering a stroke or heart attack, to slipping into a coma or ending up with no activity in the brain stem, having to be removed from life support within a matter of hours after what seemed like a successful surgery at the time. No matter how skilled a doctor, nature or undiagnosed health conditions could intervene at any moment.

"I cleared the clot," I said, being truthful. "We're going to monitor him closely over the next several days. Don't anticipate him coming home until at least Monday. I never release my patients until I'm confident that they'll be okay without standby care."

"I understand, Doctor Harris." She was fighting off tears. "I'm just glad Michael's still alive. You hear all those horror stories about people dying on the operating table and —"

I rubbed her shoulder gently. "He was a trooper. The surgery was by the book."

Mrs. McCoy smiled. "I don't know what I could ever do to repay you. You saved his life."

"Ma'am, it was my pleasure to remove the clot. You don't owe me a thing, except taking care of your husband while he recuperates, and discouraging him from doing anything that may cause another one. He is going to have to stop trying to do a lot of heavy lifting, and he needs to retire from that construction job."

"I keep telling his hard head that. Now they'll probably force him to retire. But it's for the best."

"Definitely for the best, in this case."

I reached into the pocket of my scrub pants and hit the button to turn my cell phone back on. I had retrieved it when I left out of the operating room but had neglected to turn it on, both my phone and my hospital pager.

I felt the initial vibration from it powering up and then it started going off like fireworks.

"Excuse me for a moment," I said to Mrs. McCoy and then took a few steps to the side so I could read my text messages.

All of them were from Jemistry:

CALL ME ASAP.

CALL ME WHEN YOU GET OUT OF SURGERY!

CALL ME! IT'S URGENT!

BABY, I REALLY NEED TO SPEAK WITH YOU THE SECOND YOU GET OUT OF THE O.R.

BABY, I FUCKED UP!

COURTNEY KNOWS! LOOK OUT FOR FLOYD! SHE LIT HIS ASS UP!

ARE YOU OKAY? HAVE YOU SEEN FLOYD?

I was standing there shaking my head and about to text Jemistry back when Floyd came ripping through the double doors of the waiting room. Mrs. McCoy seemed taken aback, like the rest of the people sitting there. They all looked around at one another, to see if one of them was the one about to receive bad news about a loved one. Floyd had on his white coat and had an angry expression on his face that others probably mistook for anguish.

When the majority of them realized that Floyd had locked eyes on me, they relaxed a bit.

I walked over to him. "Not here."

"I need to talk to you . . . now!"

"Floyd, I just came out of surgery." I tried to maintain my composure. "I'm consulting with a family member. I'm aware of your *issue,* and we will deal with it later."

"My issue?" he practically yelled, acting all belligerent. "Is that what you call it? An issue. How could you tell —"

I was getting pissed off. "How could you not tell me about Jemistry being pregnant?"

We stared at each other for a few seconds.

"I can't believe this shi—"

Floyd had at least enough sense to prevent that curse word from escaping his lips in front of a dozen people. He scanned the room and realized that his behavior — storming in there as he did — was inappropriate and unprofessional.

He glared at me. "I'll wait for you in your office."

"Fine by me," I said, refusing to break eye contact first.

He straightened his coat and stomped off like a child.

Mrs. McCoy walked up to me. "Is everything all right? Both of you seem upset. It's none of my business but I —"

I looked down at her and forced a chuckle. "Everything is great. He's a cardiologist and we're consulting together on a mutual patient. We'll talk about it later." I patted her on the shoulder. "I'll have the nurse come and let you know when Mr. McCoy is awake so you can go up and see him. I'll be by to check on him in a little while and give you some updates. Just remember that he's going to be groggy for most of the night until the anesthesia completely wears off. He might not quite be himself."

She smiled. "As long as he is alive, that's all that matters to me. When he gets home, I'm going to wait on him hand and foot. I'm not letting him overexert himself, no matter what."

"We're on the same page. I'm sure that I can count on you."

"Yes, Doctor Harris, you can definitely count on me."

I walked out of the waiting room, hoping that I could count on myself not to end up getting arrested a few days before Thanksgiving for ramming my foot all the way up Floyd's ass.

CHAPTER THIRTY-FOUR

"Love means to commit yourself without
guarantee."
— Anne Campbell

"What happened?" Jemistry asked, meeting
me at the laundry room door as I entered
the house from the garage. "Did you see
Floyd?"

I walked past her into the kitchen and
tossed my briefcase down on the table.

"Jemistry, I really don't want to talk about
this right now," I finally replied.

"Let me guess. You're upset with me
because I told Courtney about her husband's roaming dick."

I pulled a chair out, sat down, and pulled
the bottom of my tie out of my waistband.
Then I slipped out of my jacket.

"Can you hand me a beer, please?" I asked
politely.

"A beer?" She rolled her eyes at me.

"Sure, I'll get you a beer, Tevin. That's what wives do when their dictators come home from work."

I sighed as she crossed the room, yanked the refrigerator open, and pulled a Bud Light out of the six-pack on the bottom shelf.

"I'm not trying to be your dictator, baby."

She slammed the bottle down on the table then sat across from me. We stared at each other for a few seconds.

"Oh, my bad!" She stood back up. "Mea culpa! Let me fix your dinner plate. Sorry that I didn't have it on the table before your arrival."

Jemistry walked over to the sink, washed her hands, took out a porcelain plate from a cabinet, then walked over to the stove and started piling what looked to be spaghetti onto it. She put on an oven mitt, yanked a baking sheet out of the oven that had garlic toast on it, and then tossed two pieces beside the pasta on my plate.

She walked over to a drawer, pulled it open, and grabbed a fork, tossing it on top of everything else on the plate. I kept my eyes glued to her every move, wondering how she could be upset after throwing my ass to the wolves. If she had kept her mouth shut, or had at least warned me that she

371

was about to spill the beans to Courtney, my day would have gone much smoother.

Jemistry set the plate down in front of me and then retook the other chair. She folded her arms in front of her in defiance and glared at me.

"This is silly," I said. "All of it. You don't need to be all upset and put yourself and the baby under a bunch of stress. We don't need to be going at each other. Sure, I was upset with you earlier today. I come out of surgery and read your *montage* of texts, and then Floyd comes storming into a consultation with a patient's wife.

"He looks like he's ready to jump me, right there in the waiting room."

Jemistry sucked in a breath. "He didn't hit you, did he?"

I smirked. "He thought about it, I'm sure, but Floyd's not a dummy. I have him by eight inches and at least fifty pounds of muscle."

"So what happened then?" she insisted on knowing.

"Dinner looks delicious. You mind if I eat it while it's still hot?"

"You can eat as long as you tell me what the fuck happened while you're doing it."

I was about to sprinkle some pepper on my food when she said that. I put the

372

pepper back down and pushed my plate away. "That's what microwaves are for. Okay, fine."

"So what happened?"

"You can probably guess most of it. You orchestrated the first part of the chaos, after all."

Jemistry rolled her eyes again. "It was time for her to know. Courtney's always singing Floyd's accolades. Talking about how faithful and honest a man he is. I couldn't sit by another second and allow him to pull the wool over her eyes. I couldn't do it and still consider myself her friend.

"It's not like I gave her any details. Hell, you didn't give me any. All I said was that you had shared with me that Floyd was fucking a lot of women from work. I told her that she needed to be careful."

"How did it even come up?" I asked, not that it even mattered much. "I thought that all of that had boiled over, since you'd never said anything."

Jemistry calmed down a little. "Tevin, I met Courtney for lunch and she was just leaving her gynecologist's office. She was going on and on about how offended she was that the nurse always asked her if she wanted to be tested for STDs, since her insurance covered most of the tests. She said

373

that she felt like cursing the nurse out, but instead told her that she was married and not promiscuous like that. She said that *those kinds of tests* are for single people only."

I closed my eyes for a few seconds and allowed her last statement to sink in.

"Now do you see why I had to tell her?" Jemistry asked.

I opened my eyes. "Yes, I understand perfectly."

"Good." She paused. "It wasn't like I woke up this morning intending on turning someone's world upside down. But what if he's given her something? Or if I didn't say anything and he eventually gave her something?"

"Baby, I hear what you're saying and I receive it," I said. "I receive it and I agree with what you decided to do. Like I told Floyd, not only today but also all along, he was dead-ass wrong and it was inevitable that it would come out.

"Honestly, it's better that Courtney found out from you, someone who actually cares about her. My mother had to find out from a trifling whore who decided to accost her and throw Daddy's affair up in her face.

"That's what's so crazy about the entire thing. Time and time again, I told Floyd about how my father's roving eyes and dick had destroyed our family. How love does not equate to doing unnecessary and unwarranted shit simply because you believe you can get away with it."

Jemistry sighed. "Yeah, I know about all of that. Even though she's not married, I used to preach that same stuff about wilding out for no good reason to Winsome." She stared at me like she wanted to add something. "Speaking of Winsome, she came by the school today."

"For what?" I asked with much disdain. "She needs to stay the hell away from both of us."

"And I made that clear. She came by to wish me happy holidays. You have to understand that we've spent every holiday season together, in some way, for at least the past decade. That's not going to be the case this year.

"Winsome means well, but she has to figure out how to make better choices. I told her that I would pray for her and be there for her in spirit."

Jemistry giggled.

"What?" I asked.

"She did make one choice and she says that it's final. She's now a full lesbian instead of being bisexual. She has sworn off dick for life."

I chuckled. "Yeah, right. For life, or until she sees a man she can't resist."

"She said that she has a girlfriend. That she's committed. Some woman named Sharon that she met on the Metro train."

"Great place to pick up people. It's not going to last."

"You picked me up in a bar after I'd just finished delivering a male-bashing poem, and look at us."

"You have a point."

We both laughed.

"She also said that she's been going to counseling," Jemistry said. "To try to figure out what she wants to truly do with her life and why she keeps making irresponsible decisions."

"That's good. That's really good. I don't have anything against Winsome," I said. "I'm over it. But if you ever let her come back around on the regular, she can't disrespect our marriage."

Jemistry sucked in her bottom lip. "Maybe sometime. She's my ace and I love her and all. And I miss her. But right now, I want to concentrate on establishing our life together and having a healthy baby. We have so much to still do to the nursery."

Her statement about the nursery sounded

accusatory, not to mention the look she was giving me, as though I should have been ashamed.

I lifted my brow. "Don't look at me. You're the one who keeps changing your mind about the color scheme. And going all out by having that man paint a mural. We can't put any furniture in there until the walls are painted and dried.

"You need to hurry up. It might take me a couple of months to put that fancy crib together that you picked out."

"Yeah, I've heard some nightmares about men trying to follow the instructions to put together cribs. Even for surgeons, common sense isn't always so common."

"Oh, so now you've got jokes!" I chuckled. "There are a lot of parts but if I can put a human being back together, I can damn sure get that crib up without tearing up something."

"I can't wait to see that."

Jemistry stood up, took my plate, and walked over to the microwave to heat it up. As it was rotating on the glass base, I asked, "Aren't you going to fix yourself a plate?"

"Baby, please. I've had three servings and four pieces of bread already. I'm going for round three when *Criminal Minds* comes on at nine."

I took a swig of my beer. "What time do we have Lamaze class tomorrow?"

Chapter Thirty-Five

"To love abundantly is to live abundantly,
and to love forever is to live forever."
— Henry Drummond

We arrived in New Orleans two days after Christmas. I was lost about what to get Jemistry for a present, but the choice became obvious when her Nissan Rouge was diagnosed with a bad transmission. Rather than go through all of that, I insisted that she let me purchase her a new vehicle. I wanted to surprise her but decided against it. I wanted her to get what she wanted. She was the one who would have to drive it, and she would be carting my seed, TJ, around in it so it, had to be safe.

Being quite nerdish when it comes to wanting to know every detail about something before I make a high-price-tag purchase, I surfed the Internet and landed on the Insurance Institute for Highway Safety web site and printed off their list for the top safety picks for 2014. When Jemistry had arrived home on her last day before winter break, we went over it together, selected a few to go check out, and ended up purchasing a forest-green Acura MDX with a butter leather interior.

Jemistry surprised me with a Breitling Chronomat watch that had to cost at least six grand. I was not expecting such a lavish gift. Even though she made about a hundred forty thousand a year as a principal, I still didn't think she had to go that far.

She laughed at me when I tried to get her to take it back. "Two things," she said. "It's engraved and if you weren't so busy complaining, you would've seen that already. Secondly, you refuse to let me pay any bills around this mickey so I need to spend money on something. You already bought me a car, so I bought you a watch." She planted a kiss on my lips as we lay in bed together when she had presented me with the present. "So, Doctor Harris, read your inscription and miss me with all that."

We both laughed as I removed the watch from the case and flipped it over. It read:

Tevin, I want all of my days to begin and end with you. Always yours, Jemistry

"That's very sweet, baby."

"Glad you like it." Jemistry reached down under the blanket and started rubbing my dick. "Enough of the sappy, romantic talk. Fuck me like I stole something."

I chuckled and reached under the blanket and into her panties and started playing with her pussy. "You're always so wet."

"That's because you make me that way."

She started kissing and licking all over my chest. A lot of women sleep on the fact that men are aroused by that. Just because we don't have tits, it doesn't mean that we're not sensitive there. Jemistry knew that it excited me.

I started moaning as we continued to play with each other's privates.

"You're going to drive me insane," I whispered. And I was not even lying. Her scent was driving me wild as we played with each other's tongues.

Jemistry tossed the blanket completely off the bed, slid out of her panties while I kicked my pajama pants off, and then impaled her pussy on my dick. She started grinding on me like she was a windmill. Then she started snapping her pussy onto my dick. Crazy!

"You like that, baby?" she asked, finally breaking the kiss and coming up for air.

"You know I like it. Work that pussy, sweet-heart."

She dug her fingertips into my chest and started pouncing up and down on my dick.

She threw her head back and I watched her breasts, getting more and more succulent as her pregnancy progressed, swirl around in circles. I grabbed a hold of them and squeezed. She let out a moan of pleasure.

"Oh, Tevin!" she screamed out as she came the first time, and kept going.

I let go of one of her breasts and rested my hand on her stomach, trying to see if the baby was moving or seemed like he was under stress. Even though I had been given all of the reassurances in the world, I would be concerned until TJ made his entrance into the world. But I had stopped talking about it all the time. I didn't want to speak anything negative into existence.

Tevin Harris, Jr. was going to be the man, and Tevin Harris, Sr. was going to be the man who kept his eye on the man. I was going to make sure that he had everything he could ever want, but he wasn't going to be a spoiled brat either. I was going to have to find that perfect balance. He was going to play sports — basketball, baseball, foot-ball, soccer, and whatever else we could fit in. He wasn't going to sit on his ass playing video games all day and end up with an obesity issue by the time he hit double digits in age. He was going to learn how to read and write early. He was going to learn his math facts so he never had to struggle once more difficult things were introduced. Like I said, the man.

I was thinking all of those things when I felt him kick. Then I immediately faked like I was ejaculating so Jemistry would feel like she had done what needed to be done to please me. I was only probably sixty to ninety seconds from busting a nut anyway but, lately, I had been putting on pretenses every now and then, finishing myself off later or just allowing my dick to deflate and calling it a day.

Jemistry collapsed beside me, breathing heavily. "Nothing like early-morning dick action."

"You have a potty mouth," I said, then chuckled. "If your students heard you talking like that, they'd talk mad shit."

"My mouth is nothing compared to theirs. They are doing the most these days. When the spring semester starts, I'm going to have to crack down on kids sneaking off into vacant classrooms and closets trying to fuck or suck all over each other."

I glanced over at Jemistry. "Really?"

"It's gotten ridiculous. Parents have no clue what their kids are doing at school, or before and after school. I can only do so much and I can't prevent them from doing whatever off the premises, but I'll be damned if they continue to disrespect Medgar Evers High."

"Go on with your bad self, Joe Clark," I joked, referencing the biopic *Lean on Me* and the no-nonsense principal who turned a lot of lives around despite some parents disagreeing with his strict policies.

Jemistry laughed and started giving me a hand job.

"What are you doing?" I asked, surprised. "We just finished; you're not ready for another round, are you?"

"No, I'm not, but you can't fool me, Tevin. I know you didn't come. So I'm helping you out. Your fake nutting face is nothing like the real thing. It's a *toned-down* version."

She giggled and started moving her hand faster and faster.

"I appreciate you trying to prevent my coochie from undergoing a good dick pounding but you don't need to have to do things by yourself. Not as long as you have me."

Then she lowered her head and took my dick in her mouth.

Boy, oh boy, did she finish a brother off!

We checked into a suite at the W New Orleans-French Quarter, got settled, and then ventured out to find some good food. We had a "hit list" of restaurants we wanted to try over the next several days. Jemistry wanted to try Batch, SoBou, Iris, Restaurant R'evolution, and Sylvain. I wanted to check out Green Goddess, Criollo, Galatoire's, Domenica, and MiLa. While we did not consider ourselves official "foodies," we were damn close. I had used Jemistry's pregnancy as an excuse to pig out myself. It was not a good look. After TJ was out the basket, she and I were both going to have to hit the gym hard, but we would do it together.

We hit R'evolution up first on Bienville Street. We threw down with a vengeance. We started with Creole Louisiana Snapping Turtle Soup with deviled quail eggs and Madeira. We also ordered some Mussels and Andouille with sweet garlic and Calabrian chile rouille.

Jemistry had the Linguine and Manila Clams for her entrée while I tried out the Lamb Chops with rutabaga purée. We went hard and both ordered desserts: She had the Turbodog Stout Chocolate Cake and I had the White Chocolate Bread Pudding Crème Brûlée.

After lunch — and waddling out the restaurant — we decided to go to a couple of tourist attractions. First, we stopped by The Cabildo on Chartres Street. It was a building that had replaced an original one that burned down in 1788. It was rebuilt between 1795 and 1799 and had served as the seat of the local government during the Spanish colonial period. It was also where the Louisiana Purchase was signed in 1803.

Next, we rolled through the Beauregard-Keyes House on the same street a few blocks away. Both Confederate general Pierre Gustave Toutant Beauregard — who had ordered the first shots of the Civil War at Fort Sumter, South Carolina, in 1861 — and Frances Parkinson Keyes — author of more than fifty books and short stories — had occupied the home about a hundred years apart. So they named the historical building after both of them.

Jemistry was getting worn down so we went back to the W and took a nap. We woke up, made love, and went to the Le Petit Theatre to see a smaller version of the musical *Hair*. Jemistry had never seen it but I had seen it as a child on Broadway. Some called it "The Ultimate American Rock Musical." I felt like it was all of that and then some.

Hair is about a group of young adults in the 1960s trying to maintain a balance of love, peace, and trust during the Vietnam War era. Most of the songs are classics, like "Aquarius/Let the Sunshine In," "Good Morning Starshine," and "Easy to Be Hard."

By the end of the show, most of the audience was dancing in the aisles, including us. We had an amazing time.

We ended up staying in New Orleans until January 3rd. We brought in the New Year among the masses in Jackson Square. Allstate kicked everything off at six PM with their Fan Fest, which included a concert. At nine, Eric Lindell and the Honey Island Swamp Band performed. At one minute to midnight, the official countdown began as the fleur-de-lis descended from the roof of Jax Brewery.

Jemistry and I counted it down together.

"Happy New Year, Mrs. Harris," I said and then kissed her for a good minute.

"I really love you, Tevin," she yelled over the crowd. "This is the first of many years we will bring in together."

"No doubt." I took her hand. "Let's go find a good spot to watch the fireworks.

We walked closer to the Mississippi River so we could watch the spectacular fireworks display. It did not disappoint.

■ ■ ■ ■

JEMISTRY

■ ■ ■ ■

EPILOGUE

"Love conquers all."

— Virgil

TJ was born on Valentine's Day 2014. He was *twelve pounds three ounces* and twenty-three inches long. I ended up having to get a Caesarean. I was happy as shit about it, too. If I had had to push him out, the world would have come to an end because I would have turned Providence Hospital out.

Tevin was more excited than I had ever seen him. He was handing out cigars and you would have thought that the entire vascular unit had made a mass exodus from Sibley over there. The hallway near the nursery was flooded with people trying to get a look at the new prince. He looked like Tevin had literally spit him out instead of coming from my womb. I was definitely only the vessel. He had his miniature twin.

Estella sent me flowers but did not come

anywhere near the hospital, to my knowledge. I appreciated that. While she and I could never be friends who hung out or talked on the regular, I was sure that her thoughts were genuine. I still had never revealed her daytime visit to Tevin and it was staying that way.

Adding to the chaos was a lot of my staff and faculty members from Medgar Evers. They were all over the hospital as well. One thing was for sure. TJ was going to have a lot of love in his life, several people claiming to be his godparents, and tons of gifts. Floyd and Tevin had made amends, even though Courtney had kicked him out of the house and filed for divorce. Both of them came to the hospital separately. Winsome also came by with her girlfriend. They were still going strong. I had also decided to try again with her, after getting Tevin to cosign on it. We both agreed that since she was not lonely anymore, she had no real reason to try to sabotage our marriage. Floyd loved Tevin, Tevin loved Floyd, Winsome loved me, and I loved Winsome. Bona fide, genuine love doesn't simply die because everyone does not agree all of the time. People make mistakes. We are all flawed.

I had never gotten around to having a baby shower. I didn't really want one, to be honest. I figured that we would get a lot of repeat items, which ended up happening anyway in the upcoming weeks, and I was too anal to go through the process of trying to do registries at various stores. Even though most offered online registration, it was still too much for me. Part of being a new mother was going to be making sure that everything was the way that I wanted. I was hoping for more gift cards and cash than actual gifts. We ended up getting a mix of the two.

After all of the excitement had died down on the floor and in my room for the day, I sat up in bed, trying to get adjusted to the staples in my stomach, and asked Tevin to hand me TJ.

He was holding him in a chair by the window, staring at him like he was a piece of gold.

He brought me the baby as I lowered my hospital gown, and then held him up to my breast. I was going to have to get used to producing milk. My breasts felt like concrete slabs. I was going to have to pump several times a day while I was in my office, once I went back to work in the coming months.

Tevin wanted me to take the remainder of the school year off. I was considering it but didn't want to jeopardize my job in any way.

He assured me that he could "manage" to get me a doctor's report stipulating that I needed the time off for health-related reasons. It was a thought. Being able to spend the time with TJ until after Labor Day would be a blessing.

As TJ was figuring out how he wanted to latch on to my breast for dear life, Tevin rubbed his head gently.

"See," I said.

He looked at me. "Huh?"

"Look at his head. His big-ass head. Could you imagine what would have happened to it if I had been forced to push it out the birth canal?"

Tevin chuckled. "I have to give you that one. It would've been a mess."

"I love you, Doctor Harris."

"I love you, Mrs. Harris."

We both watched as TJ ate his dinner and then watched late-night television together. We were all looking forward to our next phase of life together. After all, it was a one-shot deal.

COMMENTARY BY ZANE

Originally, I had come up with at least three different titles for this book. I am not going to say them because they are pretty damn good and I may or may not use one, or all, of them at some time in the future. Like all of my books, I had a purpose in mind when I sat down to write it. Also, like all of my books, the story and characters began to take on lives of their own, and many of them morphed into different people.

In this case, when I started the book, Floyd and Courtney were not even on my radar. It was my intent to make this book about two people — Tevin and Jemistry — and concentrate solely on their "situation-ship." But the picture became much bigger when I decided to address other issues that plague a lot of couples.

What this book really boils down to is "a conversation." It is meant to be a discussion piece for couples, singles, and anyone who is interested in trying to figure out why there is often so much drama and strife in relationships. Why some people seemingly go their entire lives not ever finding what it is that most people crave: true love.

Despite what a lot of people try to make others believe — that they are fine being single and doing them — I am not one to buy it. Maybe it's because I receive thousands of emails monthly from both men and women seeking advice about how to make love work for them. Maybe it is because I could never imagine my life with such an eternal void in it. Maybe it's because my parents have been married more than sixty years and I realized at an early age that a healthy, nontoxic, non-dysfunctional household was actually possible if both people loved and respected each other enough to not only listen but to also comprehend.

So *The Other Side of the Pillow* is really a long-ass conversation piece. Instead of it being a nonfiction relationship book like *Dear G-Spot,* it is a fictionalized tutorial on how to communicate with emotional honesty, how to appreciate the difference between the ways that men and women view relationships, instead of fearing them, and how to either forgive or let go.

Too many people remain in unrealistic

situations that have nothing to do with one party being good and another one being evil. They are simply unrealistic. Two people might be madly in love but circumstances will likely never present themselves that would afford them the opportunity to come home each night and fall asleep in each other's arms. Two people might possess character traits that are not equally yolked and may tend to do things that are not acceptable in the world of the other person. One person may be lazy, while the other is ambitious. One person might think they are the shit while the other person believes that they are not up to par. One person might have a low sex drive while the other person wants sex several times a day. There is no right or wrong in those scenarios. They are merely unrealistic.

Jemistry signified the typical bitter black woman in the beginning of the book, to the point where I had her reciting a poem called "Bitter." A lot of women have been overwhelmed, overshadowed, and overexerted by men that they attempted to love who could never truly love them back. The reasons for the men not being able to convert to what the women needed range from lack of knowledge to lack of emotions.

Jemistry was ready to give up . . . for good.

But then when she least expected it, love walked right into her life in the form of Tevin. There is something to be said about not searching for love but allowing it to find you. Love was the last thing on her mind when she decided to express her feelings with that poem.

Now Tevin wasn't actually looking for love either. He was on the mend, even though his marriage had ended years earlier. In his mind, he couldn't fathom how he could be the total package that women always claimed to want: tall, dark, handsome, education, wealthy, and well hung, and yet be single. Sure, he could have dated women right and left, bedded them, and led them on. But that was not in his nature. He was a man who had never felt like conforming to whoredom because it was impressed upon most young men to do so. He had always yearned to be in a committed relationship and, as mentioned in the novel, he had witnessed the pain that his father's infidelity had caused both his parents. That was not a road that he wished to travel.

So I created a rare man who actually expressed his emotions without fear of judgment. A man willing to cry over, willing to fight for, and willing to sacrifice some of himself for a woman he deemed worthy of it all. Too many times women say that they want a man who will do all of these things and then turn around and make them feel bad when they open up.

Twice in the past two months, I have seen that in action on my Facebook page when I posted a couple of advice emails in particular. One from a married woman who was prepared to cheat on her husband who was "99 percent perfect" — her words not mine — with a man who had six kids by five different women. He had found her sexting and had cried instead of punching her lights out so she was convinced he had to be on the down low. Ridiculous!

Then I received an email on the weekend that I actually completed this book from a husband who poured his heart out. As I type this, there are more than seven hundred comments and counting on that thread and a lot of people calling him weak and telling him to "man up." Again, ridiculous!

All of that is to say that women need to wise up and stop overlooking the men who are capable of loving them right and chasing after the men that will treat them horribly. Most of the women cannot help that kind of mentality. If it is what they witnessed growing up, then it is their normalcy. Relationships without a bunch of drama and nonsense throw them off-kilter. They often do not know how to accept love, especially if they do not even love themselves. It has become a generational curse.

One way to sum all of this up is this way and I am going to use an analogy. We really need to try to salvage the family unit globally. It is becoming more and more impossible to do so with so many accepting so much less. Also, with men and women not being able to relate to each other. It is like this:

Image two beautiful Clydesdale horses hitched to a wagon together (a married couple). They both have their eyes on the road ahead, trying to get to the same place (a healthy marriage and prosperous life). Like most horses, they both have blinders on so that they cannot see what the other is doing (they have a lack of communication). They have two ponies attached to them from behind (a male pony behind the male horse and a female pony behind the female horse). All the ponies can see because of their own blinders are the respective adult horses directly in front of them (their parents). So the male pony will learn from, imitate, and repeat the actions of his father, and the female pony will do the same in regards to her mother. Thus, the choices

400

that the parents make, the way that they interact with each other, and the morals that they establish will be revisited on their children, and then their children's children, and so on.

That is why it is so important for people to truly lead by example. One cannot have several children out of wedlock, and then tell their kids that it is a sin to have sex outside of marriage. One cannot allow themselves to be abused over and over in the name of love, and then try to tell their children that abuse is wrong. One cannot squander their money on material things, and then try to impress the importance of saving on their children. One cannot abuse drugs and alcohol for the entire childhoods of their children, and then tell them to "just say no to drugs." One cannot sit on their ass, refusing to work — not due to health issues but just because — and then tell their kids that they need to be not only working but up out of their homes by the age of eighteen. I am sure you get my drift.

Anyway, I am not trying to write another book within a book. I will vent about the rest of the things on my mind later. All I will say is that I hope *The Other Side of the Pillow* has somehow enlightened your perspective on relationships. I hope that it has

somehow made you think about how important it is to accept that everyone has a past.
I hope that it makes your thinking mature
in some way and offers clarity on your
outlook on life. There are many more
aspects of the book that I feel could use
some elaboration. However, if I did my job
well enough, you'll be able to figure them
out.

As always, I love and appreciate each and
every one of you.

Love and Blessings,
Zane

3/2/15